She's resourceful. She's tough. She's Rachel Cord.

I heard a cracking noise behind me. The noise came from the living room. Someone had come in. I hadn't brought a gun and looked for something to use as a weapon. I picked a magazine off the floor and rolled it tightly. A man stopped at the hall doorway holding a black and yellow pry bar.

"Who the fuck are you?" he said.

He came into the room. The mess on the floor made moving uncertain. I stood my ground. Watched his eyes.

"I said, who are you, bitch! What are you doing here?"

"Protecting interests from scum like you."

He rushed me raising his arm across his body to give me a backhand with the pry bar. I stepped in beneath his swing jamming the end of the magazine as hard as I could into his solar plexus.

I jammed him again. When I jammed him a third time, he dropped to his knees. He tried to breathe. I locked my hands together smashing the side of his face with a "for the bleachers" swing.

Rachel Cord Confidential Investigations

Life's A Bitch. So Am I.

Still A Bitch

Bad Bitch Blues

Queen Of Tarts

Hangman's Oak (Short Story)

Visit Rachel Cord at www.rachelcord.net

Also by R. E. Conary

Paradise Ladies & Others

RACHEL CORD
Confidential Investigations

Queen of Tarts

R. E. Conary

Everyone Deserves An Equal Footing

Queen of Tarts

Rachel Cord
Confidential Investigations
Book Four

Copyright © 2016 R. E. Conary
Cover Photo © Tatjana Pilate | Dreamstime.com

Equal Footing Books
ISBN: 978-1-946545-01-5

First Print Edition

For Terry

One

I glanced out my office windows. Not a lot was happening. There'd been some rain overnight and it was still overcast and chilly. I had no appointments and the two open cases resting on school desks were waiting for information before I could close them out. I went back to reading an article in *PI Magazine* on interviewing people with personality disorders when Doris Garrity brought in my mail.

"There are two checks you need to endorse for deposit, Rachel. The rest is basically junk mail."

"Thanks, Doris. Just put them on the desk."

"Rachel? Are you busy?"

"Not really. What do you need?"

Doris came and sat in the other loveseat. "A neighbor of mine, Mr. Carlson, is in the hospital. He's in critical condition and in a coma."

"Sorry to hear that. What happened to him?"

"Someone broke into his home Thursday night and attacked him. He was found the next morning by Edna Duquesne, his next-door neighbor. Saw his front door open but didn't see him. She found him on his living room floor and called 9-1-1. The police think it was a burglary gone bad."

"And you're not sure?"

"I don't know. Haven't heard of any burglaries in our neighborhood. Carlson's an old man. Lives alone. Doesn't really associate with anyone except Edna. I doubt he has anything worth stealing. Nothing gets delivered there. He walks everywhere. Doesn't own a car. Why pick on him?"

"Good question. Have the police provided any information."

"Not really. According to Edna, the police have little to go on. They haven't been able to talk with him. With the house a mess, she says, it's hard to tell what's missing."

"Are you asking me to look into it?"

"Would you?"

"What do you think I can do the police aren't?"

"I don't know. Someone breaking into houses and hurting people is scary. Everyone's on edge. I'm frightened."

"I would think so. Have you spoken with the police?"

"Yes. An Officer Drake stopped by Friday evening. He was going door-to-door asking everyone about anything suspicious the night before. We hadn't heard anything. He didn't have much to tell us. He gave us a card and said to call the detective in charge if we thought of anything. But there's been no news, and it's Monday already."

"Who's the detective?"

"Detective Paul Wodehouse. Here's his card."

"I've met him. He works out of West Division. I can call him, if you'd like, but doubt I'll get anything you don't already have, if that much. My butting in isn't usually welcome."

"Anything you find out would be appreciated."

"Do you know Carlson's full name?"

"Edna calls him Mike. Might be short for Michael."

"Okay. I'll let you know what I find."

"Thanks."

Doris left and I stared at the card she'd given me. *Paul G. Woodhouse.* I'd met him twice, no, three times. The first was at Lt. Ed Montero's promotion party a few years back. Dean Lockhart introduced us. The other times were in the past year when I had information to pass along. Maybe he'd reciprocate now. I recognized one of the two numbers on the card as the police department's main line. I called the other one.

"Detective Wodehouse. May I help you?"

"Good morning, Detective. This is Rachel Cord. We haven't spoken in several months. How are you?"

"Aside from being overworked and underpaid, I'm alive. How 'bout you?"

"Doing well, actually."

"Glad to hear it. You have something you want to share with me?"

"Not at the moment. I'm hoping there's information you can give me."

"What's that?"

"Mike Carlson was attacked in his home last week, and I understand you're the lead detective. Are there any new developments?"

"What's your interest? Do you know the vic?"

"I've never met him. A woman who does secretarial work for me is a neighbor. Her family's worried they could be attacked too. Can you tell me anything?"

"Not a lot. He's still unconscious, but has been upgraded to stable. So I haven't been able to talk to him. I'll be checking on him again later today. Right now, we think the intent was robbery. He withdrew cash from an ATM at a nearby grocery store earlier in the day. Someone may have seen him and followed him home. Could be the reason. Hard to say. We didn't find any cash at his home, and his wallet is missing."

"Why is it 'hard to say' if that's the reason or not?"

"Because his ATM receipt said he only took out $40, and he spent nearly half at the grocery store. Not a big haul for such a violent break-in."

"True. But would the robber know that's all he took out? Maybe he was standing where he could see the ATM screen and thought it was $400, not $40."

"It's possible. Carlson's place was tossed as if the perp thought there was more cash somewhere. Or something else worth taking."

"Like what?"

"No idea. Most of the stuff in the house was outdated and still there. The mess makes it hard to tell what could be missing. Just keeping options open. The perp worked the old man senseless then trashed the place. That's all I know for sure."

"Do you think this was a specific attack, and others in the neighborhood aren't in danger?"

"My gut says yes. This wasn't a break-in. Carlson must have opened the door. Why, I don't know yet. Maybe he knew his attacker. Still, I can't rule out the possibility of more robberies. Depends on what the perp was really after and whether he got it or not. Patrols have been increased in the area, just in case."

"I see your problem. Anything you can tell me about the victim?"

"Name is Michael Henry Carlson, white male; turned 76 in February; Army retired. Inherited the house when his mother died in '89. Haven't discovered any next-of-kin. Seems to be a loner. His next-door neighbor, Mrs. Edna Duquesne, is his emergency contact."

"Is the house still a crime scene?"

"Why? You want to go snooping to see what we missed?"

"Who, me? Not at all. Just thought Mrs. Duquesne and some of the other neighbors might want to clean the place for his return."

"Very considerate of you. Now's not good. I may want to go back myself for another look. I'll let Mrs. Duquesne know when she can tidy up. Anything else?"

"No, thank you. I'll let you get back to work."

"Appreciate it. Oh, if you do come across anything I should know, call me."

"Definitely."

There wasn't much new, but I gave Doris the rundown, anyway.

"I'm glad to hear he's better. He's always been a good

neighbor. Never any problems in the nine years we've lived there. So you don't think there's any danger?"

"Wodehouse thinks it's a one-off. But who knows for sure."

"Any chance you can investigate it further? I can pay you." Doris took out her checkbook.

"Put it away."

"Rachel—"

"Look. My current cases are caught up except for the two I'm waiting for info on. I don't have any scheduled appointments. I can spend a few hours checking some things. I can't really interfere, but I'll try to find out what I can. There may be no need to pay me."

"Okay."

"What can you tell me about Carlson?"

"Not a lot. Edna's the best one to talk to. Except for Carlson, she's lived on the block the longest. She knew his mother. We're six doors down on the opposite side. I'd see him working in his rose garden or cutting his grass. He uses an old rotary push mower. He's always polite, but quiet. Keeps to himself. In his late seventies, I think, but spry. Strong too. Couple of years ago, Tina, my youngest, fell off her bike and hurt her leg. He carried her home. Wasn't even bothered he got blood on his clothes."

I glanced at the family photo Doris kept on her desk. The two boys had dark chocolate skin like hers but were tall like their father. The two girls were much lighter. Her husband, Bud, was white with a radiant smile."

"What's the neighborhood like?"

"Mostly quiet. I thought safe until what happened to Mr. Carlson. Capri Estates is a sought-after area. Property values are up. So are our taxes. But I wouldn't live anywhere else now. We bought before everyone else found it. Moved in on 9/11. Can you believe it? Not a clue about what happened till late that afternoon. I got a new house, and 3,000 people died."

"Somehow, I don't think the two events are related."

"No, but it sure put a damper on our excitement. Anyway, Capri was a late-forties project aimed at returning veterans. The original houses were two bedrooms, living room and eat-in kitchen, attached one-car garage and small front and back yard. Pastel colors and red tiled roofs. More than half now have converted garages for an extra room. Some, like ours, were completely renovated with a second story added. Others, like my friend Anita's, added on the back and nearly no yard. I think Carlson's is still original. I've never been in it."

"Do you have Mrs. Duquesne's number? Think she'll talk with me?"

"Maybe. She's a retired teacher. Like Carlson, she lives alone. Her husband died some years ago, and her kids are grown and on their own. Here's her home number and address. If she's not home, she may be at the hospital with Carlson."

I called Mrs. Duquesne's number and got an answering machine. I didn't leave a message. Taking the chance she was at the hospital, I drove there. There was a flower and gift shop in the lobby. I picked up a small bouquet of assorted roses, carnations and mums in a mug to cheer Carlson when he awoke. Getting directions, I went to his room on the 6th floor. An elderly black woman sat in a visitor's chair reading. Carlson appeared to be sleeping. His face was heavily bruised. He was hooked up to various machines and had an oxygen tube clipped to his nose.

"Hi, are you Mrs. Duquesne? I'm Rachel Cord. Doris Garrity sends her sympathies to Mr. Carlson."

I showed her the flowers. She rose and set the book aside.

"That's very kind of Doris, and of you to bring them. They're lovely. I'm certain Mike will enjoy them."

She placed the flowers next to a bouquet of light pink roses on a table by the window where they could be seen but out of the way. I looked at Carlson. His face was puffy and so heavily bruised he looked more black than white. Though the bruising was starting to turn a sickly yellow at the edges. His forearms were equally bruised as if he tried to defend himself, and his wrists looked like he'd been tied. I turned to Mrs. Duquesne.

"How is he?"

"Better. He opened his eyes for the first time about an hour ago. He smiled at me. His doctor checked him. He has a concussion among other injuries. Needs to rest, mostly. I was reading to him when he awoke. He's sleeping now. Rachel Cord? You're the private detective Doris speaks about, aren't you?"

"Yes, I am. Doris asked me to help find out why Carlson was attacked. May I ask you some questions?"

"I don't know I know anything that would help."

"I understand you've known him a long time. Just telling me about him could be helpful."

"He's resting. I'd hate for our talking to disturb him."

"We could talk in the visitors lounge or go to the cafeteria. Have you had lunch? I'd be happy to buy."

"Thank you, but I brought sandwiches. We could have coffee, though. The nurses will keep an eye on him."

We sat at the cafeteria windows looking at a courtyard. Mrs. Duquesne with her tuna salad sandwiches and coffee, and me with a burger, fries and diet soda.

"How long have you known Mr. Carlson, Mrs. Duquesne?"

"Call me Edna. I stopped being Mrs. Duquesne when I retired. Horus and I bought our home in 1984. That's when we met Mike and his mother, Abigail. She had Alzheimer's. Mike took care of her."

Had he always lived with his mother?"

"Oh, no. He retired from the Army, in 1980, I think. He mentioned Arizona. He moved home a couple years later when Abigail needed help. She was a sweet lady. On good days her mind was still sharp. She taught English at Horace

Mann High School in the fifties, sixties and early seventies. I taught English and literature there for three years until they closed it in '86. Then I moved to John F. Kennedy High School until I retired. Abigail and I shared many memories of Horace Mann. She loved it so. It's a business plaza now."

"I know. My office is there."

"Really? Which room is yours? Maybe it was mine."

"Room 222. Actually only half of the room. The developers split many of the larger classrooms into two offices."

"Two-twenty-two was Pete Haynes' old room. He taught history."

"I love the large windows. How long did Carlson care for his mother?"

"Let me see. Abigail died in 1989. I remember it was Mother's Day. She'd been in hospice only six weeks. I was there with Mike when she passed. I guess about seven years."

"Must have been hard for him."

"It was. Hardly left the house for more than a year after. Let the yard go to pot. Then one day, all of a sudden, he was out in the yard mowing, trimming, pruning and all. Asked me if there was anything of his mother's I'd like to have. Said Salvation Army was coming to take everything else. She had a pair of vases she knew I liked. I took those and a large photograph of Horace Mann High. I still have them. He gave everything else away, even the furniture. Bought all new everything. Painted the house inside and out."

"And he's stayed there ever since?"

"Pretty much. Went several times to Arizona in the nineties for a couple of months at a time. We watered his plants and mowed the lawn for him then. Since 2000 he hasn't gone anywhere. We've kind of looked out for each other after my Horus died."

Edna filled me in on family history as told to her by Abigail on her good days and brought me up to speed on Carlson's day-to-day activities.

His house was among the first in the development built in

1948 during the post-war boom. His parents, Henry and Abigail, bought it new after moving from Ohio. His father was a World War II veteran, who completed his engineering degree on the GI Bill, and moved the family here for the local aeronautical industry. Michael was 14.

Over the decades the neighborhood went through changes from exclusively white to predominantly black to mostly Hispanic by the late nineties. Local businesses changed hands many times, and many closed giving the area a rundown feel. In 2003, its tree-lined streets piqued new interest, and affordable prices created a resurgence luring businesses back. The Carlson home was one of very few still owned by the original family.

Michael Carlson was a creature of habit. Kept primarily to himself. When he worked in the yard or was on one of his daily walks, he'd nod and smile, maybe wave, to people he saw; might even offer a "Good morning" or a rarer "Hi, how you doing?" But that was about it. He rarely stopped to chat. If he did, it would be about everyday things. Never about himself or his military experience.

Besides his walks around the neighborhood, he'd walk to Amigos twice a week for lunch. Edna would join him sometimes. The staff there knew him as *Señor* Mike. He spoke passable Spanish. Once a week, he walked to the local library, and twice a month, the twelve blocks to Piggly Wiggly with his handcart. He often used the ATM there, have lunch next door at Paula's Café or at the Kabob House across the parking lot, do his grocery shopping and then walk home.

Edna had no idea why someone wanted to hurt or rob him. We went back upstairs. A nurse came out of Carlson's room and spoke to her.

"He's awake but will probably nod off again. Doctor Adams will check in around four."

"Thank you."

Carlson's eyes opened when we entered the room. He tried to smile slightly and his hand raised a few inches. She took his hand in hers.

"You're going to be okay. Mike, this is Rachel Cord. She's a friend of Doris Garrity, from down the street. Brought you these pretty flowers. She's going to help find who did this to you."

Carlson's eyes shifted to me.

"I'm sorry to bother you, Mr. Carlson. I know you need to rest, but do you know who did this to you?"

He shook his head 'no.'

"Do you know what he wanted?"

He raised his hand to show two fingers.

"Are you saying there were two of them?"

He nodded.

"Both men?"

He shook his head; held up one finger.

"One man? The other was a woman?"

He nodded.

"Black or white?"

He held up two fingers.

"White?"

He nodded then held up one finger.

"One was white but the other one wasn't black?"

He nodded.

"Hispanic or Asian, maybe?"

He nodded and held up one finger.

"Hispanic. Was the man or woman Hispanic?"

He raised two fingers.

"Okay. The man was white and the woman Hispanic, is that right?"

He nodded.

"Young or old?"

He waggled his hand back and forth.

"Middle-aged? Thirties or forties?"

He pointed downward.

"Thirties?"

He nodded.

"And you didn't know them, never met them, right?"

He nodded.

"Do you know what they wanted?"

He nodded.

"Was it cash?"

Carlson shook his head then licked his lips. He tried to speak. Nothing came out but a couple grunts. He looked over to the counter and tried to point. Edna went and poured some water in a glass and held it for him to sip through a straw. He nodded to her and smiled. He looked at me.

"G-g-go-o," was all he managed. He began breathing heavily and closed his eyes for a moment.

"It's all right, Mr. Carlson. Don't strain yourself. Can you still nod?"

He nodded.

"Okay. Did they get what they wanted?"

He shook his head and shrugged slightly.

"Is that 'no' or 'you don't know'?"

His eyes drooped and he closed them for several moments before opening them again. He held up two fingers.

"Then, you don't know, correct?"

He nodded. His breathing was still labored and he closed his eyes again. In a few moments it was obvious he had fallen asleep.

"Edna, any idea what he was trying to say?"

"I'm not sure. It sounded like 'go' and an 'O'."

"That's what I heard too. But 'go-O' what? Go out somewhere? Go over somewhere? Go on something? Maybe he was trying to say a single word. He was stuttering trying to get it out. Maybe something like 'goal' or 'goat'. Doesn't look like he can tell us right now. Did you notice anything in particular missing from his house?"

"No, I didn't think to look with Mike lying there like that. Everything was a mess. After the ambulance took him away, the police closed the house up. I haven't been able to go back in."

I looked back at Carlson. His breathing seemed normal again and he was sleeping soundly. It was frustrating he couldn't communicate better. What did the thieves want if not cash? I really wanted a look in his house.

"Edna, do you have a key . . .? Never mind. Excuse me a moment, please."

I went out in the hall and called Wodehouse.

"This is Rachel. If you haven't been told yet, Michael Carlson has regained consciousness. He's weak and can't communicate well."

"I was just leaving to go see him."

"He's sleeping again. No idea when he'll reawaken. I found out two people attacked him: a white male and an Hispanic female in their thirties."

"Great. A white male with a Hispanic female isn't much help in this town, but it jibes with what we already know."

"What's that?"

"There were two people involved. Most likely a man and woman because of the shoe prints and fingerprints we found. Unfortunately, their prints aren't in the system as far as we know yet."

"Too bad. Anyway, I don't think they wanted cash."

"What makes you say that?"

"Carlson could only communicate by nodding or shaking his head. When I asked if it was cash, he indicated no. He wasn't able to tell me what it was though or if they found it. I think my questions wore him out."

"Probably, but they should have been my questions — not yours."

"Sorry. Look, if it's all right with you, I'd like to take Mrs. Duquesne back to Carlson's house and see if she can see what's missing. And if nothing is, it's possible his attackers may return."

"Good point. We've had patrols checking the house regularly but not under constant surveillance. I'm glad you're asking permission and not sneaking over there."

"You said not to. Said you planned to look again. I'm hoping you'll let me tag along."

"Okay. I'll wait until later to speak to Carlson. Let's meet at his house in half-an-hour but don't go in without me."

"Wouldn't think of it."

Two

Edna had me park in her driveway. I told her I'd drive her back to the hospital after we looked at Carlson's house. Capri Estates was a large complex. The homes were mainly stucco painted in Mediterranean colors with red-tiled roofs. As Doris had said most had converted garages to extra rooms while some had added a second story. Towering trees provided shade along the streets. Many of the trees showed their age. Some were missing all together while others had had limbs removed.

Carlson's home was white stucco with the front door and garage door painted a brilliant Mediterranean blue. There was some grass in the small front yard but mostly it was well-tended rose bushes. I realized the ones in the hospital room came from here.

Det. Paul Wodehouse arrived a few minutes later. We reintroduced ourselves, and he addressed Edna.

"Nice meeting you again, Mrs. Duquesne. Thank you for going through the house with us. I know it must be difficult after the way you found your friend, but I'm hoping you can see what may be missing."

"I'll try, Detective."

"I hope you weren't upset when we asked for your fingerprints last week?"

"Not at all. It was explained why you needed them."

A concrete walk led to the small, covered porch. In front of the large, square picture window sat two rockers and a small table the same blue as the door. Wodehouse made a note in his pad of the date and time and who was entering, cut the police seal, and unlocked the door with what I presumed was Carlson's key. I noticed parts of the frame had been dusted for prints. There was no entryway. We walked directly into the small living room.

To my left was an upended loveseat in front of the picture window and an end table in the corner. The left wall had two single windows. Between them was a very nice reproduction Impressionist painting of a garden hanging askew. Beneath the painting was an overturned couch matching the loveseat and another end table in the far corner. The linings of the loveseat and couch were ripped out. Their cushions lay slashed on the floor. The drawers of the end tables were pulled out and the contents spilled on the floor. There was fingerprint powder on the drawers and on an overturned coffee table next to a spilled ceramic vase of roses. Table lamps had fallen over. Another Impressionist painting of a poppy field was on the far wall above a wide bookcase. Books and VCR tapes were on the floor. The tapes pulled out of their cases. Ahead of me was the opening to the kitchen on my right. Beyond that an old TV/VCR combo unit on a low table, then the opening to a tiny hallway and the open door to a bedroom. I could see stuff on the hall floor from a linen closet. Someone had gone to a lot of trouble looking for something. The kitchen entryway was coated with fingerprint powder.

Edna wandered through the mess and picked up a wooden jar and an old meerschaum pipe. I saw three other pipes on the floor. I sniffed but didn't get the impression this was a smoker's home. Edna turned to me.

"These belonged to Mike's father. They still hold their tobacco scent. Mike said he would sit and hold this humidor to his face for hours and remember his dad. I'm sorry, Detective. I shouldn't have picked this up, should I?"

"That's all right. We're finished here. I just want you to see if there's anything missing."

Edna turned, at a loss, looking for somewhere to set the humidor. "It's such a mess."

She placed it on the bookcase. I picked up the other pipes, held them to my nose and was instantly transported back to my father sitting in his chair after a long day watching the evening news; April, our red and white springer spaniel, going grey at the muzzle, lying beside him, her head on his feet.

"I'm sorry, Detective. I don't believe Mike kept anything valuable in here."

"That's okay. We'll keep looking."

I followed Wodehouse into the kitchen. Along the left wall was a narrow floor-to-ceiling cabinet, counter, single sink, and more counter with cabinets above and below. There was no dishwasher. A coffee pot sat at the end of the counter. The cabinets were open and the goods from them either pushed around or on the floor. There was more fingerprint powder on the counter, the cabinet doors and some of the canned goods. Facing me, an open door led to what looked like a laundry and storage room. Next to the door was a gas stove. It had no hood. The wall and ceiling was yellowed with age and grease. To the right of the stove was another door that locked from this side. It was closed. Two kitchen windows faced the front of the house. In front of the windows was a dinette set with four chairs. A ceramic vase of roses was turned over on the table. The roses wilting. One chair was turned over. Beside it was dried blood. Several bloody footprints marked the floor. Two distinct patterns of different sizes. Beside me was a microwave on a rollaway cart. Next to it the refrigerator. Beyond it was an open shelf unit. Everything from it was on the floor.

Wodehouse and I checked the entire kitchen and found no indication of anything hidden or missing. Same with the laundry/storage area. The garage was through the door to the right of the stove and had stuff scattered about and boxes emptied. Looked like Carlson used it mostly as a ceramics workshop. There was an electric kiln and shelves filled with molds. Several of the molds were broken.

The house had no basement. Though we get snow, and winter freezes, and spring floods, Capri Estates homes were built on slabs.

The hallway was so small the three of us couldn't stand in it together. Everything from the linen closet was on the floor. Edna picked up what she could and carried it to the living room. The two bedroom doors were side-by-side and the single bathroom was across from the second bedroom.

The bathroom was a simple toilet, sink, shower/tub arrangement with the plumbing sharing the same wall as the kitchen sink. A small window was over the tub. The hamper had been emptied and thrown in the tub. The thieves had pulled the medicine cabinet out of the wall to see if there was hiding space behind it. There wasn't.

I looked at Wodehouse. "These people were seriously looking for something."

"I agree, and from the looks of the mess, I don't think Carlson told them where to find it."

The left hand bedroom had two windows. One in the back wall facing the doorway, and the other on the side wall near the back corner. There were two nightstands, a ripped apart double bed, a five-drawer chest and a rocker by the far window. The drawers were pulled out and belongings strewn around. Everything in a large closet with folding doors was on the floor. Still-life paintings of flower arrangements were on the walls.

Fingerprint powder had been used liberally. That stuff can be a bitch to remove. I hoped Edna wasn't planning to do the cleaning herself.

Edna searched around before turning to us. "His mother's jewel box is missing. It sat on top of the chest. It was a gift to Abigail from her husband."

"What did it look like?" Wodehouse asked.

"It was walnut with an inlaid flower design and two inner trays. About this large."

"Was her jewelry valuable?"

"Mostly sentimental, I think. Some costume jewelry, a few family heirlooms — old gold with sapphires and small diamonds — and his parents wedding and engagement rings."

Wodehouse made a note. "Anything else."

"I think Mike kept their wedding and death certificates in there as well. Maybe their birth certificates too. I'm not sure."

I picked up a lamp and set it back on the nightstand.

"Doesn't sound like it'd be worth all this mess."

Wodehouse nodded.

The second bedroom was mostly a mirror image of the first, except instead of a window in the side wall there was a single glass door leading to a patio. The room was also set up as an office/den. An overturned, comfortable chair by the back window had its lining ripped out. There were empty bookcases and two desks. One was a beautiful antique oak slant top with two storage drawers. The drawers were pulled out, as were the small ones inside the cubbyhole. Fingerprint powder was on several items. The thieves hadn't pulled out the support arms for the slant top. I did it to relieve stress on the hinges.

The other desk was a modern computer desk. There was no computer and the pulled out drawers were empty. A filing cabinet with its drawers left open leaned over unbalanced. Stuff was scattered all over the floor and we were careful where we stepped.

"Mike had an iMac and an Epson all-in-one printer."

Wodehouse made another note in his pad. I righted the filing cabinet pushing in the drawers being careful not to get fingerprint powder on me. Then I looked in the top drawer. The file folders had been gone through. Some lay on the floor. Carlson was methodical and labelled his folders. There was no way to tell what was missing without his help. Among the folders on the floor, one was marked "Receipts" and another

"Military." I flipped through the "Receipts" folder and found the purchase and documentation for the computer and printer. I gave those to Wodehouse.

Out of curiosity, I went through the "Military" folder. Carlson retired a Sergeant First Class from the Army in 1977 at Ft. Huachuca, Arizona. He was in Vietnam in 1971, the year of my birth. Before the Army, he was in the Marines for three years during the Korean War. He had a fistful of decorations listed. One document said he was married.

"Edna? Did you know Mike was married?"

"Yes, but they divorced a long time ago he said. They had two daughters. He's shown me pictures of when they were little. There should be an album here somewhere."

I put the folder in the cabinet and turned to look at the room. This was the only room without flowers or paintings of flowers on the walls. Instead, the walls held large topological maps. Actually, two were made up of smaller maps pieced together. One of these showed Ft. Huachuca, the town of Sierra Vista, and the surrounding area. The other was of the Superstition Mountains centered on a place called Weaver's Needle. The other maps gave me no clue of where they were. Carlson retired at Ft. Huachuca so I sort of understood that map, but why the others?

"Edna, do you know why Mike has these maps?"

"He was interested in treasure hunting. Said those showed where legendary lost mines and buried gold were supposed to be."

"Gold? Mike tried to say 'go-O.' Go-Old. Gold. That may be what he was trying to tell us?"

Wodehouse looked confused. "What are you talking about?"

"Carlson tried to tell us something, but all he could manage to say was 'go-O.' I thought he was stuttering. Maybe he was trying to say gold. Edna, did Mike have any gold?"

"I hadn't thought of that. It's possible. He had two large nuggets he found panning for gold in Arizona. Laughed about it. Said they were his *big* strike."

"Where did he keep them?"

"One he gave to me years ago. I haven't looked at it in ages. The other was attached to his key ring."

Wodehouse pulled keys from his pocket. There were only two on the ring: the key to the front door and a padlock key.

"It wasn't here when we found these on the living room floor. Can you describe the nugget?"

"It was an irregular blob shiny where it had been rubbed a lot. Weighed more than an ounce and about so big. It was attached to a short chain."

"At today's prices," Wodehouse said, "that nugget alone is worth a lot."

He made notes in his pad. I made a mental note to check out area gold dealers. Especially pawn shops that bought gold. The thieves could hock the computer, jewel box and other stuff at the same time. As far as Edna could tell, nothing else was missing. Leaving the room, Wodehouse stopped and looked up. I followed his gaze.

"Does the attic access look like it's been moved to you?"

I shook my head. "Not at all."

"Hang on a moment."

Wodehouse went to the kitchen and came back with a stepladder he must have gotten from the garage. He set it up and climbed it pushing the access panel in the ceiling out of his way. The attic was no more than a shallow crawlspace for insulation. Wodehouse didn't try going fully into it but just felt around. He came down holding a small blue metal box. The box was locked. It had three tiny dials on the front. A thousand possible combinations. How long would it take me to go through—

"This may be what they wanted. Mrs. Duquesne, have you seen this before?"

"No, I haven't. I have one similar where I keep my insurance papers and passport."

Wodehouse shook the box. "Sounds like paper. Too light

to be filled with gold. Still, Carlson hid it up there for a reason. Think I'll hang on to this until he can tell us what they wanted."

We didn't discover anything else missing. We went back to the porch and Wodehouse closed and locked the door. He made another note in his pad.

"Thank you, Mrs. Duquesne. This list of missing items could help us a lot."

"You're welcome, Detective. Do you know when I can start cleaning up?"

"Anytime you'd like. We're finished." He handed her the keys and entered a note on his pad. "You might want to get a professional cleaner to do the job for you. It can be a challenge. Especially the blood on the kitchen floor. Rachel, where are you off to now?"

"I'm taking Edna back to the hospital then I'm not sure what my plan is."

"I'm going there. Hopefully Carlson will be awake and can answer my questions. Mrs. Duquesne, I'd be happy to drive you. No reason for Rachel to be inconvenienced."

"Thank you, Detective."

I smiled at Wodehouse's attempt to cut me out. "Guess I'll head back to the office then. Edna, it was a pleasure meeting you."

"And I, you. Give my regards to Doris, please."

"I will."

Three

I watched **Wodehouse and Edna** drive away. I found most of what Doris wanted to know. She didn't need to fear for her family. This was a one-off. Carlson was specifically targeted. It looked like buried gold was the motive. There was no reason for me to do anything more.

Still, recalling that stubborn old man lying in a hospital bed so badly beaten made me mad. I wanted to find who hurt him. See they paid for their greed. And, admittedly, the idea of a treasure hunt was tempting as well.

Instead of getting in my car, I went to the house on the other side of Carlson's and knocked. Nobody home. I went across the street to the three houses opposite.

At the first, I met a young mother with three-year-old twins. She and her husband had been home Friday evening but hadn't heard any disturbances nor seen any suspicious people or vehicles. The house directly across from Carlson's was empty with a "For Sale" sign and a box of flyers planted next to the sidewalk. Now a three bedroom because of the converted garage, they wanted $199,500, claiming that was a bargain. At the third house, an SUV had just parked in the drive. A woman about my age and a girl in her mid-teens got out.

"Excuse me. I'm Rachel Cord. I'm a private investigator. May I ask what you know about the break-in across the street last Thursday?"

"We spoke with the police."

"I understand. I've been hired by one of your other neighbors to see if I can discover anything new."

"Who would that be?"

"Doris Garrity. She lives just down the street there."

"Trish's mom?" the girl asked.

"That's right."

"She's my best friend. I'm Abby. Is Old Man Carlson all right?"

"Abigail! I've told you not to call him that."

"But everyone calls him that."

"You're not everyone. I apologize for my daughter's rudeness. She knows better."

"I've heard people called worse."

"Still no excuse. I'm Laura Whelan, by the way. We don't know a lot about what happened, but you can come in if you'd like. I've got groceries here I need to get in the fridge."

"I'll be glad to help."

Loaded down with bags, we went in the house and were greeted by barking. The original layout was similar to Carlson's house except I could see straight through that the first bedroom opened out to some sort of family room or sunroom. On the other side of glass doors was the biggest, shaggiest dog I'd ever seen. That is, if it was a dog. It was standing with its front paws against the doors. Its huge head brushed the lintel. We went in the kitchen and put the bags on the counter.

Laura took a box out of a cupboard. "Abby, give Brighid a treat and take her out back. We'll take her for a run later."

I helped Laura put the groceries away.

"Thanks for the help. Would you like a drink? There's lemonade, tea and soda."

"Lemonade sounds good, thank you."

We carried our drinks out to the sunroom. Passing through, I saw that the first bedroom had been changed into a TV room/den. The sunroom spanned the entire back of the house. Two more sets of glass doors probably attached to bedrooms. What was left of a backyard was small with privacy fencing and a large tree in the corner. Abby was sitting astride the dog—still didn't believe it was a dog—lying on the ground.

"Is that really a dog?"

Laura laughed. "Oh, yes! Brighid's an Irish wolfhound, the largest breed. She's as gentle as a lamb, but her size and bark scare off unwanted visitors."

"That, I believe. As to unwanted visitors, what do you know about what happened to Mr. Carlson?"

"Not a great deal, as we told the police. Liam, my husband, our son John, and I watched the college basketball tournament. If you didn't see the game, my Bobcats beat Georgetown 97-83. Abby was with Brighid at the dog park with some friends. She's not a basketball fan. Liam says she must have been a changeling." Laura smiled. "Anyway, we knew nothing of the break-in until the next night. Although Abby said she saw a dark van in front of his house when she came home."

"Did she say what kind of van it was?"

"No. Just dark blue or black and tinted windows. And, no, she didn't notice the license plate or see anyone. She told the police the lights were on at Carlson's place. But that's to be expected. It was only about 8:30 when she came home. I've seen lights on there as late as two in the morning."

"How well do you know Mr. Carlson?"

"About as well as anyone on the block except Mrs. Duquesne across the street. He's basically friendly but a loner. When we moved in he came over and offered to help unload. He took a shine to Abby when he found out she shared the same name as his late mother. He brought us take-out from Amigos later that day. We took him to dinner after we were settled as a thank you, and I give him baked goods on holidays. Occasionally, Brighid and I meet him on a walk and go along together."

"Ever talk about his interests, hobbies?"

"Mostly about his roses. He has several varieties and they're all beautiful." Laura laughed. "Told me he uses only aged horse manure for them. Said it was the best for roses."

"Did he ever talk about lost gold mines?"

"Gold mines? I don't think . . ." She paused. "Yes. Once. I can't recall how long ago or how we got on the subject. Let me think. I know. He mentioned he lived in Arizona once. I'm a big Wild West fan and asked if he'd ever been to Tombstone. Said many times. It was just a half hour away. I was jealous. We got talking about gunmen and outlaws and such and then about silver and gold mines. He mentioned looking for the Lost Dutchman and others and panning for gold. Even showed me a nugget he had on his key ring. Wow. I'd forgotten all about that. Do you think that's why he was attacked? Someone thought he had hidden gold?"

"It's a distinct possibility. How long have you lived here?"

"Seven years come August. Moved in before the start of the school year."

"Thank you for the lemonade. I enjoyed it. And for taking the time to speak to me."

"You're welcome. I hope it helped. Do you know how he's doing?"

"Better, I think. He woke up today but is still in poor shape. No idea when he'll be released. Edna, Mrs. Duquesne, will most likely know how he is. She's there now. I'd better be going."

"I'll check with her on when we can see him. Think I'll bake some cookies. I'll see you out."

As much of a loner as Carlson was, he shared knowledge of his gold nugget and interest in gold mines. With how many, though? Had someone shared that information with someone else? Someone who wanted to know more? As for the van, how many dark blue or black vans are there in the area? The city has more than 300,000 people. Count the greater metro area and we're talking two-and-a-half million. So what would be reasonable? Fifty vans? A hundred? A thousand? Talk about needles in a haystack. No way was I going to track that. Leave it to the cops.

Laura mentioned Amigos, and Edna said Carlson ate there regularly. Maybe he talked about gold there too. Worth a try. Might as well catch an early dinner. Wendy and Clare had daughter/mother plans for the evening.

Amigos sits on the corner of 73rd Street and Cutter Avenue a few blocks west of the Capri Plaza Shopping Center where Carlson shops at Piggly Wiggly and uses the ATM. It shares a parking lot with a strip of small businesses, a Burger King and a Popeyes. The scent of hot fried tortillas and grilled meat permeated the lot and made my mouth water. Hoped they had good guacamole. Too many places gum it up with additives and make it spicy. I like it best as a cool creamy complement to salsas and spices with the clean taste of ripe avocado holding sway and just a bite of lime. As I went to the side entrance, a reflection in the window caught my eye. I turned.

At the other end of the parking lot, a black conversion van pulled out of a spot and went out onto 74th Street to the light at Cutter. What were the odds it was the van sitting at Carlson's house? Practically nil, but I was going to check it anyway and hurried back to my car. I hoped I'd get there before the light changed.

As I neared the end of the lot, I saw the last business was a pawnshop. Had the people in the van been in there? The light changed and the van turned west. I took the chance of losing it, parked, and went into Lou's Pawn & Loan.

The older man behind the counter was writing down something in a notebook next to an Apple iMac. Next to it on the counter was a printer. I was betting Epson. I pulled out my PI license as I approached.

"Excuse me. Did two people just drop off that computer and printer?"

"Yes, why?"

"Did they also have a wooden jewelry box, about this big, with a floral design?"

"Yes. Is something wrong?"

"A man was beaten in his home several blocks from here and those are among the missing items."

"Damn! The woman said they were hers. Said the box belonged to her late mother. They needed money to help with her funeral expenses. Gave me a real sob story. Damn! I gave them $625 because of the computer and a couple a nice diamond and sapphire pieces. Most of the jewelry was junk."

"Did you get her name?"

"Damn straight! Made a copy of her driver's license too. Always do. Can't be too careful in this business."

"Could I see the license?"

"Sure thing."

He turned the notebook he was writing in around and flipped a page. There was the photocopy of the license. Miranda Vega, 38, 15855 West Camellia Drive. I took a picture with my smartphone then plugged the address into my map app. It was about eight miles west just beyond the Outer Loop. The same direction the van was heading.

"I suggest you call the police and let them know this stuff may be stolen. Was the man with her a white male?"

"Yes, he was. What are you going to do?"

"Try to catch them if I can."

"If you do, and if you get my money back, I'll give you a 25 percent reward. Damn, I hate getting ripped off."

Four

I headed for my car and called Wodehouse. "This is Rachel. You're not going to believe it, but the bastards who beat Carlson just hocked his stuff at Lou's Pawn & Loan in the 7300 block of Cutter Avenue. They're in a black conversion van headed west less than ten minutes ago. I'll send you a picture of the woman's driver's license."

"That's great news. I'll get the word out and send a unit to her address. Then again, maybe a patrol will spot them if that's not where they're headed."

I sent him the photo as I left the parking lot, ran the red light—there was no traffic at the moment—and headed west. Traffic was light but I knew it would get heavy pretty soon as everyone left the city at the end of the workday. The speed limit along this part of Cutter was 45 miles per hour. I edged my speed up to 54 hoping the thieves wouldn't want to be stopped and were staying within the limit. As Wodehouse pointed out there was a big question mark about whether they were headed home or not, and chances slim I'd catch up.

Still, my chances of spotting them in the first place barely registered on any scale, yet it happened anyway. Maybe I'd get lucky again.

Traffic ganged up a bit as I neared the Inner Loop and the Galleria Mall. There was also Mercado Verde, an older mall of mostly Hispanic shops and fresh produce. The van could have pulled in to either, or gotten on the Loop. I kept going. Traffic thinned and the speed limit rose to 55. I jumped mine to 64. Years of local driving convinced me I could get away with nine miles above the limit but not to try for more than ten.

Near the Outer Loop it got crowded again. The Loop was the Interstate bypass around the city for destinations north, west and south. The north entrance was at a standstill. Maybe an accident on the freeway. Didn't see a black van waiting in line. Only thing to do was head for Miranda Vega's address.

My GPS sent me north on 158th Street then west on Camellia Drive. This was a working class neighborhood of small but mostly neat homes. Many of the houses had bars on the windows and doors, and several of the yards had ornate wrought iron fences. The house at 15855 was one of these. I didn't see the black van, nor had the police or sheriff's deputies arrived. I wasn't sure whose jurisdiction this was.

I'd come all this way and saw no reason to sit and wait. I went through the gate and rang the bell. A minute later a short, elderly, Hispanic woman came to the door. She gave me a look up and down through the iron screen door, and her sour expression made me think she didn't like my suit. What can I say, it was my best Phillip Marlowe look, a powder blue suit and tie with a dark blue shirt and a snap-brim Panama. I smiled.

"We no want," she said with a thick accent and started to close the door.

"*Perdóneme,*" I said using my limited Spanish. "I'm looking for Miranda Vega. Is she here?"

The woman looked behind her and called out, "*Rosita. Por favor.*"

"*Si, Lita. Un momento.*"

A young girl about 10, wearing jeans and a pink blouse with a Disney mermaid on it, looked up at me.

"Sorry. My *Lita* doesn't speak much English. Can I help you?"

"I'm looking for Miranda Vega."

"That's my mom. She's not here."

"Do you know where she is?"

The woman and girl spoke to each other in Spanish.

"Why are you asking? Are you a bill collector?"

"No, I'm not a bill collector, but it's important I find your mother. She's in big trouble."

"What kind of trouble?"

The woman interrupted again and they argued back and forth. Then the woman tried to close the door waving me away.

"¡Marchar!"

"She sold some stolen goods," I tried to say before the door closed. The girl reopened the door.

"You're a liar! ¡Mentiroso! My mother wouldn't do that!"

I pulled out my phone and showed her the driver's license. "Is this your mother?"

She looked carefully at the picture and glared. "Yes, but my mother doesn't steal!"

"This woman sold a stolen computer at a pawnshop less than an hour ago."

"Impossible! She's at work. She starts at two and doesn't get off until ten." Tears welled in the girl's eyes. "You're lying! Lying!"

I saw the reflection of blue flashing lights on the wall. I turned. A Hispanic man in a green, deputy's uniform came up the walk.

"What's going on?"

Before I could answer, the girl and the woman began speaking to him rapidly in Spanish. This was way beyond the six-week class I had in fourth grade. Considering the number of Hispanic clients and people I've interviewed over the years, I really should take some current classes. Thankfully, the deputy managed to calm them down and turned to me.

"Who are you?"

I showed him my PI license. "I'm Rachel Cord, a licensed investigator. A man was beaten and his house robbed last week. An hour ago," I showed him the picture on my phone, "this woman sold the stolen items at a pawnshop. I'm trying to locate her."

"My mother's not a thief! She's at work." I think the girl repeated it in Spanish.

The deputy looked at me unconvinced. "This is my area. I know this family. They're hard-working and honest."

"Maybe so. I'm not trying to make trouble or accuse someone unnecessarily. This is the license the pawnshop owner copied when the goods were pawned. Detective Wodehouse at West Division can vouch for me."

The deputy turned back to the woman and girl. They spoke for several minutes then he turned back to me.

"Look, I know you think you're right and that *is* Mrs. Vega's license, but they insist she's at work."

"Where is that?"

"Amigos Mexican Restaurant on Cutter. She's one of the managers."

"That's where the pawnshop is. How . . .?"

I tried to think back. I saw the van leaving the parking lot. I didn't see anyone in the lot or walking toward the restaurant. Did I only assume two people were in the van? Exactly how long had it been since they left the pawnshop before I went in? Did Vega get back to the restaurant before I parked?

"She must have gone back to the restaurant and I missed her. I followed the van."

"Never! Never!" The girl screamed, ran up and hit me. "You lie! ¡Mentiroso!"

"*Rosita, venga a la casa. Ahora.*"

The girl went in the house and the woman closed the door. The deputy shook his head.

"I don't know. Let me check something."

He moved away to make a call on his phone. Another car pulled up and Wodehouse got out. I went to meet him and filled him in on what I knew. The deputy came over holding his phone.

"Detective, I'm Deputy Agular. I don't know what's happening, but I've got Mrs. Vega on the phone and she insists she's been at work since before two today and has never left. She also says she's never pawned anything in her life. She wants to talk to you."

Wodehouse gave me a dubious look and took the phone. "Mrs. Vega? This is Detective Paul Wodehouse of the City Police Department." He moved away where I couldn't hear the conversation. When he came back he gave the phone to Deputy Agular.

"We're going to meet Mrs. Vega at the restaurant and see if we can clear up a few mysteries. Deputy Agular, I spoke with your shift commander. She agreed to let you be there too as you know the family and, if necessary, translate for some of the staff. I'd sure appreciate it."

"No problem."

Wodehouse, Agular and I convoyed back to Amigos. When we arrived I saw two patrol cars parked at the restaurant and another one parked down by the pawnshop. There was a "CLOSED" sign on the door and no customers inside. The staff was seated at three tables on one side of the main dining area and Mrs. Vega and a man were at a table on the other. There were four uniformed officers and a plainclothes detective I didn't know. The detective walked over to Wodehouse.

"Hey, Paul. Everyone says Mrs. Vega was in the restaurant all day. Never left. Even ate here. At least one staff member can account for her presence at all times."

"That's a problem. Who's the guy sitting with her?"

"Arnold Weinstein. He's a lawyer. He and his wife were having dinner — apparently they're regulars — and they overheard some of what was going on. He volunteered to advise her, if necessary."

"It is what it is. Is the pawnshop owner available?"

"Yes. Do you want him now?"

"Not yet. Let's see how Mrs. Vega reacts when I ask if she's willing to be identified. Any problems interviewing the staff?"

"Three have very little English. Another staff member translated."

"Interview them again separately. Deputy Agular, would you assist Detective Young, please? Thank you. Rachel? I'll let you listen, but if you say anything you're gone. Understand?"

"Perfectly."

"Good. Let's get started. Good evening, Mrs. Vega. Mr. Weinstein. I'm Detective Wodehouse. I apologize you had to close early. I know it's inconvenient?"

"Monday nights are slow, Detective. The biggest loss will be the waiters' tips. What I don't understand is why I'm being accused of selling stolen property. I've never done that nor would I." She looked at me. "Are you the woman who frightened my daughter?"

I glanced at Wodehouse before answering. "That wasn't my intent. I—"

"But it happened nevertheless. And you told her I was a thief. Arnold here thinks I should sue you. What do you think?"

"I didn't *say*, 'you were a thief.' I merely—"

"Enough!" Wodehouse said. "Mrs. Vega, how well do you know Michael Carlson?"

"Michael Carlson? Who is he?"

"I understand he eats here frequently. White male, age 76, retired military, speaks Spanish fairly fluently. I think he's known here as *Señor* Mike."

"*Señor* Mike. Of course. Everyone here knows him. A fine gentleman and generous tipper. I read he was attacked and in the hospital. We're all very worried for him and hope he recovers soon, but what has that to do with my being called a thief?"

"Where were you last Thursday evening?"

"As usual, I was here until after we closed. We close at ten on Thursdays. Then I went home, as usual. Mid-week traffic is usually light that time of night, so I was probably home around ten-thirty or so. I had a glass of wine with my husband and we watched the news at eleven before retiring. Why?"

"Do you or your husband drive a black van with tinted windows?"

"No. I have a silver Lexus. Juan a gold GMC Terrain. We don't own a van of any color. You haven't answered my questions. Why are you asking me all this, and why are you interrogating my staff?"

"What time did you get here today?"

"One-thirty. Why?"

"Where were you before that?"

Vega rubbed her eyes with her thumb and forefinger and pinched the bridge of her nose with irritation. Weinstein looked as if he wanted to interrupt. He was a teeth clencher.

"I got up at six-thirty to help my mother-in-law fix breakfast and get my son and daughter off to school. I then had coffee with my husband before he left for his office. I worked in the garden until ten then left for a lunch meeting with colleagues from *Latinas Unido*. We're a non-profit dedicated to furthering and advocating Latino/Hispanic culture and enhancing the lives of all *Latinas*. Then I came here."

Weinstein butted in. "Detective. Mrs. Vega has patiently answered your questions. She deserves to know of what she's being accused."

Wodehouse ignored him. "Mrs. Vega, have you ever been in Lou's Pawn & Loan? It's located at the other end of the parking lot."

"I've been in all of the businesses in the neighborhood from time to time to ask them to display posters of Hispanic events. So, yes, I've been in there. In fact, several times last month, as well as all of the other businesses sharing the parking lot, to coordinate a Mexican *Carnaval* celebration we held outside here March sixth."

"But you weren't in there today?"

"That is correct."

Something was odd. Carlson said he didn't know his attackers, but Vega knows him well. She's been in the pawnshop many times, yet the owner didn't say he knew her. Wodehouse took out his smartphone and showed Vega the picture I sent him.

"Is this your driver's license?"

"May I see that, Detective?"

Weinstein butted in again and reached for the phone. Vega put on a pair of glasses and they carefully studied the picture and whispered to each other. Weinstein returned the phone and Vega removed her glasses.

"It *looks* like my license."

"Then can you explain how *your* license was used *this* afternoon at Lou's Pawn & Loan to sell items stolen from *Señor* Mike's home?"

Vega's eyes widened and shifted from side-to-side. She looked across the room.

"Consuela. *Venga aqui por favor.*"

"*Si, Señora.*"

Vega removed a key from her jacket pocket. "*Vaya consiguen mi monedoro de mi escritorio, por favor.*"

"*Si, Señora.*"

Vega looked very unhappy, closing and opening her eyes and drumming her fingers on the table. I thought I heard her mumble "*puta.*" I looked across the room to the staff. Four were women but none could have been mistaken for Vega. Consuela returned with the purse.

"*Gracias, Consuela. Usted puede ir.*"

Vega searched through her purse but didn't find her driver's license. She took several deep breaths to contain her growing anger. She took a picture from her wallet.

"Detective, this is a picture of me and my sister, Angela Herrera. It was taken five years ago. As you can see, we look a lot alike. Many people have thought we are twins but she is two years younger. She used to work here but moved away three years ago. For '*una mejor vida,*' a better life, she said. Last week she came back.

"She visited and brought presents for the children. I think it was Tuesday. I was working. Wednesday afternoon she came here with the man she lives with."

"Do you know his name?"

"Gary Mic-something. McBride. That's it. Gary McBride. They stayed for lunch. I didn't see her again until today . . . about three, I think. They had lunch and then she asked me privately for some money. Said Gary's check was late but she could pay me back by Friday. I was very busy, a server was late, so I gave her my key and said there was a hundred dollars in my purse she could borrow. She must have taken my license too."

"Do you know what they're driving? Where they're staying?"

"I never saw their car. She mentioned the Sunrise Motel, though, when they were here last week."

"Does she have a cellphone?"

"Not that I know of."

"Just a moment."

Wodehouse went across the room and spoke with Detective Young, Deputy Agular and another officer. The three of them left and Wodehouse returned.

"Thank you, Mrs. Vega, for the information. I believe what you've said. However, to be absolutely sure, would you mind if the pawnshop owner comes in and looks at you?"

"Detective, this is absolutely ridiculous," Weinstein said. "It's insulting and—"

"It's all right, Arnold. The detective is only doing his job. No, Detective, I have no objection."

Minutes later the man I'd spoken to at the pawnshop came in with an officer.

"I'm sorry, Mrs. Vega," he said. "Of course I know you. I didn't realize that woman was using your ID. I thought she looked familiar, and of course I should have recognized the name, but I didn't. Her story was convincing and—damn—it just didn't make me think of you." He turned to Wodehouse. "Mrs. Vega, here, is definitely not the woman who sold me that computer and jewelry. I'm so sorry, Mrs. Vega."

"Quite all right, Mr. Murray. Thank you for helping. How is your wife doing?"

"Better, thank you. The physical therapy is going good. Well, goodnight."

Wodehouse gave Vega his card. "If your sister contacts you, please call me right away. Anytime. Thank you for your cooperation."

Wodehouse walked away and Vega stared at me. Weinstein still clenched his teeth. I felt the need to wipe the egg from my face but resisted the urge to raise my hand.

"My apologies, Mrs. Vega, for a false assumption."

"You know what they say about 'assume', don't you?"

"Yes, and I certainly have this time. I'm very sorry for causing your daughter and family any distress. Goodbye."

Outside, Wodehouse was on the phone. Everyone else was gone.

"We're making progress," he said as he put the phone away. "They're registered at the Sunrise as husband and wife. Haven't checked out yet. Young's waiting on a warrant to check the room for prints and possibly other evidence. They're driving a black Chevy Express with Arizona plates. We put a BOLO out on it."

"I know where the Sunrise is, and they left here in the opposite direction. Maybe they skipped."

"Possibly. The highway patrol's been notified and Traffic is checking major intersection cameras. Just have to wait it out."

"Was Carlson any help to you earlier."

"No. He'd been given a sedative to make him rest. The doctor says he getting better and stronger. I should be able to see him tomorrow and have pictures for him to look at."

We parted company and I slinked over to Popeyes with my tail between my legs, picked up some take-out and headed

---

home for a night of Scotch and mindless TV.

Five

Mindless **TV turned out** to be *Antiques Road Show* and more interesting than expected. One of the Keno brothers evaluated an antique desk that looked a lot like Carlson's. Besides the high value Keno gave it, the most interesting feature was a hidden drawer and I wondered if Carlson's desk had one too.

It was no longer my business, but curiosity is a hard cat to tame. With no pressing engagements, I called Edna if I could take another look at Carlson's house in the morning. She said she'd leave me a key under her front mat as she was going to the hospital early.

At 8:30 a.m., I entered Carlson's house and locked the door behind me. It was as messy as yesterday. There'd been no time to clean up. I carefully stepped around stuff and headed straight for the back and the antique desk. I turned on the overhead light. The desk was just as I had seen it last. The two main storage drawers pulled out and on the floor, as were two of the small shallow drawers from the cubbyhole. Another two small drawers lay on the desktop.

I felt inside the openings where the small drawers fit for a hidden catch. Yes! I found two. The first was in the top of the left hand drawer. The catch released a section of the pigeonholes above it. I removed the section and found two small hidden drawers. Inside these was a bag filled with gold nuggets and another bag with a dozen or more tiny gold bars.

The bars were shiny, looked new but had no markings.

My brain boggled over how many thousands of dollars worth I was holding when I heard a cracking noise behind me. I quickly put the bags back, slid the drawers in place and closed the slant top then turned around. The noise came from the living room. Someone had come in. I hadn't brought a gun and looked for something to use as a weapon if needed. I picked a magazine off the floor and rolled it tightly. Then took out my smartphone and dialed 9-1-1 but didn't press, "call." I considered sneaking out the side door to the patio when a man stopped at the hall doorway holding a black and yellow pry bar.

"Who the fuck are you?" he said. A woman behind him looked an awful lot like Miranda Vega.

"I'd ask you the same thing, but I'm pretty certain you're Gary McBride. And you must be Angela Herrera, Miranda's sister."

The woman's eyes bulged and her voice went tight and nervous. "Gary. Let's get out of here."

"No! We haven't got what we came for."

He came into the room. The mess on the floor made moving uncertain. I stood my ground. My finger ready to make the call on the phone I held behind me. I watched his eyes.

"I said, who are you, bitch! What are you doing here?"

"Protecting Mike Carlson's interests from scum like you."

I pressed, "call," heard a ring and a male voice asking, "Nine-One-One, What's your emergency?"

I yelled "Intruders!" and shouted the address. He rushed me raising his arm across his body to give me a backhand with the pry bar. Herrera yelled "Gary!" I dropped the phone behind me and stepped in beneath his swing jamming the end of the magazine as hard as I could into his solar plexus.

I jammed him again and he dropped the pry bar. He grasped my shoulders trying to stay standing, his legs wobbled. When I jammed him a third time, he dropped to his knees. His face turned purple, his mouth gaped. He tried to breathe. I locked my hands together smashing the side of his face with a "for the bleachers" swing. He lay sprawled on the floor.

Herrera and I stared at each other. My breath came hard and she had her hands covering her mouth. I didn't look for my phone. I faintly heard the dispatcher saying something. I called out the address again and McBride's and Herrera's names.

"You might as well sit down, Angela. You've no place to go."

She folded in the hallway, wrapping her arms around her knees, and buried her face. I looked at McBride. His eyes were fluttering and rolled up so I couldn't see the irises. He took shallow breaths. He lay curled in a fetal position, his arms clutching his middle. I picked up my phone and told the dispatcher we'd need an ambulance. I stayed on the line until a patrol unit arrived. EMT arrived shortly later. Wodehouse came in as they wheeled McBride out and as I finished making a preliminary statement.

I repeated my story to him. He told the officers he'd take me in to get a signed statement. After they left, he looked around the floor.

"As I came in, I heard the EMT telling the hospital McBride may have internal bleeding. What in hell did you hit him with?"

I pointed to the partially unrolled magazine on the floor.

"You've got to be kidding."

I picked it up and rerolled it tightly. "Think of it as a piece of broomstick."

Wodehouse shook his head. "So they came back to find Carlson's gold. Do you think he really has any?"

I smiled, opened the desk, pulled out the hidden drawers and showed him the nuggets and gold bars. On the other side of the desk were two more hidden drawers with bags of nuggets and a key that looked like it went to a bank safety deposit box.

"Think Carlson actually found a lost goldmine?"

I hefted a bag of nuggets. "Looks that way to me, but I can't explain the gold bars. They look new but have no markings."

Wodehouse held up a tiny bar, thinking. Then he looked off in the distance.

"Carlson has a ceramics kiln in the garage. Gold melts at a fairly low temp. Maybe he made these himself."

The gold was fascinating. Shiny. Tempting. We looked at each other with gleaming eyes. Smiled. Blushed. Then laughed. We put everything back in the secret drawers, rehid them behind the sections of pigeonholes and closed up the desk. We made a silent pact to never reveal what we'd found. Then I followed Wodehouse to his office so I could write out my statement and sign it.

After going home for a change of clothes and stopping for a slaw dog at Charlie's Chicago Hot Dog Stand, I finally made it to my office by mid-afternoon. Doris and Mary Farr were at the round reception center at the top of the stairs.

Mary handed me a note. "This lady called earlier, Rachel. Sounded anxious to hear from you. Said she could be reached at that number all day."

"Thanks. I'll give her a call."

"Also, we put your mail on your desk. One item was sent Express Mail."

"Good. Thanks. Doris? Have you got a minute?"

We went to my office and I gave her a rundown on what happened and the capture of McBride and Herrera.

"Oh my God!" Doris sat on one of my loveseats. "He attacked you? Are you all right?"

"I'm fine. He's not."

"Oh, Rachel. I'm so sorry. I never expected when I asked you to—"

"Not a problem.

"But you could have been hurt. Maybe even . . . I don't know."

"It's all right, Doris. I'm fine and they were caught. The important thing is there isn't someone breaking into homes in your neighborhood. Carlson was targeted."

"Why? He's an old man. He doesn't have anything."

"No, but they thought he did. He has a gold nugget and sometimes shows it off. And he talks about lost goldmines and prospecting in Arizona. One of the thieves knew this and they've been in Arizona. They thought he had more gold. Hell, they may even have thought he had a map to some mine. I don't know. But it's over. That's all that counts."

"Thank you, Rachel. Thank you. I'm so sorry this happened. What do I owe you?"

"You don't owe me anything. I said I had some hours to spare."

"But you put in all that time yesterday, and what happened this morning. It's not fair."

"Hey, I decide what's fair with my time. This wasn't official. We didn't have a contract. Just a favor between friends."

"Okay. I don't like it, but okay."

Doris left and I looked at my mail. I opened the Express Mail envelope from Gwen Ivers, a Tampa, Florida PI.

Inside was a cover letter, a 10-page report detailing her investigation, six witness depositions attesting that Milton Arthur Franks was at the Vinoy Renaissance St. Petersburg Resort & Golf Club continuously from Thursday, Dec. 3, 2009, to Monday, Dec. 7, 2009. Two of the depositions were from friends of Franks and four from hotel staff, including a waitress who served Franks breakfast every morning of his stay. There were several, date and time-stamped, grainy photographs taken from hotel security footage showing Franks in the hotel during the same period as well as four receipts with Franks' signature. Gwen included a flash drive with video of the hotel's security footage, as well as an invoice of her billable hours and expenses.

I made copies for my files and put everything in a messenger envelope, then called Speedster Messenger Service for pickup. I called Truman Pfeiffer at Andrews Pfeiffer & Associates, my lawyers, to let him know the documents were on their way. That left me only one case pending, and, hopefully, that would be resolved soon also.

I looked at the note Mary gave me. Just a name and local phone number. No message but Mary thought the woman was anxious. *Stephanie Grimes.* I didn't recognize the name or associate it with any of my recent or past cases. Only one way to find out what she wanted.

"Good Afternoon, I'm Rachel Cord. May I speak with Ms. Stephanie Grimes, please?"

"This is she, but it's Mrs. Grimes. Thank you for returning my call."

"How may I help you, Mrs. Grimes?"

"You can find whoever murdered my husband."

Six

It's not everyday I'm asked to find a killer. That's usually left to law enforcement. Though I do investigate criminal activity for clients, most of my business involves finding people—particularly runaway teens. Stephanie Grimes' comment caused a momentary brain-freeze. I wasn't sure how much time lapsed before I responded.

"Excuse me, Mrs. Grimes, but why do you think your husband was murdered?"

"My husband is not a drinker, and he doesn't drive at night, yet he supposedly died in a car accident while driving drunk. That's impossible! The police won't believe me. I need someone to find the truth. You were recommended to me. Please help me."

"I certainly understand your stress, and this isn't something to discuss over the phone. Let's set an appointment to—"

"Can you come to my home, now? I'd like you to start right away."

I glanced at the clock. It was 4:15. There was nothing on my schedule, and Wendy's and my dinner reservation wasn't until 8:00. Whether I took the case or not, Grimes needed to speak with someone and I was elected.

"Yes, I'm available. What's your address?"

Her home was in a gated community near Cramer College. The guard at the entrance checked his list, gave me a visitor's

pass to display on my dash and directions. I passed many
stately homes on one and two-acre lots, a country club and
golf course — it felt like a maze — then the street I wanted
seemed to disappear over a low hill. At the crest, I could see
the road ended about half-a-mile ahead in a shallow valley
with three or four private estates. I was amazed to see this
much open land so close in. However, the address I had was
to a house on the hillside overlooking the valley.

House was a misnomer. It appeared to be two low, wide
buildings fitted in and part of the hill. I'm not architecturally
inclined, but *Prairie Style* came to mind as I followed the
winding, private drive. Terraces and walls were native
sandstone, long sweeping balconies railed with some rich-
colored red wood complemented the stone, and tons of glass.
The drive led me around to the back of the buildings. The
smaller building had a two-car garage and the larger a three-
car. There was additional parking for another half-dozen cars
or more.

I turned off my phone, as I didn't want to be disturbed
during an interview. A blonde woman in her twenties was
waiting for me by the walk.

"Miss Cord?"

"Yes."

"I'm Yvonne, Mrs. Grimes assistant. This way, please."

Along the path to the entrance was a garden of low
ornamental grasses with a small sitting area and a tinkling
fountain. Situated between the house and the hill behind it, it
made for cozy privacy.

The entryway was as large as my living room, and it
stepped down to a vast living area easily larger than my entire
three-bedroom condo. Beyond it was a wall of windows that
immediately drew the eye to the valley below and a
cinematographic sky. It was an hour or two before sunset, but
the rays of sunlight peaking through heavy, dark clouds were
so captivating I missed seeing the woman seated in the room.

The woman rose. I guessed her in her mid-forties despite

the dark circles around her eyes. Her short, styled hair was a deep brown with auburn highlights. She had good muscle tone and a deep tan. She wore a gray tunic and slacks with gray flats.

"Miss Cord. Thank you for coming. I'm Stephanie Grimes. May I offer you something to drink? Coffee? Wine? Anything?"

I noticed a glass of wine on the low table where she was sitting. It was a bit early in the day for me, but knowing how stressed she seemed during our brief conversation, I knew sharing similar tastes could ease anxieties.

"Wine would be fine. Thank you."

"Please join me."

The mission style furniture lent a spare elegance to the room. The butter-soft, leather cushions were a warm comfort.

"I'm amazed by your view. You must have wonderful sunsets."

"We do, but I love best the fierce storm clouds as they race by, lightning flashing."

Yvonne came and set a glass of wine and a plate of cheeses and crackers on the table then departed. The wine's color was dark ruby. As I held it to my nose, I caught intense fruity hints and spices. Its texture rich on my tongue. I didn't want to know what it was because I was sure it was beyond my budget.

"This is very nice."

"I'm glad you enjoy it."

We sat quietly for several moments sipping our wine. Mrs. Grimes probably trying to decide how to start. I saved her the trouble.

"Mrs. Grimes, why do think your husband was murdered?" It was the same question I asked earlier.

"Call me Stephanie, please."

"Very well. I'm Rachel."

" As I said on the phone, Douglas wasn't much of a drinker. More than a couple of glasses of wine or beer and he was apt to fall asleep. He rarely drank anything stronger. And he wouldn't drink and drive. Never. A drunk driver killed his mother when Doug was 13. He would never — never — put himself in that situation. Also, he hated driving at night. He's — he was — only 49, but he was already developing cataracts. So, the idea he was drunk and drove off the road at night is ludicrous."

"But the police didn't see it that way?"

"No. It was ruled an accident. But, you see, I wasn't here and didn't find out the details until after his funeral."

"Where were you?"

"In Mexico. A small village in the mountains east of Oaxaca. Quite isolated. By the time I found out about the accident, got back and made funeral arrangements, I was a total wreck. I really didn't understand how it happened."

"When did you find out?"

"Yesterday. I was finally getting resolved to his being gone. Trying to catch up on what I had missed. I was going through old newspapers — I always do that after a trip — and saw . . . saw the articles about Douglas. I couldn't believe it. An accident, okay. They happen. But driving drunk? At night? It made no sense."

"What did you do?"

"I called and spoke with Sheriff Ward who was quoted in the paper. We talked for quite awhile. I tried to convince him Douglas wouldn't have done that, but he didn't believe me."

"What did he say?"

"He was polite. I believe he was trying to be as helpful as possible to a distressed widow. He tried to assure me that the investigation and autopsy reports were thorough and complete and read me several parts. Basically, he said the matter was closed without more substantiation than my personal belief."

"I see. When and where did the accident occur?"

"After midnight on the 14th in Washaw County."

"That's pretty far west. What was he doing there?"

"He and his partners take a week to go fishing every year to get away from business and clear their heads."

"Were they in the car with him? Had they been drinking?"

"No. That's strange too. Usually they all ride together. But this year Doug took his own car. I believe the others went with Rashid. Anyway, they were all at the cabin when Doug left on his own."

"What kind of car was he driving?"

"A Subaru Legacy sedan. Two thousand eight. He bought it new."

"How many partners are there?"

"Four counting Doug. They own Gimmicks. It's a high-tech software company. Doug and Darren McManus are the lead program designers. Harold Cochran handles marketing and Rashid Suliman is the company's chief financial officer."

"And they were all together on this trip?"

"That's correct."

"Have you spoken with them?"

"Yes, but they say pretty much what the sheriff told me. That all of them drank heavily that night, including Doug. That he insisted on leaving and they couldn't stop him."

"But he doesn't normally drink heavily."

"That's right."

"Did they explain why they drank so much?"

"That's confusing. They claimed they were celebrating the sale or merger of Gimmicks. But I know that can't be true. Doug loved his company. It was his idea. He never wanted to be a cog in a larger conglomerate again."

"What exactly would you like me to do?"

"Find the truth. I don't believe it was an accident."

"You realize if it wasn't, his partners would be suspects?"

"Yes, I know. I can't believe that either. They're like family."

"And if it was an accident, will you be satisfied knowing that?"

"I think so. I just want the truth."

"I'd like to help you, Stephanie, but this could be more complicated than I can handle alone. Have you talked with your lawyers about it?"

"No. They also represent the company, and I'd rather not involve them."

I thought a moment. I didn't think Carmen Andrews or Truman Pfeiffer was a large enough firm and I was their main investigation choice. I took out another card and handed it to her. "There are things I can do, but I suggest you contact Marston & Marston to represent your interests. This is their card. They're a very good firm and they have their own in-house investigating team. I've worked with them before. I'd totally understand if you chose to use only their services. If you'd like to hire me, I charge $100 an hour plus expenses with a $1,000 retainer. I can start tomorrow morning."

"I would like to hire you, and I will call Marston also." She pressed a button on a remote lying on the table. Yvonne returned. "Yvonne, please make out a check to Miss Cord for $1,000 from my personal account and bring that package also."

"Yes, ma'am."

"Thank you, Rachel. I'm starting to feel a bit more in control already. What else do you need?"

"A list of people I should speak with, to start. I'll have more questions for you once I've an idea which way I'm headed."

I left with Stephanie's check, a long list of names, and a package she said was a gift. Inside I found two bottles of Beaune Grèves Premier Cru 2005. If it was the same wine I had earlier, it was probably worth two hours on the clock. A very nice gift, indeed.

I turned my phone back on when I got in the car and found one message from Edna. I called. She said Carlson was doing much better and may be released by the end of the week. I wished them both well. I headed home to get ready for dinner with Wendy. We were going to Aubergine, a vegan gourmet restaurant. The things one does for love.

Seven

Who knew textured soy faux meat could taste like the best *Chicken Parmesan* I'd ever eaten. Even the fake cheese tasted right. And in keeping with the restaurant's name, every dish included eggplant in one form or another.

Wendy and I had an excellent evening with delicious food and talking over our workdays. Things were hectic in her division at the bank with tax time coming due.

"I haven't noticed any red flags, which is good, but we need to pick up the pace. The number of clients using our tax return assistance program is greater than last year already."

I told her about my morning at Carlson's.

"Rachel, you could have been hurt. I don't want to lose you."

"The bad guys got caught and I'm okay. What more can we ask."

"Well, it's come too close in the past, as you well know."

"Can't deny that. I'll try to do better. By the way, have you heard of a company called Gimmicks?"

"A software company, right? They have a large office park on the Southside. Why?

I filled her in on what my new client hired me to find out.

"How awful. Do you think his death was intentional?"

"Too early to say. At this point, anything's possible. Just have to see what I can find. Does your bank handle their accounts?"

"No, but I wish we did. They're worth somewhere in the hundreds of millions. But, if they were our clients, you know I wouldn't divulge their affairs to you or anyone without a court order."

That was a given. While I knew Wendy could dish with the best when it came to talking about problems at work, she had a way of never revealing who or what the problem really was.

Later at home, we opened a bottle of the Beaune Grèves. It was as delish as it had been earlier, and while it didn't provide any insights into my new case or get Wendy to expose any workplace scandals, it did lead to some very satisfying, down and dirty, hanky-panky.

I spent the next morning running around town speaking with people who knew Douglas Grimes well. Most were still shocked by his death. Comments like, "Such a waste" and "He was so young," were on many tongues, but the commonest thread was confusion over how he died. Nearly everyone said he wasn't a heavy drinker, and most knew of his aversion to driving at night even if they didn't know the reason.

With Stephanie's permission, his ophthalmologist told me Grimes' developing cataracts weren't severe enough to need immediate surgery but did cause him occasional problems driving at night from glare. She said Grimes was embarrassed about having cataracts so young, but was reluctant to have the surgery for the same reason. He told her he avoided night driving as much as possible.

At the library, I went through back copies of the *Daily Record* and found three articles about his death. One was his obituary that appeared the morning of his funeral, and one was an initial brief story of the accident mentioning alcohol may have been involved. That story ran in the Monday, March 15, edition as a side item on the local section front page.

The third article, headlined "Local Software Giant Dies in Car Crash," made the bottom of the Thursday, March 18, edition front page with a jump to page 6. The gist of the story was Douglas Ulysses Grimes, age 49, died when his car failed to make it around a sharp curve and went off a bluff early March 14. According to the autopsy report, his blood alcohol level was 0.18, way above the state limit of 0.08. Grimes was alone in the car. The accident occurred about three miles from a cabin Grimes was staying at with his business partners. They were there on a fishing trip and drinking heavily before Grimes left alone. No explanation was given as to why he insisted on leaving.

Several people quoted in the story included Washaw County Sheriff Jasper Ward, Deputy Carl Tucker, County Medical Examiner Winfield Scott Horton and Harold Cochran, Grimes' partner. Neither McManus nor Suliman were quoted but were named as partners in Gimmicks.

The software company, formed in 2006 to produce and market applications primarily for business and entertainment, started with six employees, including the four partners, in a storefront of a dilapidated strip mall. Last year, the company moved into its new headquarters on a 160-acre campus south of the city employing more than 300 people. A private company, Gimmicks' estimated value was between $350 million and $700 million.

That's a whole lot of shekels even without the possibility of the company being sold. There was no mention of a "sale or merger." I looked back at Cochran's quote. "It was a good week. We decided to party that last night. Too much, it seems. Should have stopped him. Didn't realize he was so drunk."

According to his obituary, Grimes was born January 10, 1961, in Puyallup, Washington. He graduated from Stanford University with B.S. and M.S. degrees in Computer Science and joined Microsoft in 1985. Leaving Microsoft in 2002, he founded Grimoire Cybernetics, which later became Gimmicks. Grimes was survived by his wife, Stephanie (nee Miller), and his children from a former marriage, Jason and Penelope Grimes. Apparently, he had no living parents or siblings.

Stephanie believed her husband was murdered. The available evidence indicated otherwise. Would further investigation prove it one way or the other? Grimes' actions were out of character, but why kill him? My ever-cynical mentor would have asked, "Who benefits?" Was there a profit motive? I hadn't spoken with the partners yet, maybe—

My phone rang. Two people sitting close by gave me dirty looks. I shrugged apologetically, got up from the table and answered as I headed for the door.

"This is Rachel Cord. Hold a moment, please. Okay, how may I help you?"

"Rachel. John Cartwright. I understand you're working for Stephanie Grimes. She hired us this morning as her attorneys of record."

"Glad to hear it. I recommended she call you."

"She said that. Thanks for the referral. I think you and I should talk. Are you available?"

"I can be. Your office? In an hour?"

"How about an hour-and-a-half? Say, three o'clock?"

"See you there."

I went back in the library to clean up my mess then headed for a quick burger and fries before going downtown. I called Stephanie.

"This is Rachel. How are you doing?"

"All right, I think. Friends and acquaintances keep offering condolences and help. I swear if I get one more casserole I'll need another freezer."

"You could donate them to a homeless kitchen."

"Good idea. I will. Have you found out anything yet?"

"Not a lot. John Cartwright at Marston & Marston called and said you'd hired them. I'm meeting him shortly. Is there anything you don't want me sharing with him?"

"No, nothing. He said many good things about you. He suggested you could work for him on this instead of working directly for me. What do you think?"

"Let me discuss it with him. May I call you later?"

"Yes. I'm not going anywhere. I'm . . . I'm still trying to reconcile Doug being gone. I walk in a room, and I half expect to . . ."

"Are you alone?"

"No, Yvonne's here. She's been great."

"All right. I'll call later.

"Thank you for helping me. It's greatly appreciated."

"We'll talk later, bye."

The law offices of Marston Marston & Associates occupy two floors of an office tower overlooking City Park. I was shown directly into John Cartwright's office. Another man was with him. They both stood when I entered.

"Rachel. Thank you for coming. This is Bob Hammond, head of our investigative department."

Hammond was a short, balding, kindly looking man in a gray suit. His handshake was firm and dry.

"Pleased to meet you, Ms. Cord."

"Same here, Mr. Hammond."

Cartwright pointed to a sitting area by the windows.

"Why don't we relax over here? Rachel, would you like anything?"

"No, thank you. I just finished lunch. I spoke with Ms. Grimes and have her authorization to discuss my findings with you. Will this be a two-way street?"

Cartwright smiled. "For the most part, yes. We've been retained to look after Ms. Grimes' interests in her husband's company as well as to the possibility his death may not have been accidental. I suggested we take you on as an adjunct to that part of our investigation. Would you be amenable?"

"I get paid either way, and your resources are an advantage, however, I like being my own boss."

"And your methods are often unorthodox," Hammond said. His voice was soft, but he had a mischievous crinkle around his eyes.

"Sometimes."

Hammond turned to Cartwright. "John, I recommend we

share information, as needed, but keep our investigations separate. No offense, Ms. Cord."

"None taken. I agree. Where do we go from here?"

Cartwright sat forward. "Have you spoken with the partners yet?"

"No. They're on my list, as are the two wives. Suliman is single. This morning, I talked with eight people who knew Grimes well and read the newspaper accounts of his accident. What I've been told and what I've read give me two very different pictures of Douglas Grimes. That makes me suspicious, so I'm sort of circling around the partners at this point to get a feel of why one or all of them would want him dead. My first instinct is money. Stephanie mentioned a possible sale Grimes would have been dead set against. No pun intended."

"Have you spoken with anyone in Washaw County?" Hammond asked. "Or requested the accident and autopsy reports?"

"Not yet. It's a long drive. I plan to do it tomorrow as I prefer face-to-face conversations, and I want to look at the scene and the cabin."

"Save your energy," Hammond said. "We've already requested copies, and after our forensics team reads those they'll be going out there."

"Good. I wasn't looking forward to the drive. What else are you doing?"

"Getting ready for an audit," Cartwright said. "Gimmicks is a privately held LLC with surviving partners retaining sole ownership in the event of a partner's death."

"Ah, the money angle."

"Exactly. I haven't seen a copy of the partnership agreement yet—I'm waiting on a callback—but according to Ms. Grimes, in the event of a partner's death his family receives a percentage of the company's worth at the time of death. She thinks it's 25 percent but isn't sure. Four partners. Four-way split. Sounds logical, but we'll need to see what's written. An immediate audit determines the exact amount. I'll be arranging that."

"So with Grimes dead, the remaining partners get the company, and if they sell the company later, they keep the profits. Right?"

"That's my understanding."

"Stephanie said her husband would never sell. What's a tech company go for?"

"Who can say? One billion? Two? More? Depends on what they do and what another company wants."

"I can't think that high, but it looks like motive to me."

I stared out the window.

"What are you thinking, Rachel?"

"Grimes died on the 14th. The autopsy report was released on the 17th. Some tox screens may not have come back that quickly, if they were tested for at all."

"That's what our team will be looking for also," Hammond said.

"If tests were missed, would Stephanie let you exhume his body?"

Cartwright shook his head. "Grimes was cremated per his request and his ashes scattered in the lake at Gimmicks."

"If we need it done," Hammond said, "the examiner's office may have tissue and blood samples we can retest."

"Looks like you guys have got it covered. I'll go back to talking to people and see what comes up. It was nice meeting you, Mr. Hammond."

"Call me, Bob. Everyone around here does."

"I'm Rachel. John, I'll keep you informed on what I find."

Rather than head straight for my car, I walked over to City Park and sat by the empty fountain. Nearby trees were starting to bud and sprout new leaves. Building shadows blocked the sun making the chill breeze feel colder. Most of the walkers hurriedly cut through on their way from one warm spot to another. Two homeless people sat bundled on a bench in a stray ray of sunlight on the far side of the park. I took out my notepad and added what I had learned from John and Bob. I called Stephanie.

"Any news, Rachel?"

"Not enough. I spoke with John Cartwright. We'll be running separate investigations, but sharing information. He said he's arranging for an audit of Gimmicks' assets."

"Yes, I know. That's supposed to happen if a partner dies. The family gets a settlement, but not a stake or say in the future of the company."

"Sounds a bit unfair."

"It's the way Doug — all of them — set it up. It doesn't matter to me. I'd rather have Doug."

"I understand. When you say family, does that include his children?"

"Yes, I'll share whatever settlement there is equally with Jason and Penelope. Beyond that, I'll continue receiving royalties on Doug's copyrights."

"Don't those belong to the company?"

"No. Doug developed his original programs prior to the partnership. We lease exclusive rights of use to Gimmicks. The company was originally created to market those programs and develop new ones. Which they've done quite successfully."

"You said you were surprised the company was being sold or mergered?"

"Yes, of course I was. Doug said many times he wasn't interested in selling or merging."

"Did you know there were offers to buy the company?"

"Yes, and some sounded very lucrative, but Doug laughed them off."

"Did he have the final say? Or could his partners outvote him?"

"Doug could be outvoted. But it would have been to the company's detriment. His original programs are among the most popular and profitable, and probably of greatest interest to a buyer. If outvoted, we would have pulled the leases and formed a new company. The partners were well aware of that possibility."

"Could his children continue the leases or sell the copyrights as part of their inheritance?

"No. I own the copyrights outright. Doug developed them during our first three years of marriage. Said I was his inspiration. He made me co-owner of the copyrights with right of survivorship."

"Do his partners or his children know this?"

"I would think so. It wasn't a secret, but I don't know if Doug told anyone or not. I haven't."

"So the partners and his children could believe the copyrights are available?"

"I suppose."

"That could be a serious motive your husband was murdered."

"Do you believe he was murdered?"

"I'm not sure which way I'm leaning yet, but I do see profit as a possible motive. I think you considered it when you hired me."

"True. I don't want to believe it, though. These are his partners. Our friends. But I know Doug could not have died under those circumstances any other way."

"I'll stay in touch."

"Thank you."

I glumly stared at the empty fountain. I couldn't understand killing someone for money. I know it happens, even paltry amounts, but I don't understand it.

As I stared, my mind wandered. The shallow pool of the fountain filled, twinkling lights and colored streamers waved in the branches of the trees, crowds of people sang in jubilation, and I breathed in the hot fragrance of frying funnel cakes.

Six years ago, on a gay, spring night, hundreds of us gathered in this park, before this fountain, to watch 50 of our friends step into the waters to make vows of love and marriage. It was glorious and audacious.

It was a wonderful memory. Gay marriage was illegal then. Still is here. But someday. Someday.

I got up from the bench. The two homeless people were still sitting across the park even though the sunshine was gone. I walked over and saw they were a man and a woman with a small dog huddled between them. I gave them $40 and wished them well

Eight

"**E**xercise is good," echoed through me. If it hadn't, I'd stop. Exercise is sheer drudgery. To be endured. Stoically. Like it or not. I'm not against exercise, per se. I just don't find it fun. Others do. Like Wendy.

Wendy's particular passion is running. I hate it. Always have. But she gets that runner's high, that feeling of euphoria. I've never felt it, but hers often leads to passionate cuddles afterward. Which is the only reason I go along, achy knees and all. Ah, the sacrifices we make for love.

Luckily — yay — it was a cold and drizzly morning, and Wendy opted for working out in our home gym instead of running along the river. I used the rowing machine while Wendy hit the treadmill. One advantage of exercising at home is dressing any way you choose. We usually choose naked. Though Wendy wears a tight sports bra while running to avoid the jiggle jiggle.

My preference for the rowing machine, besides being easier on my knees, was it gave me a wonderfully erotic view of Wendy running. Nine years my senior and nearly six years my lover, and I never get enough of her. I closed my eyes thinking of what I'd love to do with her gorgeous, glistening—

"What?"

I'd been lustfully fantasizing and discovered Wendy, no longer on the treadmill, had said something to me. I blushed at her raised eyebrow and teasing grin.

"Sorry. I was daydreaming."

"So I see."

"Er, did I miss something important?"

Her smile broadened, and I felt myself get redder.

"You might think so. What I said was, 'Yes, Rachel, I will marry you.'"

"What?"

She laughed. I was speechless. I'd asked many times the past couple years—and again last night—only to be put off without a definitive "yes" or "no." And now—

"You still want to marry this old lady, don't you?"

"What? Oh, yes! Yes! Yes to infinity and beyond!"

I jumped up, hugged and kissed her. I couldn't have been happier. I wanted to make love right then and there to celebrate. Wendy, being more practical, said, "Showers first." We lay cuddled together later on our bed.

"We need to tell Clare. Think she'll come with us?"

"Definitely. Mother wouldn't miss it."

"Should we combine names? Like Cord-Devlin? Devlin-Cord? Cordev? Devord?"

"Never liked hyphenations. Cordev? Don't think so. Why bother with all the stupid paperwork? What's wrong with staying who we are?"

"Okay. So, where? Massachusetts requires residency. Unfortunately, California's out. There's Connecticut, Vermont, New Hampshire. How about D.C.? The Lincoln Memorial?"

"You forgot Iowa. It became legal there last year. It's only a five-and-a-half hour drive. Some of our friends could come too and help celebrate."

Five-and-a-half hours? Bullshit! Try nearly 21 years. I hadn't forgotten. I knew where Wendy was headed. I burned those bridges long ago. There was no going back.

"Keokuk is only three hours. We could go there."

"Rachel, my love, I'll marry you anywhere. But if we're going to marry, I'm meeting your family first. Warts and all.

That's my deal."

I sat in my office going over the Grimes case and getting nowhere. I reread the same note several times. *Who benefits?* I couldn't think straight. My head was still back with Wendy's ultimatum of meeting my family.

Family. Right. My family had a conniption when rumors started about me being lesbian. My father and oldest brothers, Frank and Al, took the accusations personally, feeling I besmirched the family name. My nephews and nieces teased me constantly. Except for my brother Wally and calling Mom on her birthday and Mother's Day, I'd totally cut off everyone else since turning 18. I ran off to the Army then because being lesbian in rural Iowa — or rural anywhere — wasn't acceptable. It wasn't acceptable in the Army either, but those of us with a like bent served faithfully anyway and kept it on the down low.

Damn it to hell and back again. What does Wendy expect? To be greeted with open and loving arms? Not going to happen. Not with those troglodytes. That's unfair to Mom and Wally.

Mom loves me unequivocally and nothing would change that. Her only concern was my happiness. Wally said he knew all along, and that was why he gave me his *Playboys* when he left for West Point. But Wally's probably back in Iraq. No support there. What to do? What to do? Shit. Put up with the trogs for a day or not get married?

"Cord residence."

"Hi, Mom. When are you going to get Caller ID?"

"Pumpkin! I'm glad you called. Did Walter contact you about Dad?"

"No. What happened to Dad?"

"Your father fell and is in the hospital, but he's all right."

"Fell? How?"

"He fell from a ladder and broke his hip and right arm. He'll be home in a day or two."

"What was he doing on a ladder? He's 79, for gosh sakes."

"As if that would stop him. A limb fell on the roof. He climbed up to check damage and missed a rung coming down. As Walter didn't call you, you must be calling about something else. Are *you* all right?"

"I'm wonderful. I'm getting married."

"Congratulations. It's about time."

"You do realize I'm marrying a woman, don't you, Mom?"

"Of course. Why would I presume otherwise? Does she make you happy?"

"Wondrously happy."

"Have you set a date?"

"Not yet. That's the catch. She insists on meeting the family first."

"Good for her. I like her already."

"But will anyone else? I doubt they've changed."

"True. Most are set in their ways, but things are changing, dear. Gay marriage is legal here now. We even have gay couples in Decatur County."

"Really? So, you don't think we'll be tarred and feathered?"

"Pumpkin, I won't allow it. What's her name?"

"Wendy Devlin."

"Pretty name. When are you coming?"

"Haven't decided yet. We both have busy schedules right now."

"Well, Easter's little more than a week away. Everybody'll be here. Might as well get it over with as quick as possible. 'Sides, I miss you."

"Me too, Mom. Me too."

"Let me know when you and she decide. I'll take care of everything."

"Thanks, Mom. Oh! One more thing. Wendy's vegan."

"You mean that tofu stuff?"

"That, and no meat, eggs or dairy of any type. That means no bacon in the beans, mayo in the potato salad, or butter on the corn. Maybe Easter's not a good idea."

"No. No. I'll work it out. I'm not letting a menu get in the way of seeing you. It's been too long."

"Thanks, Mom. You're right. It's been too long. You're the best. I'll call when I know we're coming. Love you. Bye."

That went pretty well. Guess I'm stuck. Too bad about Dad, but he shouldn't be climbing ladders at his age. Hope he recovers well. Many old people don't. Hate to think of him as an invalid.

I called Wendy with the news to make her happy. We agreed to discuss when we would go that evening.

Nine

Jason and Penelope Grimes, adult children from a former marriage, had flown in from Seattle for their father's funeral. According to Stephanie Grimes, they were emotionally upset by his death. The ex-wife, now Beverly Norton, remarried and living in Vancouver, B.C., had sent condolences and made a charitable gift in Douglas Grimes' memory.

It was unlikely they had any involvement in his death but might know something useful. The brother and sister had returned to Washington. Stephanie gave me their numbers. I called the daughter first and got voicemail. I left a message to please call me. I tried her brother's number.

"Fish & Wildlife. This is Jason."

"Hello. I'm Rachel Cord. I'm an investigator working for your stepmother. My sympathies for your loss."

"Thank you. Why has Stephanie hired an investigator?"

"She doesn't believe how your father died."

"I can understand that. Seemed strange to me too. Then again, I wasn't very close to my dad since the divorce. I remember he wasn't much of a drinker. He never drank when we'd go anywhere. A drunk driver killed his mother. He only drank tea or soda when he drove."

"That's good to know. Has anyone contacted you about your father's copyrights?"

"No. Didn't realize he had any. Though he did own a software company. I guess there should be copyrights or patents. Anyway, nothing was mentioned in his will. Stephanie said something about Pen and me receiving some kind of settlement from Dad's company. That's all, besides what he left in his will."

"Yes. There's an audit next week to determine the amount you, your sister and Ms. Grimes will share. Are you sure none of his partners spoke with you?"

"Just at the funeral and at his home after. Nothing about business, though. Spent some time with Darren reminiscing. He and Dad were longtime friends. Our families used to hang out together all the time. I still see his son, DJ, regularly."

"How long were your dad and McManus friends?"

"Before I was born. They met at Microsoft. Hired the same day. When Mom and Dad were divorcing, Darren and Nasha tried to smooth things over to no avail. Pen and I stayed with Mom. Everyone stayed friends, though. Dad moved east a year later and met Stephanie. Darren joined him three, four years ago to start Gimmicks. That's about all I can tell you. As I said, Dad and I weren't close. I was really pissed by the divorce."

"Well, thank you for your time. It's very helpful."

"You should talk to Pen. She probably knows more. She and Dad stayed close. Visited him and Stephanie often."

"Thanks. I left her a message to call me. Her phone wasn't answering."

"Yeah. That's right. She's really upset about Dad's death. She's cocooning at Mom's. Luckily she's on spring break. I can give you Mom's number."

"That would be appreciated."

Death affects people differently. I had no idea how Penelope Grimes would react to my calling, but I had to try. Maybe speaking to her mother first would help.

"Norton residence."

"Good afternoon. I'm Rachel Cord. May I speak with Ms. Norton, please?"

"I'm sorry. Mrs. Norton is unavailable. Would you care to

leave a message?"

"Actually, I'd like to reach Penelope Grimes. Is she there?"

"Miss Grimes is also unavailable."

"Do you know when she'll return?"

"I do not. Is there a message?"

"Yes, thank you. As I said, my name is Rachel Cord. I work for Stephanie Grimes, Penelope's stepmother. I realize this is a trying time for her, but I need to speak with Penelope about her father. It's very important. I would appreciate hearing from her as soon as possible. Here's my number."

Not exactly a dead end; just a minor roadblock. I looked at the list Stephanie gave me. I'd talked to nearly everyone but the partners and their wives. I wanted to know more about them first as they could be suspects. Stephanie emphasized I speak with Nasha McManus. I wasn't sure it was a good idea. Still, McManus knew Grimes a long time and might help me understand him better. Have to see how it plays. I called her and made an appointment to see her later in the day.

I was feeling hungry and called my police friend, Frank Taylor, to see if he'd had lunch yet. We agreed to meet at Charlie's.

For a change I arrived first at Charlie's Chicago Hot Dog Stand and put in our order: Frank's usual two Chicago dogs and fries, and one for me with a side of slaw and drinks.

Charlie's version of the classic Chicago hot dog is a bit of heaven. An oversized all-beef grilled hot dog nestled in a toasted poppy-seed bun surrounded by neon green relish, onions, chopped cucumber, tomato wedges, Greek peppers, and yellow mustard with a dash of celery salt. And his slaw is a festive mélange of green and purple cabbage, carrots and red bell pepper bathed in a non-mayo creamy sauce made from cucumbers, olive oil, lemon juice and secret seasonings. I often took a quart home to share with Wendy.

Frank arrived as Charlie finished the order. We sat at a table beneath the spreading oak tree. Frank's a big, cuddly bear with polished chocolate skin and short kinky hair that's more salt than pepper these days. His soft demeanor fools a lot of people, but underneath he's hard as rock and not one to be messed with. Unfortunately, he's retiring this summer. He and Lorraine are returning to his native Chicago. The city will be less without him, and I'll miss both of them terribly.

"What's happening, Rachel? Got problems with a case you couldn't discuss on the phone."

"Nothing like that, Papa Bear. I am trying to find out if a man was murdered or simply died in an accident, but that happened far from here and doesn't concern the city police. What I wanted to see you about is a much happier subject."

"What's that?"

"Wendy and I are getting married."

"Good for you. When?"

"The date's not set, but soon, I hope. I have business to finish, and Wendy does too. Also, she insists on meeting my family first."

"I bet you're looking forward to that."

"Right. Like looking forward to swimming with alligators."

"How long since you were home?"

"Twenty-one years this summer. I always believed like the man said, 'you can't go home, again.' But Wendy's adamant. No family, no marriage. So I guess I'll find out. Anyway, we're getting married in Iowa whether at home or somewhere else."

"It'll work out. You'll see. Let us know when and where, and Lorraine and I'll be there."

"Thanks, Frank."

We spent the next half hour enjoying our hot dogs and jawing about city issues and people we liked and some we didn't. We parted with a hug, and I headed for my appointment with Nasha McManus.

Driving along North River Drive, I suddenly realized why the address Ms. McManus gave me seemed familiar. I'd been there years ago when it was the home of Carl Cheswick. My eyes blurred and my breathing became labored. I stopped my car at the side of the road. I took deep breaths trying to relax as buried memories returned.

Cheswick and his partners, John Thornton and Gwen Archer, were involved in child pornography and money laundering. Archer and her accomplice, Calvin Tierney, raped and tortured me before I was able to kill them. The two of them were the ones providing the pornography and were also responsible for killing 11 young teens and burying their bodies at Tierney's place across the river.

Cheswick and Thornton went to Club Fed on laundering and conspiracy convictions. They managed to beat the pornography and child killing charges by laying the blame on Archer. There was no proof they knew of the porn or the where and how of its making, and she wasn't alive to defend herself.

I hadn't had a debilitating flashback in several years. My memories were mostly under control and no longer haunted me. Though my rape didn't happen at Cheswick's, it took some minutes before I could continue. I wasn't sure how I'd react when I arrived at 8715 North River Drive.

The gates were open and there was no longer a gatehouse. I headed down the winding drive, came around a curve and saw the redbrick mansion, the 18 windows on the second floor and the balconies at each end. Beyond the house a broad lawn led to a gazebo, dock and the river.

A young black man answered the door. He was so tall and lanky I couldn't tell if he were still a teen or in his early twenties.

"Good afternoon. I'm Rachel Cord, here to see Ms. McManus."

"Mom's out back on the patio. Follow me."

On my previous visit the house was total chaos. A couple hundred teens and young adults partying like no tomorrow. Music blasting from darkened rooms. Sweet smells of popcorn, marijuana, strawberry margaritas, beer and sweat.

Today was a 180-degree difference. The entry still seemed infield-sized, but there was a large mahogany table in the middle covered with plants and vases of flowers. The walls were covered with African sculpture and African-American paintings. I realized one was an original collage by Romare Bearden.

We passed through the horseshoe arch of the double staircase to the banquet room. Floor to ceiling windows the length of the room afforded panoramic views of the gardens and river. Two large statues were in the middle of the room, while at one end was a sitting area and at the other a dining table for twelve. Art covered the walls and there were more vases of flowers. Some florist was doing a blooming business. We went out through sliding glass doors to the patio beneath the second story balcony in the rear.

Nasha McManus sat at a wrought iron glass-covered table. She wore an ankle-length loose gown bare at the shoulder in a Kente cloth, multi-colored, strip-woven pattern. Her hair was cut close to the head. She had high cheekbones, deep brown Hera eyes and a sensuously long Modigliani neck. What is it about older women? If I weren't already in love and getting married . . . calm down, girl, calm down.

"Thank you for seeing me, Ms. McManus. I'm Rachel Cord."

"It's Nasha. Join me. I was expecting to see you at some point. There's iced tea and the banana bread is freshly baked. If you'd like something else, Polo will be glad to get it."

"This is fine. Thank you. Please call me Rachel."

Polo left us as she poured me a glass of tea and set a slice of banana bread on a plate. Spring flowers bloomed in the gardens, though it would be weeks before the azaleas and rhododendrons flowered. A rose garden reminded me of Michael Carlson. Have to ask Doris if he's home yet.

"You have a beautiful home. I can see you've done wonders with it."

"Thank you. It's really too large for just the three of us, but we have room for everyone for family gatherings. Have you been here before?"

Oops. Didn't mean to give that away.

"Once, many years ago for a party. I much prefer your taste to the former owner's."

"Thank you. This was his family home, I gather. I understood he had to sell because of legal problems."

"To pay his lawyers and fines. I'm not sure if he's still in prison or not. Ah, you said you were expecting to see me? Did you know about me before I called?"

"Yes. Stephanie is a close friend. She didn't believe how Douglas died. I recommended she hire you."

"Really? You realize your husband and the other partners are prime suspects if Grimes' death was not accidental?"

"Certainly. Yet that's what happened."

This was a new development. I hadn't expected a suspect's wife to suggest an investigation.

"Then why encourage Stephanie to have it investigated?"

"For her peace of mind. I agreed with her that county sheriff's department wrote it off too quickly. The examiner's report may have been incomplete. I don't want her having lingering doubts."

"How did you think of me?"

"Sonny Tristan and Jeremiah Browne recommended you."

"You know Brownie and Sonny?"

"Yes. Darren and I love the blues. We first met Sonny in Seattle. When we discovered her appearing here, we had to see her. Now we catch her whenever she's in town at Brownie's Basement Blues. In fact, we're going Saturday night."

"I didn't know she was back. Thought she was still touring Europe."

"She returned last week."

"I'll have to go see her act. I love her, too. So, what do you think of Grimes' death?"

"Of course, I can only tell you what Darren told me. He's been in knots over it. They were friends for 25 years. Started together at Microsoft in '85. Douglas left in '02 after his divorce from Beverly. When Douglas wanted to start a new company, he called Darren. Darren was ready to leave Microsoft, and we were ready for new adventure. Do you know how the company was named Gimmicks?"

"No."

"It's from the initials of the partners' names. G for Grimes. Double M for McManus. C for Cochran. S for Suliman. Add an I for ingenuity and another for invention, and a K to kick start the whole shebang."

She smiled. I bet this was an oft-repeated anecdote.

People tell their stories in their own way and time. There's little point in rushing them or trying to lead the questioning. They may forget something or hide something. Be patient. Nod and smile appropriately. Make small comments to keep the narrative flowing. There'll be plenty of time for follow-up, if needed, to steer the conversation.

"Douglas and Darren are the prime programmers. There are 26 other programmers now. Ray handles the books, but he does have two accounting programs he designed. Harry is the marketing guru. His genius sent them global. Which is one reason other companies want to buy or merge with us."

"And everyone gets obscenely rich if the company sells."

"Not obscenely. You're thinking Bill Gates and Paul Allen, or Mark Zuckerberg. Selling Gimmicks won't raise any of us to that stratosphere. And before you ask, selling or merging *was* a bone of contention. Harry and Ray were most in favor. Darren saw advantages both ways. Douglas didn't want to be eaten up by larger fish in a bigger pond."

"And the fishing trip?"

"The trips are to get away from business and recharge batteries. No work. No decisions. Enjoy life for its own rewards. Thinking up new needs and coding is both exciting and exhausting.

"This year, however, they got an offer in excess of two billion just before the trip. Harry and Ray wouldn't leave it alone. Darren said they were pissing their pants with excitement. Kept discussing it the whole trip, apparently. They wore Douglas down and he finally agreed. That Saturday night they celebrated. At least Harry and Ray were celebrating. Darren wasn't feeling any pain either. He said Douglas seemed morose and agitated, but was drinking as much as — if not more than — everyone else. They all drank much more than usual, I'm sorry to say."

Nasha paused to sip her tea.

"Darren told me that around midnight, Douglas said he was leaving. They tried to talk him out of it but couldn't. None of them were in any condition to argue or drive. Before Darren passed out, he saw Harry go out the door with Douglas still trying to keep him from leaving. The next morning they were packing when a deputy arrived to tell them of the accident and get statements. That's all I know."

"And your husband truly believes it was an accident?"

"What else could it be? But it's an accident he feels terribly guilty about. He thinks if they hadn't pressured Douglas so much all week, and if he — Darren, that is — if he hadn't drunk so much too, he could have stopped Douglas from leaving."

"Guilt weighs heavily even for things one can't control."

"Very true. And Darren is the type to have guilt trips."

"Even though Grimes was stressed, do you think he would really have drunk that much and driven? I mean, everyone I've spoken with says he didn't drink much and never drove after drinking. It seems out of character."

"It's not like Douglas, I agree. The only time I knew him getting that drunk and unreasonable was when he divorced Beverly. The divorce itself was amicable. The children never knew how much stress was on their parents. Douglas was despondent. Felt he had failed. He spent several weeks in a drunken stupor. But he never attempted to drive in that condition back then. I can't imagine how upset he must have been to drive drunk now."

"You've known Douglas Grimes a long time. What else can you tell me about him?"

"Douglas' passions revolved mostly around his work. Family often took second place. Darren can be like that too at times. I think that led to their divorce and a period of estrangement with his children. I felt he recognized it and learned from it. His marriage to Stephanie was more solid. He became closer with his daughter but not his son. Gimmicks was his other child. He didn't want to lose it. I know that."

"With his death, do you think this deal, whatever it is, will still go through?"

"I'm not sure. Darren's expressed second thoughts. Feels the deal contributed to Douglas' accident. I suppose eventually."

"Does your husband know I'm asking questions?"

"Yes. I told him when I recommended you to Stephanie, and called him when you made the appointment today. We have nothing to hide, Ms. Cord. I hope your investigation gives Stephanie closure and helps ease Darren's guilt feelings. Is there a problem?"

"To be honest, I wanted to catch the partners unaware. I was leery when Stephanie insisted I meet you. Now I understand why. I'll just have to approach things differently. Thank you for seeing me."

Ten

Stewing that McManus knew of my investigation and had probably told his partners, I headed toward my office. My phone rang. I pulled over to answer it.

"Rachel, this is Lil. You still looking for Amber Lind?"

Amber Lind was a fifteen-year-old runaway from across the river. Her parents got caught possessing and dealing drugs. Mom was in a deferred sentence drug rehab program while dad was serving three-to-five. Amber and her younger sister, Ruby, were bounced around the system before landing in the home of Jabba the Hutt.

Detective Wayne Jablowski and I weren't friends even though he helped me out of a couple tight spots. As a result, I try not to get caught on his turf across the river. I've never figured out if his dislike was my being lesbian, a female, or if he just didn't like private investigators. Whatever it was, it didn't stop him from hiring me when Amber ran away two months ago. I'd searched and put out feelers to no avail. This was my first lead.

"You better believe it, Lil. Have you heard something?"

"I know where she might be. A girl we just rescued recognized Amber's picture on the wall here."

A former prostitute, Tiger Lil runs The Lillith Society, a local organization helping children and young adults exit the sex trade business. Lil was similarly saved years earlier in New York City. This was her way of giving back.

"What's her story?"

"Tara's seventeen. Been in the game four years. Decided today to make the break and we rescued her. Said the girl in the photo is calling herself Kandy Kane. Won't tell you what Kandy's come-on line is."

"I can well imagine."

"Anyway, Kandy arrived from Dallas a week ago with two other girls."

"She out on the streets?"

"Not yet. Tara says they're getting the VIP treatment working out of a condo. Doubt it'll last long."

"Does Tara know where they're staying?"

"Would you believe a rooftop condo in your complex?"

"What?"

Lil gave me the address. My condominium complex consists of five buildings. The two nearest the river are four stories high; the three stretched out behind them are seven stories. The seventh floor of each of those buildings consists of four condos with gardens and patios. I've heard at least two of them have a swimming pool.

My and Wendy's corner condo is a spacious three bedroom, three bath on the top floor of the northeast building by the river. It was expensive, but I got a good rate years ago with a VA loan. When we became a committed couple, we refinanced with both of us on the deed. Wendy's hefty payment for her share freed funds for my personal downsizing. The idea someone was using one of the condos for prostitution was abhorrent.

Lil said Tara was scared of getting involved. That wasn't much help. The authorities needed probable cause and warrants to go in and rescue Amber and the others. If it took too long, the girls could be gone.

"Lil, can you convince Tara to tell the police what she told you so they can get an emergency warrant?"

"I'm not sure. Would her name have to be revealed?"

"She could be an anonymous CI, I think. I'll check."

I needed to call Jabba, but called Frank Taylor first. He and Jabba started out together in uniform in Chicago and stayed friends.

"Frank, it's Rachel. I've got a serious situation needing quick action."

I filled him in and he said he'd help, but didn't have any pet judges for a quick warrant. He suggested Lt. Trujillo at Sex Crimes who I should have thought of first. While we talked, Lil called back and I put him on hold. Tara would help, but only if her name wasn't released. I told Frank and called Kerri Trujillo.

"Rachel, I know you want this to happen immediately, but I need time to talk to Tara and then Judge Warner. Call you back."

I called Jabba.

"Detective Jablowski, how may I help you?"

"It's Rachel Cord. I've located Amber."

"Where? She with you?"

"Not yet, but I know where she's staying. Apparently she went to Dallas and is now here. I hate to say it, but it looks like she's involved in prostitution."

"Oh, for crap's sake! You sure?"

"'Fraid so. My tip came from another prostitute that knows her. I'm sorry."

"Where is she? I'll come get her."

"You don't have jurisdiction here, and you know it."

"As if that ever stopped you on my turf, damn it!"

"I know. I know. Look, Frank's on it as well as the head of Sex Crimes. They'll get her out."

"Yeah, in a month of Sundays, maybe."

"Leave it to the good guys."

"Says the bitch who always follows her own advice. You owe me. Tell me where she is."

I didn't answer right away. This was wrong in so many ways.

"You're right. I owe you. Meet me at Riverside Park across

from Miss Kitty's Kathouse Kabaret on River Drive. I'll take you to her. Hopefully, Frank and Lt. Trujillo will be set by the time you get here."

"I doubt it. The wheels don't run that smooth. I'll be there in an hour."

Jabba the Hutt was on the warpath, and I didn't want to be the one standing in his way. I also didn't want to be responsible for endangering his job and pension. I called Frank.

"I understand, Rachel. Wayne's thinking like a dad, not a cop. He and Sophie spoil the kids they foster and love every one like their own. He won't back off. I'll meet you and help keep him leashed."

I drove to the parking lot across from the Kathouse to wait for Frank and Jabba. On my way, Lil called to say Tara was talking with Kerri. Just as I pulled into the lot, Kerri called to say she had her team on alert and she was taking warrants for child endangerment to be signed by Judge Warner. I could only hope the cavalry arrived before Jabba went Rambo.

While I waited, I studied the new Kathouse, a sleek modern building and far cry from its former warehouse at the same location. It sported its original green neon winking cat sign and was still a popular nightspot. The Kat puts on a nightly, song, dance and comedy revue heavy with political satire and sexual innuendo. The performers are drag queens and transsexuals.

The former manager, Margo Lane, has his own club in New York's Tribeca district. A few years back, he and I had a weird, obsessive relationship despite his only liking men and me women. We discovered his voice could hit a particularly low pitch that not only turned me on but brought on orgasmic ecstasy as well. When he moved east, he gave me a CD of erotic poetry with him narrating in that special voice. Wendy and I listen to it occasionally when we're in a particularly randy mood. The mere thought of it made me tingle.

Frank arrived a few minutes later, and not long after, Jabba roared into the lot. The man that got out of the car surprised me. I hadn't seen Jabba in years. He hired me over the phone and emailed Amber's photos. When we first met he must have weighed well over 300 lbs. This version was half the man he used to be.

"Hey, Frank. Didn't expect you here. You got the warrant, or did tits for brains call you to hold her hand?"

"Make nice, Wayne. Lt. Trujillo's getting the warrants signed now. We're doing you a favor letting you be here."

"Yeah, right. It's my girl jammed up. No way I'm not freeing her."

"Wayne, my turf, my rules. Otherwise, go home."

"Okay. I'll play nice, but Trillo better be quick with his warrant."

"Kerri Trujillo's a she," I said, "and she doesn't waste time when kids are involved."

Jabba looked at me. "Better hope you're right. Say, what happened to you? Get your tits caught in a wringer you couldn't get out of?"

"Something like that, Jabba. I had reduction surgery. And you, you're half the man you used to be. May have to stop calling you Jabba."

"Diet and doctor's orders. Figured if that Subway guy could do it, so could I. And what's always with the Jabba crap?"

Frank was laughing. "Wayne, you ever see the *Star Wars* films?"

"I don't watch sci-fi crap."

"There's a character in them called Jabba the Hutt. A gargantuan slug."

Jabba looked at me again. "Thanks. Okay, time's wasting. Where's Amber?"

I looked at Frank. He nodded. I told Jabba where we were going. Frank rode with him and I led them to my condo complex. There was no sign of any police. Frank called Trujillo who told him it might be another hour.

"Frank, we may not have an hour. My girl's in there. We gotta move now."

"We have to wait, Wayne."

Jabba shook his head and headed for the building entrance. Frank and I caught him in the lobby at the elevators.

"Wayne, be reasonable. We can't barge in. It isn't legal."

Jabba nodded and looked at me. "This the only in or out?"

"Stairs down the hall and others at the ends of the building."

"Shit! Too many exits to cover."

A cleaning lady who was washing the lobby windows came over.

"Actually," she said pulling a police badge from her coveralls, "all exits are covered. We have officers in the stairwells and the elevators. Hi, Detective Taylor. Glad you're here."

Frank shook her hand. "Officer Sterling, isn't it?"

"That's right. The lieutenant said to waylay you if you got here too soon."

Her phone rang. She answered, listened and hung up. "That was the lieutenant. She has the warrants and will be here in 15 minutes. If you would, please, wait in the office there so as not to cause suspicions until she gets here."

It was a slow fifteen minutes, but Lt. Kerri Trujillo arrived on the dot.

"Officer Sterling, everything set?"

"Yes, ma'am. No one's left or gone up since we got here."

"Good. Hi, Frank. Rachel. You're Det. Jablowski?"

"Yes, Ma'am."

"Pleased to meet you. I'd like you to go up with us to identify your foster daughter. Rachel, sorry, this is a police only affair. You'll have to stay down here. Let's do this."

Ninety minutes later, Jablowski and three police officers came out of the building with Amber and three other teenaged girls. They went to a waiting van. As Jabba came over to my car, more officers came out with three adults in handcuffs followed by Frank and Kerri.

Jabba shook my hand. "Thanks for all you done. We gotta go to the station for processing and statements, but Trillo says I can take Amber home tonight."

"You're welcome, and her name is Trujillo, not Trillo."

"Right. Have to remember that. She was great up there, low key but totally in command. Made the kids at ease. Thanks, again. Send me your bill. You were worth it."

"No bill. I owed you. Glad I could help."

Wendy filled our glasses with more Beaune Grèves before cozying beside me on the balcony. The day ended well and it felt good to kick back and relax with a loved one. I hoped Jabba — Wayne — and Amber were home safe with Sophie and Ruby. Wendy and I drank a toast to them.

The night was cool, the chimenea fired up, the wine warming, and we shared a large afghan. Her body felt achingly seductive. My fingers searched for an opening in her robe to caress the inside of her thigh. Her hand stopped me. She whispered in my ear.

"Later, love. We have decisions to make first."

I sighed deeply. "Right."

"How long is your Grimes investigation going to take, do you think?"

"Hard to say. Hopefully, not more than a week. There's really no way to predict how long a case takes. It sets its own schedule. I spoke with John Cartwright this afternoon. His team of forensic and auto accident experts are going to Washaw County early tomorrow. I'm trying to decide how to get info on the partners now they probably know about me."

"It does seem strange a suspect's wife suggested the investigation."

"I know. That was weird, but Nasha McManus seems legitimately concerned for Stephanie Grimes. I think she sincerely believes her husband's account of what happened. She's told him about me, but I don't know if he's told his partners. That's my problem. Cartwright suggests I keep snooping and show up Monday with the audit team. See how it plays out." I sipped my wine. "What's your schedule like?"

"It's three weeks to April 15. I had to hire five more CPAs to help with our tax return assistance program. It's that popular, and we've opened 93 new accounts so far because of it. Everything else is kosher. Bart's bugging me to use some of the six weeks leave I haven't taken, but I don't want to be gone a lot before tax day. Unless some disaster occurs, I'm free any time after that but could squeeze out a day here or there. It's really dependent upon how soon you finish."

"I want it as soon as possible too. How about we elope this weekend?"

"Sounds good to me. Right after I meet your family. That's the deal."

"Okay. Okay. It was just a thought. Mom thinks Easter is good because everyone will be there. We'll get it over in one fell swoop while they're on what passes for best behavior."

"Easter seemed good to me too, when you told me earlier. We can set a wedding date after that. Mother agrees and she'd like your mother's phone number."

"Not a problem. Now, can we concentrate on something else?"

"Stop that! You'll make me spill my wine."

My fingers had gone searching again. I leaned over to kiss her. She sighed.

"You're incorrigible."

"Randy too."

Eleven

Early the next morning and feeling pleasurably contented, I walked up to the second floor of the Mann Avenue Plaza. Doris and Mary were busy at the round reception desk.

"Good Morning, Rachel. Why the big grin? What's happening?"

Mary turned and looked at me. "Wow. Someone's happy."

My smile broadened and I felt a slight warming of my cheeks.

"Indeed I am. Wendy and I are getting married."

"Great!"

"When?"

"Soon. Wendy has time off coming, and I just need to finish up a few things. I won't be taking on any new clients until after our honeymoon."

Mary handed me my messages. "Tell that to the Rizelli brothers. They want to hire you immediately."

"They've got a lot of nerve. It took a year to get paid last time. Call them and say I'm not available. Refer them to Dan Cook or Norm Fields. I think they're looking for new clients. In fact, refer all new queries to them for the time being. Thanks."

"Have you decided where you're going for the wedding?" Doris asked.

"Iowa. Wendy wants to meet my family. If that goes well,

we'll probably get married at my parents. If not, we'll find some place closer like Keokuk or Broomfield. Either way, you're both invited. I'll keep you posted."

I went down the hall to my office, put my bag on my 1930s oak teacher's desk and pulled my laptop out of the drawer. I sent an email to Fields & Cook Detectives letting them know I'd be referring clients to them. Then I started research on Douglas Grimes' partners.

IRBsearch is my main go-to for finding out anything about anybody, but I also use sites like *Whozat* and *fefoo*, and social media like *Facebook*, *MySpace* and *Friendster*. You never know what obscure bit of info will pop up where.

After four boring hours, two diet sodas and an apple fritter, I knew more about McManus, Cochran and Suliman than I cared to—and not much I wanted or needed.

Speeding tickets and misdemeanors for youthful drinking and pot—hey, who didn't—weren't exactly red flags. All were financially secure in the seven figures due primarily to the success of Gimmicks. McManus had an additional cushion— as had Grimes—from being with Microsoft when it went public. Still, $2 billion split three ways instead of four is an enticing incentive. The cliché "what rich people want is more" is a cliché because it's so often true.

My only interesting discovery was Harold Cochran being married five times and declaring bankruptcy in 1997 after his third divorce. He married his current wife, Amanda King Cochran, 29 and 22-years younger, three months after the death of wife number four. Kimberly Walcott Cochran died in a car accident in Southern California in 2003. I'd check that out later. I needed a break.

I walked the 10 blocks to Phil's English Tearoom on Cutter Avenue. The fresh air felt good and cleared my head.

As I entered, I put on a pair of two-button shorties. Phil's dress code requires ladies to wear gloves and gentlemen ties. As I tend to prefer men's suits, I could get away without wearing gloves, but I think of myself as more of a lady. The rule is silly in a way, as etiquette says to remove your gloves when eating and drinking. Common sense dictates it also as you wouldn't want to ruin a good pair of gloves. I always carry an extra pair in my bag in case of soiling. Still, Phil's rule does set a certain tone. The Tearoom is femme heaven.

Today's hostess was Twyla Wetherby, a 20-year-old beauty from Devon in the west of England. Twyla was one of several college women the Tearoom hires from the UK on one-year work/study programs in conjunction with Cramer College. She'd be returning home in the summer, then finishing studies at Cambridge.

"Hello, Ms. Cord. Nice to see you again. Would you prefer inside or the patio?"

"Patio, please. It's turned into a beautiful day. Are you looking forward to going home?"

"Yes. It's lovely here, but I miss family and friends. This way."

There weren't many dining inside. Six lipsticks jabbering away in the sitting area by the hearth with tea and cakes; a nattily dressed butch and her femme at a table in back by the black-draped portrait of Princess Di. Sitting by herself next to the French doors was Dr. Jacqueline Losey.

"Hello, Rachel. Long time no see."

True. I met Jackie and her husband, Dr. Dorian Losey, a gynecologist, more than five years ago while searching for a missing person. They were into kinky, group sex and knew the missing man intimately. Jackie made a pass at me then and later at my lover Karen Tanaka's memorial service. Karen had been an assistant professor of Fine Arts, and Dr. Jackie was a professor of psychology at Cramer. They'd known each other slightly.

"It has been a long time. What brings you this far from campus?"

"I've the afternoon off, and I'm looking for someone to nibble. You available?" She gave me her cat eating the canary grin.

"'Fraid not." Not now. Not ever.

Twyla led me to a quiet table next to the garden.

"Ms. Cord? The lady you spoke with was chirpsing me if I wanted a bit of a do later. What's your take?"

Twyla was wearing a cameo on a black ribbon choker. Tearoom code for a staff member amenable to dating. What to tell her?

"Up to you. I really don't know her that well. She's married, but I understand she's not particularly exclusive with her playmates, their gender or practices."

"Hmm. Maybe I'll pass. Would you like the waitress to bring you tea when she comes to take your order?"

"Yes, thank you. What flavors of oolong are available?"

"If you want iced tea, I recommend the Golden Oolong. If hot, the Competition Grade Taiwan Beauty is particularly good. Very creamy and peachy tasting. It's my favorite."

"I'll have that."

While I awaited my tea, I looked at the menu and decided on a BLT on rye for a light lunch. Wendy would prefer the TLT with smoked tempeh strips instead of bacon. But as she wasn't here, she didn't need to know.

The patio was about half full of couples and foursomes. Fortunately, there were no men. It was too soon for the tourist trade who flock here — dragging their husbands along — for high tea and English atmosphere. In the garden behind me, I heard muffled laughter. I smiled as I recalled some of my own nuzzlings with willing partners in one of the secluded, trysting corners. Too bad Wendy wasn't here.

Across the patio, Elspeth Glencannon, co-owner of Phil's, was seated with three young ladies wearing the standard staff outfit of black tuxedo pants, vest and white frilly blouse. One of the women wore a cameo choker. They were probably new, as I hadn't seen them before. When they finished talking, the young women left and Elspeth saw me. She came over as my sandwich arrived.

"Rachel, love. Great to see you. How are you?"

I loved her Highland tones and the way she rolled the R in my name.

"Fine, Elspeth. And you?"

"Doing well, thank you."

"Sit, please. I've exciting news. Wendy and I are getting married."

"Good on you! When?"

"Soon. Home in Iowa."

"That's grand. Can we throw you a party?"

"When we come back. That'd be great."

"Phil will be disappointed to miss it."

"Where is she?"

"I think she and Ellen Durant are still in Shanghai. Phil's impossible to keep track of since she retired. I'll text her the good news."

There was more laughter followed by sighs coming from the garden. Elspeth and I shared a knowing smile. We traded small talk as I ate. The waitress returned with hot water to add to my pot. The re-steeped tea was quite good and I picked up flavors of vanilla and honey I'd missed the first time. I shared it with Elspeth.

Back at the Plaza, Mary had a message for me.

"A Barbara Lange called. Said she didn't need to hire you. Just wanted to get in touch. Said she's staying at PJs and would love to see you."

"Thanks, Mary."

The only Barbara I knew from PJs was several years ago. A 14-year-old trying to look 21. She and a younger friend had helped me find another girl. I later saved Barbara from a tragic incident with a pedophile. I never knew her last name. Was this the same Barbara? When I got to my desk, I called PJs.

"Duffy's Tavern. Duffy ain't here."

I laughed. "This is Rachel Cord. Where do you guys get this stuff?"

"Hi, Miss Cord. PJs has a stack of old record albums with comedy routines and old radio shows. Do you want to speak with her?"

"I had a call from a Barbara Lange who said she's staying there. Is she in?"

"Yes. She's out back with PJs and Miss Ruth. I'll get her."

PJs and her eldest daughter Ruth run an unofficial home for runaways and tossedaways. They and the girls and boys who stay there have often helped me in locating children I've been hired to find. PJs and her family also helped me through personal issues.

"Miss Cord? This is Barbara. I don't know if you remember me. I was that mixed-up kid with black hair and purple makeup."

"I seem to recall an outrageously short red sheath too."

"That's me. I've changed a lot since then. I got back with my family and I'm now a sophomore at the University of Illinois, Springfield. I came down on spring break to thank everyone for putting up with that snotty brat. I'd love to see you, if possible."

"I can stop by before six if you'll still be there."

"I'll be here. I'll let PJs know. Seeya. Bye."

You never know how the people you meet will turn out. Looked like Barbara may be one of the lucky ones.

I rebooted my computer and searched for information on the death of Kimberly Walcott Cochran. There were three newspaper items: two on the accident and her obituary. It was a one-car accident late at night. There was no passenger. The first only described the accident without identifying the single victim and indicated alcohol was suspected. The next included her name and her blood alcohol level as 0.14. There was no indication of any other vehicle being involved. It concluded she lost control while driving drunk and had gone over a cliff on a winding road.

The articles didn't explain why she'd been drinking. Harold Cochran had been at home and offered no explanations, either. The accident occurred near their hillside home. Coincidence? Kimberly Cochran and Douglas Grimes both dying in similar drunk driver accidents? I called John Cartwright.

"Hi, John. Rachel. Is your team out at Washaw County?"

"Yes. They got there this morning and are going over the reports. Why?"

"I came across some articles saying Cochran's fourth wife, Kimberly, died in a car accident quite similar to Grimes. Thought it too coincidental. Wanted you to know. I'll email you the articles."

"I see. You think there's a connection?"

"Just a suspicion. He married his current wife pretty quickly after the death. And with Grimes' death, he stands to gain a third of $2 billion or more. Also, there's a strong possibility he left the cabin with Grimes that night."

"Thanks. I'll have my people check it out. See if they can find anything near the cabin. I doubt the county people looked. You still plan to join us Monday morning?"

"Definitely. I'll let you know if I discover anything else. Bye."

I emailed the articles to Cartwright then went back over my notes. Why had Kimberly been drinking and driving that late at night? Was she upset about something like Grimes had been upset? A niggling at the back of my brain sent me relooking at Amanda Cochran.

She was a social networking butterfly. She had accounts on *Facebook*, *MySpace* and *Friendster*. I wasn't able to access her *Friendster* account, but *Facebook* and *MySpace* were open books. She left everything public. The sites were flooded with selfie photos neatly dated and captioned and what she was doing when. I don't understand the current mentality of totally exposing your life to scrutiny by anyone and everyone. What happened to modesty and privacy? Are we all becoming Narcissus? Still, it provides a field day for investigators and voyeurs.

There was a lot of repetition. It looked like Amanda deleted nothing. I found selfies of her and Harold at Lake

Tahoe, casinos in Reno, and other places that predated Kimberly's death. Had Kimberly known about them? Was that why she was drunk that night? Had she and Harold argued? What happened then?

I had no answers. I printed out several of the photos in case I needed them later and bookmarked the site. I also printed a recent photo of Amanda with her brand new Bentley Azure. Having money has its perks. Finished for the day, I headed for PJs.

Twelve

I barely recognized the young woman who rushed to hug me. Gone was the ink-black dyed hair, purple eyeshadow and lips, the red sheath barely covering her crotch. This Barbara Lange was a complete makeover. Clean face, soft brown shoulder-length hair, jeans, and a loose UIS sweatshirt. She had grown several inches and was taller than me.

"Miss Cord, I'm so glad to see you."

"Please, you're old enough to call me Rachel. You look good."

"Thanks." She stepped back with a quizzical face. "I know it's been several years, but . . . ?"

"I look different? Must be my hair. It was much shorter back then."

She shook her head while staring at my bosom. "No, that's not . . . That is . . . I thought . . ."

I smiled. "That my breasts were so large they entered the room before I did?" She blushed. "They did. I had them cut down to a more comfortable and manageable size."

"I'm sorry. I shouldn't—"

"Posh! Forget it. They were huge. They were a heavy weight—both physically and emotionally—I'm happy to do without."

Barbara, PJs, Ruth and I sat around the kitchen table drinking lemonade, nibbling freshly baked ginger snaps and catching up. Ruth's daughters Shoshana and Rasheena were out in California at UCLA working on master degrees. Jennifer, Barbara's younger friend from years back, had been adopted by her foster family and would graduate from high school at the end of May. I made a note to be there.

Barbara said, "I've decided to major in social work because of all the help I've received. It's a hard program to get into. I'm still working on the prereqs, but as a 'been there, done that' example, I think I can make a difference in a lot of lives."

PJs and Ruth were beaming with pride. I didn't blame them. I squeezed Barbara's hand.

"Good for you. I wish you the best of luck."

"Thanks." Barbara bit a ginger snap.

"You've done well, young lady," PJs said, "and we're proud of you."

"That we are," Ruth added. "Hang in there. You'll make it."

"And I have good news too," I said. "I'm getting married."

"When?"

"Just as soon as I finish a current case. Not more than a few weeks, I hope. Wendy and I will be going to visit my parents in Iowa first."

PJs gave me a knowing look and smiled. "'Bout time you went home. You've been runaway long enough."

I nodded and smiled back. Probably blushed too.

"I'll let all of you know when and where the wedding will be if you'd like to come."

We talked a bit more and then I left to get home to Wendy. As I waited for the light at Martin Luther King, Jr. Avenue and South River Drive, a blue Bentley Azure with its top down streaked past going south. The woman driving was Amanda Cochran. Curious, I followed her and called Wendy to tell her I'd be late for dinner.

Traffic was light after leaving the city and hitting the interstate. Amanda Cochran was driving steadily ten miles over the posted limit. It didn't take long to reach the twin cities of Porcius and Quartz where she pulled into a Comfort

Inn and parked. I parked at the Hardees across the lot.

She entered the motel and I followed. She wasn't at the reception desk checking in, and no one was at the counter. I went through the lobby to the elevators and glanced down the first floor halls. She was halfway down the hall to my left and a door was just opening. A man, about 30, with blond hair, nicely built, wearing a blue tee and chinos, scooped her up with a long hug and passionate kiss. Definitely wasn't her husband and I didn't think they were related, unless they were *kissing* cousins. They closed the door. I walked down to check the room number then went over to Hardees.

I ordered a drink and large fries and took enough ketchup to qualify as a vegetable then sat by the window so I could watch the motel. I didn't believe Amanda Cochran's actions had anything to do with Douglas Grimes' death. I wasn't hired to see if she were cheating on her husband or not. I was just satisfying a curious itch. The Nosey Parker streak we all share. Especially detectives. I called Wendy again to say I'd be awhile and not wait dinner.

Ninety-eight minutes later, it was dark and the last of my fries were cold. Amanda Cochran and the man came out of the motel and went to her car. She turned and kissed him. He said something and pointed toward Hardees. She shook her head and kissed him again.

As she got into her car to drive away, movement in a black SUV parked in the Hardees lot caught my eye. What looked like a large zoom lens was sticking out the window. Was someone else interested in Amanda Cochran's activities? Or interested in the guy in the motel room?

Moments later, the SUV pulled out. As it went past, I saw a man driving and could see a glowing screen on the dashboard. Had someone placed a GPS tracker on Cochran's car and was following her? I hadn't noticed anyone on the trip down. Then again, I hadn't been looking. I dumped my trash in the bin and hurried to my car. This was getting interesting.

I caught up with the SUV a few miles north. It was going

the same, steady ten miles over the limit Amanda had been doing earlier. As we came over a rise, I thought I saw the Azure's taillights about a mile ahead. I made a note of the SUV's license plate. We kept our positions for several minutes when I decided to pass.

If I was right that he was following Cochran, he might get suspicious of another car dogging his tail. All I could see of the man as I passed was his silhouette against the glow of the screen on his dash. Couldn't recognize him.

The 30-minute drive back to the city was uneventful. I maintained a spot about halfway between the vehicles. The SUV never made a move to get closer. Friday night traffic began getting heavier and slower as we neared the city limits. Once back on South River Drive, I moved up to within a few car lengths of the Azure. I couldn't see where the SUV was behind me but felt sure it was still there. When we reached Riverside Park, I pulled into the parking area across from Miss Kitty's and turned off my lights.

A minute passed and the black SUV went by. I pulled in behind and followed. As I suspected, the SUV drove directly to the Cochran residence and stopped. I parked a couple blocks back. The SUV sat for a few moments then pulled away. I followed it downtown where it pulled into a parking garage between the Federal Building and a high-rise office complex. I did an online search of the two buildings' directories from my smartphone. The Justice Department and the IRS both had offices in the Federal Building, and the office complex contained several law firms as well as the Latimer Agency.

Edward Latimer and I move in different circles. We've only met at state conferences, and I rarely bump into one of his detectives on a case. He offered me a position once, but I prefer being independent. At last count he had more than a dozen operatives working for him fulltime. I also heard he had branch agencies in Oklahoma City and Dallas.

So who was investigating the Cochrans? The license I'd

written down wasn't a Fed plate, but that didn't mean anything.

I waited 15 minutes then drove through the garage. There was a closed off area for Federal vehicles that required a special access card to enter. I saw several black SUVs parked there. There was no way to check for the one I followed. I continued up through the parking levels. On level four, three black SUVs were parked in an area marked *Latimer Agency Only*. One had the license plate I'd written down.

Why was Latimer following Amanda Cochran? The SUV had hung far back so it was reasonable there was a tracker on the Azure. The police and Feds can do it with a warrant, but otherwise you need the owner's permission to be legal. Was Harold suspicious of his decades-younger wife? Not really my concern, but an interesting tidbit, nonetheless.

I headed home for some quality time with Wendy.

Thirteen

Saturday morning I made apple and cinnamon waffles. Wendy's favorites. I watched her dribble syrup on them and thought of how the syrup would taste if I dribbled it over her beautiful—

"Rachel! Get your mind out of the gutter. I know what you're thinking. Wasn't last night enough?"

"Is it ever?"

She didn't answer. After breakfast, we relaxed and talked some about our trip to meet my family. I was getting used to the idea, but still felt shivers when I thought about it. My phone rang. There was no name, just a local number.

"This is Rachel Cord. May I help you?"

"Good morning, Miss Cord. This is Michael Carlson."

"Mr. Carlson, good morning. You sound much better than the last time we met."

"I am. Thank you. I'm back home. They released me yesterday."

"Good. What can I do for you?"

"Could you come over here?"

"Is something wrong?"

"No. No. Nothing's wrong. I have some questions, is all."

"Sure, I can come over." I looked at Wendy. She shrugged and nodded. "It's just after eleven. Is now all right?"

"That would be fine. Thank you."

"Okay. It'll be about 40 minutes. Bye."

"What's he want?"

"Said he had some questions. Seems like a nice old man. Hope he doesn't want to pay me for anything I did."

Carlson's roses were blooming and the small front lawn had been cut. He answered my knock. The swelling was gone and the bruises on his face had faded to a jaundiced yellow. He was using a walker.

"Thank you for coming, Miss Cord. Let's go back to the office. I have a hard time getting off the couch. Doctors say I should be able to do without this walker in a couple weeks. Got a therapist coming in to help get my strength back."

The living room was totally cleaned. There was a new couch and loveseat, and a recliner had been added. Books and videotapes back in place. Paintings straightened. A vase of roses on the coffee table. I glanced in the kitchen as we passed. It was bright and cheery and newly painted.

The door to his bedroom was closed. The office was back in order and clean. His computer and printer where they belonged. The antique desk was closed and had been polished. I hadn't seen any lingering trace of fingerprint powder anywhere. That stuff's a bitch to clean up if you don't know what you're doing.

"Have a seat by the window. That chair's real comfortable. I'll take my office chair. It's easier to get out of. Got a pitcher of tea here. Would you like some?"

"No thanks, Mr. Carlson. I'm fine."

"Wanted to thank you for getting my stuff back."

"Glad I could help."

"Yeah, Detective Wodehouse told me you caught the thieves coming back in my house too." He gave me a penetrating stare. "Said you thought they came back for something they didn't find the first time."

"Well, you had indicated they were looking for gold."

"Did they find any?"

"No."

"Did you?"

"Me? How could I—"

"By being nosy."

He smiled. It was a disarming smile meant to catch the unwary. I didn't know how he could know I'd found—

"Why don't you just show me what you found, Miss Cord?"

I could argue and deny but didn't think it'd do any good. Somehow I'd made a mistake. I opened the antique desk pulling out the runners to hold the slant top. All the small drawers were back in place. I pulled out the left hand drawer, reached into the cavity, and felt for the hidden latch. When I heard the release, I slid out the section of vertical pigeonholes. I pulled out a hidden drawer and lifted out the bag of gold nuggets.

"You're right, Mr. Carlson. I was nosy. I saw a similar desk on *Antiques Roadshow* and it had a secret drawer. I *had* to know if yours did too. Thought I put everything back the way it was."

He shook his head. "You put the bag of gold bars in the wrong drawer. I figured it had to be you as nothing was missing and the thieves didn't have it. Edna didn't know about it. Nor did the police say anything about finding it."

"I'm sorry. I had no business searching."

"Water under the bridge as they say. Why don't you sit back down and let me tell you a story, Miss Cord. Sure you won't have some tea?"

"Tea would be fine and call me Rachel."

"Okay. Rachel." He settled back in his chair. "You ever hear the legend of the Lost Dutchman Mine?"

"Yes. The state park is on one of your maps there. Don't tell me you found it?"

"That's part of the story." He took a sip of tea. "Back in the mid-fifties, I was a machinist at Convair in San Diego. Great company. Great planes. Before that I was in the war—the Korean War—with the Marines. Basically, I was a seagoing bellhop on the Kearsarge, but that's another story.

"Anyway, back then I saw this movie on television about the Lost Dutchman Mine. Don't remember the title, but Glenn Ford and Ida Lupino were in it. Really good film about Spanish treasure and greed. Made me want to pack up and head for Arizona, but I had a wife, a kid, and another on the way. So the dream fizzled. Couple of years later I went back in the service. Army this time. Stayed until I retired in '77. Twenty-two years in all counting the three in the Corps.

"Lucky me, I spent my last three years at Ft. Huachuca in Arizona. Knowing I was going to retire there, I bought a small house—sorta like this one for my second wife, Shirley, and me—in Sierra Vista. I got gold fever again. All my free time those last years and a couple years of my retirement, I traipsed around searching for lost gold stories like the Dutchman's mine and other legends or doing a little panning. Think that's why Shirley left me back then. I couldn't get that gold out of my head. Shirley died in '95 of lung cancer. Went to her funeral."

Carlson turned his head rubbing his eyes, lost in thought. Drank some tea. Refilled his glass.

"Sorry. Would you like more tea?"

"I'm fine, thanks. So, did you find the mine?"

Carlson grinned. "No, the Dutchman stayed lost."

"But you found gold somewhere."

"Not exactly found. More like given to me."

"What?"

"Surprised you, didn't I? Surprised me too at the time. This was the Jones Gold Discovery on Ft. Huachuca."

"Never heard of it."

"Not surprising. Most people thought Jones made up the story or was crazed. Others thought he was mistaken about where it lay buried. The gold's existence never was officially proven or unproven."

Carlson paused to drink some tea. "In June 1941, Private Robert Jones, a black man, was with the 25th Infantry at Ft. Huachuca. On days off, he and Private Robert Mayes—some accounts say his name was Sam—would go for hikes in the canyons. One day along the Huachuca Creek streambed, Jones fell in a hole that opened under him. The hole opened a tunnel that led to a walled room stacked with metallic bricks. It was too dark to see what they were. Mayes helped Jones climb out and they went and got ropes and a flashlight. According to his story, the room was filled to the ceiling with gold bars. Some accounts include bags of gold nuggets and black bars that could have been silver.

"Jones told his story then to a lot of people, but no one believed him. He went back and chopped off a hunk of the gold with a hatchet before covering the hole and carving his initials on a large rock. He also made note of an old springhouse nearby. Supposedly he sold the chunk in Douglas down by the border and threw a big, expensive party for his friends.

"As no one believed him, Jones stopped telling the story and it faded away. When Pearl Harbor happened at the end of the year and we entered WWII, it was clean forgotten. Jones didn't go back to the site during the war. Late in the fighting, his unit went to the Pacific, while Mayes was transferred and died in combat in Italy. In 1959, Robert Jones returned to Ft. Huachuca, told his story, and asked permission to dig for the gold."

Carlson paused. "Still interested?"

I glanced at the bag of nuggets on the desk and nodded.

"Believe it or not, the Army said okay. Even provided some equipment to help him dig. Jones found the rock with his initials and the old springhouse. Using those as reference, he located what he thought was the spot he fell in and commenced digging. Found nothing, but Jones insisted it was real.

"The story made headlines. Was even written up in *Life* magazine. All in all, there were five attempts to find that room of gold. All failed. Jones died in 1968 or '69. I heard and read the stories when I first got stationed there. Even went out and looked at the site myself.

"The last search was in 1975 by a private company called — let me think now — called Quest. A lot of us would go out and watch when we had the chance. Quest used new electronic search methods. They first set out a grid search pattern over the entire area. Used metal detectors and other equipment that made a picture of what was under the ground. Their electronic search revealed what appeared to be an old shaft leading to a large chamber closely resembling what Jones described. They drilled core holes into this chamber and lowered probes to detect metal. All they discovered was the chamber was filled with silt and fill material. Probably caused by flooding after dynamite was used in an earlier search."

Carlson stood up and stretched. "Back in a minute. My bladder's not what it used to be. Help yourself to the tea."

I didn't know what to believe, but the bag of nuggets and the others hidden in the desk eased my suspension of disbelief. I freshened my tea, sat back and waited.

"Sorry about that." Carlson sat in his chair. "Where was I? Oh, yeah. You know, when Jones found that cache of gold and later went back to recover it, it wasn't like the old gold rush days where a man could stake a claim and make it rich. No, from 1933 to 1974 it was illegal to own gold bullion. Jewelers had special permits for what they used. I figured the best Jones could have got was fame and a big finder's fee. I learned later he made a deal in 1962 with Treasury for a fifty-fifty split.

"Anyway, as I said earlier, I lived in Sierra Vista. My next-door neighbor, Albert Long, retired from the Army in '46. He saw action in France in WWI and was a senior supply sergeant at Huachuca during WWII. He worked as a civilian at the post before retiring in '66. He used to laugh about my obsession over gold, but we were still friends, shared beers and swapped war stories.

"He admitted when he was younger he prospected as a hobby. Never thought about getting rich. Showed me the best finds he kept." Carlson took out his keys. "He gave me this nugget on my keychain saying, 'Here's your first gold. Hang onto it.' Then he laughed. You know, the day he gave this to me it was worth about $230. The next year the price dropped to $174. Today I could get more than $1,700. That's how crazy it can get."

He put the keys back in his pocket and sipped his tea.

"When the Jones Gold story reignited with the Quest exploration in May '75, Al told me he knew Robert Jones. Both when Jones was a private in 1941 and when he came back in 1959 as a civilian. Said he personally heard Jones talk about it outside the supply warehouse about a week after Jones fell in that hole. And spoke with him after that.

"'I never saw that chunk of gold,' Al told me. 'But tell me this,' he said. 'Where does a private who makes $21 a month get the hundreds of dollars he spent on parties and other stuff? Sure made me think he knew something.' Then Al said to me, 'But these people' — pointing toward the fort and meaning Quest—'these people aren't going to find anything. There's no gold there.' Four years later, I learned how he knew."

Carlson paused, stood and stretched. I was getting used to his breaks before revealing his next surprise. I still didn't know why he was telling me all of this. He sat back down.

"Need to move or my muscles seize. Al and I were both born in February. He on the fifth in 1900, me on the ninth in 1934. We were Aquarians. As Shirley had left me two years before, we were also both alone. Al's wife died during the thirties giving birth. The baby, a girl, died also. His only son, a year older than me, died in the Korean War. Guess that's why we were so close.

"Even though our birthdays were close together, we celebrated on each other's day. I mean why party once when you can party twice, right? For his birthday on the 5th of February 1979, I gave Al a bottle of Jameson Irish Whiskey. I hadn't paid a whole lot for it as I'd bought it at the Class VI store, but it was Al's favorite. As we enjoyed a taste that evening, Al said he'd noticed I hadn't been talking about gold or hunting for it for quite some time. I replied I hadn't noticed but it was true just the same. He asked, 'So are you over your obsession?' I thought about it awhile and finally said, 'Yeah. I guess I am.' Al said, 'Good,' and we toasted each other.

"Four days later, Al called me over to his house. When I walked in, on the kitchen table was an oblong box all wrapped prettily and tied with a bow. As I was partial to Johnnie Walker Black in those days, I figured he did me as I did him. He greeted me with a smile and said, 'Mike, I been saving this for a long time. Happy Birthday.'

"His wording didn't register at that moment, and I tried to pick up the box. I was surprised I could barely lift it. I couldn't imagine what was in it. 'What in hell is in here,' I asked. Al said. 'Open it and find out.' So I opened the box.

"When I pulled all the wrappings off, I looked at a heavy metal bar of what I first thought must be brass a foot long by about 4 inches wide and two inches thick. One end was ragged with what looked like hatchet marks. I just stood there staring at it dumbfounded. I don't know how much time passed before Al said, 'Well? What do you think?'

"I didn't have an answer. My brain couldn't absorb the possibility it could be real. Finally, Al burst out laughing. I was thinking he'd played a joke on me, when he said, 'Do you remember that chunk of gold Private Jones sold over in Douglas?' I slowly nodded, and he pointed and said, 'That's the rest of the bar.'"

Carlson tilted back in his chair and stared at the ceiling. I couldn't tell from his expression if he was serious or not. I knew his gold came from somewhere, but the idea of a room of gold was astonishing. An Aussie friend of mine would have said I was gobsmacked. Carlson looked at me.

"I know it sounds impossible, Rachel, but it's true. Al found that gold cache. Guess some would say he stole it.

"Al checked out the area Jones talked about until he found

what he was sure was the hole Jones fell in. Then he waited through the war years visiting the site occasionally to be sure it wasn't disturbed. By September 1945, Germany and Japan surrendered. Everyone was coming home and mustering out. Jones and Mayes were gone. Hardly anyone remembered that supposed stash of gold. Al wasn't ready to dig but moved the rock Jones carved his initials in to another location just in case someone else went looking.

"The next year, rumors started the fort would be deactivated. Al decided to see if the gold was really there. It was and he improved the entrance to the hole so he could get in and out easily and cover it with only a few inches of dirt to keep it hidden. From that point until the fort closed, he removed the gold nuggets and gold dust only. He retired then and got a job on post as a civilian. After the fort closed in '47, he started *prospecting* and selling off the bits of gold he claimed he *found* over in the Superstitions. When the fort reopened in '51, he got his civilian job back and began removing the gold and silver bars from the cache. By 1957, he had it all and returned the hole to a semblance of the way it was when he found it."

"So when Robert Jones returned, the gold was gone?"

"That's right, and because Al moved and reoriented the rock Jones carved his initials on, Jones dug in the wrong location. It wasn't until 1975 that Quest using new techniques located what was probably the original storage space."

"What became of the gold?"

"Al hid it. As I said, it was illegal for individuals to own gold bullion before 1974. Al had no way to dispose of it. That's why he only got rid of some of the nuggets and dust through his prospecting ploy. But even after it became legal to own, how do you unload a 50-pound bar of gold without arousing suspicions? Can't be done."

"Where is it now?"

"Most of it's still where Al hid it. Al and I continued selling the nuggets and dust. We also sold a lot of the silver.

After Al died, I've continued on my own. Which is where you come in."

"How's that?"

"When I joined the Marines, I went for training to the Marine Corps Recruit Depot in San Diego. While there, I met the sister of a buddy I trained with. Her name was Juanita Alvarez and she was 16. Her family lived down in Chula Vista just south of San Diego. We liked each other and stayed in touch after I went to Korea. When I came back, Nita and I married and I got out of the Marines. We had two daughters, Abigail and Margaret.

"I had a decent job but missed the military. I went in the Army in '58, trained at Ft. Ord and got sent to Germany. I didn't have enough rank to have my family with me officially, but I brought them over anyway and we had a tiny apartment in a little village nearby. Nita hated it there. She only lasted six months then took the girls back to California. My next assignment was to Ft. Bliss. We tried to make a go of it again, but Nita didn't like the life, and I did. We divorced in '63.

"I kept in touch for several years, but eventually lost track of them. Tried again several times to no avail. That's what I'd like you to do. I want to hire you, Rachel. Find my daughters for me, please."

"Mr. Carl—Mike, it's been more than 40 years, getting closer to 50. They probably have grown families of their own. Have they ever reached out to you?"

"No. And I understand they may not want contact. But I need to know where they are. I'm not getting any younger. This recent incident made me realize how short time can be. Look, I lead a quiet, mostly happy life. I have no debt. I own this house and two in Sierra Vista I rent to soldier families. I have my pension and Social Security and some income from selling reclaimed gold I (Carlson made air quotes) *recover* from cellphones and such. I want to know if I can help them or their children."

"If you have as much gold as you claim, you can help a

whole lot of people."

"True. I'm exploring some ideas along those lines. But I need to make contact with family. Will you help?"

"I'm currently working an important case and then taking time off to get married. It could be a month before I'm available. I could recommend someone else. I even have a good contact in California."

"I'd rather wait till you get back. I'm not going anywhere. Neither's the gold. You know things about me no one else does. I'd like to keep it that way."

"All right. In the meantime, if you'd gather any records you have, like birth certificates, social security numbers, old health records, schools attended. Mailing addresses are a big help. Even old ones. Also any letters you've kept. Pictures."

"I'll see what I've got. Social security numbers are out. They weren't issued at birth back then."

"That's okay. Whatever you have will get me started. I'll keep in touch and let you know when I'm back."

"Thank you. You say you're getting married. Have you picked out rings?"

I held up my right hand. "We plan to use the ones we already have."

Carlson got up from his chair and went to the antique desk. He opened the secret compartment on the right side and removed a bag. He handed me two tiny gold bars.

"If I may, I have a goldsmith friend who could make these into very unique rings for you and your fiancé."

"That's very generous, but I can't—"

"Please. You did a lot for me. It's my gift. Ed Buchanan's a real artist and you won't be charged as he gets any leftover gold."

His face was serious. "Thank you. Wendy and I greatly appreciate it."

Wendy stared with awe at the tiny gold bars as I told her their story. It seemed extravagant the two small bits of yellow were worth more than $3,000, but the idea of having rings made from buried treasure was enticing. We called the number Carlson gave me and made an appointment for early Sunday afternoon. In the evening we caught Sonny Tristan's act at Brownie's. We promised we'd let them know the exact date of the wedding and where.

Ed Buchanan was as old as Carlson. We introduced ourselves, and he led us out to his home studio saying, "Call me, Ed." In one corner of the studio was an antique dentist's chair. Behind it on the side walls he had old dentist equipment displayed. "Was a dentist 34 years, before I decided to retire." In the middle of the room was a large, well-lighted worktable and stools.

"Pull up a stool and set." He took two binders off a shelf and brought them to the table. "Mike says to do you something special for your wedding rings. You can look through these to see if something catches your eye. They're all my designs."

We started flipping pages looking at drawings and photos of finished rings. I pointed to one with micro beads along the edges, but Wendy shook her head. She showed me one that was okay, but didn't thrill me. I glanced up. Buchanan was sitting back on his stool, arms folded, watching us.

"If you don't see exactly what you're looking for, don't think I'll be insulted. Eighty percent of those designs are one-offs made for a specific person or couple. I don't mass-produce. Tell me this: before Mike intruded himself, so to speak, what were your plans?"

We held out our right hands. "We gave these rings to each other three and a half years ago as symbols of our love and commitment. We thought we would move them to our left hands to signify our marriage when we take our vows."

He nodded. "So these rings are already special to you."

"Very special," Wendy said.

He picked up a visor with magnifying lenses and put it on. "May I see your ring?"

Wendy slipped hers off and handed it to him. He flipped a switch on the visor and lights came on. He examined the ring carefully.

"Rose gold. Fourteen karat. 'R heart W.' 'Rachel loves Wendy,' right? You gave this to her." I nodded. "And the ring you're wearing says 'W heart R', right?" I nodded again. "May I see yours?"

Mine was snug coming off. I handed it to him. He examined it then held them together. I could see mine was a little out of round. He laid them on the table and removed his visor. He just sort of stared at them. He picked up a drawing pad and pencil and began to sketch. He worked very quickly adding color with other pencils.

"Here are a couple ideas to consider."

He laid the pad on the table. There were sketches of four rings in two patterns. One pattern showed our rose gold bands set between two bands of yellow or two bands of greenish yellow gold. The other two were in a twisted cord pattern with our rose gold as one of the spiral strands between spirals of yellow and green. I touched the cord pattern sketch.

"Is this an allusion to my name?"

He smiled. "Caught that, did you? Biggest problem I see with this pattern would be losing too much metal from your original rings to keep the bands to a comfortable size. Would hate to do that. Of course I could incorporate the leftover into some other pieces of jewelry if you'd like. Something like Celtic eternity knot brooches, perhaps. That other design would keep your original bands intact. The final rings would be a little wider but still look nice on your hands. I liked the symbolism you want to proclaim by transferring your rings from one hand to the other, so I'd like to incorporate these into any design you desire."

I nodded agreement and looked at Wendy. "That's sweet," she said. "We'd like that. Why the greenish gold?"

"First of all, I think it goes well and enhances the rose color. Symbolic meanings of green include spring, nature, and harmony. To the Japanese green represents eternal life. Take your pick."

"And yellow gold?"

"Some of the better meanings would be wisdom, enlightenment, passion, love, magic; generosity and compassion."

"As much as I'm flattered by the 'cord' design, I like the simple clean lines of the band design better, and keeping these intact."

Wendy nodded. "But I'd like to include the symbolism of both the greenish and yellow gold too."

Buchanan measured our bands width at 2mm then picked up his pad and turned to a clean page. He quickly drew more rings, colored them and showed them to us. All were five parallel bands with our rose gold as the middle followed by yellow and green on the outside. The first had bands of equal width. On the second, the outer green and middle rose bands were equal and sandwiched between them were two half-width bands of yellow. The third showed the middle rose band as the widest, the outer green bands as half-width and the inner yellow bands slightly thinner again. He marked the designs: 10mm, 7mm, and 5mm, put a star by the third and an X across the first.

"I think a variety of widths looks best," he said. "And anything greater than 7 millimeters would be too wide for your fingers. Personally I'd stay between 5 and 6 or 6.2 millimeters overall. We can play with it to see what works best."

We agreed with him and realized we'd just designed our wedding rings. He asked for the gold Carlson gave me and held the two tiny bars in his hand.

"Can you believe," he said, "that I could make enough gold leaf to cover this whole tabletop and the legs with just one half of one of these bars, or that one bar here could be stretched into a wire more than a thousand miles long? Isn't gold amazing?"

He explained our 14kt rose gold rings were an alloy of 14 parts gold and 10 parts other metals for hardness and that the color came from the amount of copper added. "More copper and you'd have red gold." He'd be doing the same to Mike's bars to bring them down to 14kt but would be using silver to get the greenish effect. "Silver and gold make a natural alloy called electrum. Been used for thousands of years. Could use cadmium for a darker color, but for me it's not worth the health risks."

His excitement was catching. The only downer was they wouldn't be ready before we left for my parents.

"I do everything myself. No helpers. Were you planning on getting married at Easter?"

"No. We'll be deciding when and where after the visit."

"Well, I might be done by," he looked at a calendar, April 7th, but I'll guarantee April 11th, two weeks from now if that'll work for you. And I've got some gold bands you can wear while you're waiting so your right hands don't feel naked."

He measured our ring fingers for both the right and left hand to be sure of a comfortable fit after we transferred them. My right ring finger was a half-size larger than my left.

"Just afore the ceremony use a tiny drop of olive oil so it'll slide off easily."

Unknowingly, we'd spent the whole afternoon with Ed and were nearly late to dinner with Clare, my rape survivor sister as well as being Wendy's mom. Which made her doubly special to me. I truly believe she and the others in our survivor group saved my sanity, if not my life. Several of us still meet to share our good and bad days and to help other survivors face their trauma.

She loved the sketch of the rings and couldn't be happier for Wendy and me. That she was thrilled to be meeting my family as well was more than I could say about myself. I was still afraid it would be a disaster. But the rings and a pleasant day with people I loved pushed back the darkness.

About 9:00, Sunday night, my phone rang. I didn't recognize the area code or number. Caller ID said, "Norton."

"Rachel Cord. May I help you?"

"Good evening, Ms. Cord. This is Beverly Norton. I hope I'm not calling too late."

"Not at all, Mrs. Norton. I appreciate your getting back to me. Is Penelope with you?"

"Not at the moment. That's why I'm calling. I was given your message when I returned and I've spoken with Jason about you."

"Then you understand why I'd like to speak with your daughter."

"Yes. I also checked you out, Ms. Cord, and know what you do for a living. I've been told you have some *unique* methods of conducting your investigations, but that—basically—you're honest, thorough, committed to your clients and caring. I also verified with Stephanie that you do—indeed—work for her. That's why I'm returning your call."

"I appreciate that. Jason told me his sister was still upset over her father's death. It's why I wanted to speak to you first. From firsthand experience, I know how even an innocent comment can cause re-experiencing a traumatic event."

"True. The person, who researched you for me, told me what happened to you several years ago. I sincerely hope you've recovered from that ordeal."

"Mostly, thank you."

"Therefore, I hope you understand why I would prefer you not speak with Pen. She and her father were very close and her emotions are still too near the surface. She's not returning to school immediately and may not finish the semester."

"I'm sorry to hear that. I wish her well. Of course I won't speak with her."

"I doubt she would be much help to you anyway. No one mentioned Doug's copyrights or talked to her about the accident."

"I admit I've been on a bit of a fishing expedition, Mrs. Norton. I'm trying to reconcile the man most people have described to me with the man who died in a drunk driving accident, and I'm not having much success. So far, only Nasha McManus has hinted to it."

"I understand. I didn't see that side of Doug either throughout our marriage or during the divorce proceedings. Washington is a no-fault state, and I thought our divorce was amicable. There were no contentious issues or infighting. It wasn't until afterward I saw how much of himself he kept bottled up inside and couldn't handle. I'm afraid Pen is too much like him in that way."

"So you wouldn't have been surprised by his actions?"

"By the man I was married to, most definitely surprised. By the man he was that following year, not in the least. I do know he started counseling before leaving Seattle. And as I've stayed in touch with Nasha, I understand his marriage to Stephanie has been more emotionally balanced than ours was. I know how much his company would have meant to him, and how much it would have eaten at him to share or lose it. He really was a good man, Ms. Cord. I only wish he had shared himself more fully when we were married. I hope that helps you."

"It does. Thank you."

"I truly hope for everyone's sake it was that part of him that led to his accident, and not some nefarious conspiracy."

"I agree. Thank you for taking the time to call. It's greatly appreciated."

"Goodnight, Ms. Cord."

"Goodnight, Mrs. Norton."

Fourteen

Monday morning, **I drove** out to Gimmicks, a mostly-glass building I thought resembled a Rubik's Cube. It sat on a rise overlooking 160 landscaped acres and a lake. From the parking lot, I saw several small sailboats skimming across the water in the morning breeze. There was a dock where two motorboats were moored. Beneath an open pavilion were racks with kayaks and canoes, and more sailboats.

I met John Cartwright and his audit team in the lobby. We were all given visitor badges. John took me aside.

"Checking out the cabin was a good idea. Bill Roberts, our forensics expert, found traces of blood on one of the steps to the porch. Probably wasn't noticed by the deputy who notified the partners as no investigation was made there. We'll need to wait for DNA confirmation, but the blood type is the same as Douglas Grimes. O positive. That leaves the possibility he was hurt or unconscious before leaving the cabin. So someone could have driven him to his death."

"Do you think it happened that way?"

"Well, unfortunately, the tire tracks of Grimes' Subaru were inconclusive. It swerved back and forth on and off the shoulder, and the brakes were used several times leaving short skid marks. It's a very windy road. However, Bill says it didn't look like Grimes used the brakes where he went off that bluff.

"Bill says if someone else was driving, they did an

extremely good job of making it look like a drunk driver running off the road. He also said the sheriff's people did a thorough investigation of the crash site and the autopsy was first rate. The car was a total wreck. We'll check it again, though, in case something was missed because it was assumed to be a drunk driving accident. The blood samples weren't tested for anything besides alcohol either. We're redoing those."

"I spoke with his former wife last night. She described a part of him I can see getting that drunk and driving off, but it'll be best if the physical evidence continues to support that theory. And I'm still leery of getting full cooperation from the partners now they know why I'm here. So, what do we do now?"

"Just as we planned. We do the audit. You snoop around as best you can."

The elevator opened. Two men and a woman came out. We went to meet them. The very tall black man in the middle held out his hand and smiled.

"Good morning, Mr. Cartwright. I'm Darren McManus. This is my partner, Ray Suliman, and Margaret Wilson is our head of HR. Our other partner, Harold Cochran, is running late. He sends his apologies and looks forward to meeting you later."

Cartwright shook their hands. "Thank you. It's a pleasure meeting you all. I look forward to meeting Mr. Cochran. As you know, we're here to do an audit on behalf of Mrs. Grimes. We'll try to be as minimally disruptive as possible."

Suliman and Wilson momentarily stared at me. If I still had my double-H bosom, I'd better understand their interest. I was as conservatively dressed as the rest of Cartwright's team in a pale gray business suit with my hair back in a neat bun. I carried a clipboard for note taking.

McManus still smiled. "Not a problem. Douglas was Gimmicks. Not only did he bring us all together as a family, he inspired us to be the company we are today. We miss him dearly, and Stephanie is a dear friend. We'll help in any way we can. Ray is our CFO as well as partner. He and Margaret will see your team gets settled and has everything they need. I'd like to invite you and Ms. Cord to my office for coffee."

Cartwright didn't miss a beat, but I'm sure my eyes widened a bit. I hadn't expected the direct reference, as we hadn't been introduced.

"Thank you. We'd like that."

McManus looked down at me from above with a Cheshire grin and held out his hand. It had to be the size of a baseball glove.

"It's a pleasure meeting you, Ms. Cord. My wife told me many things about you. If you're wondering, I'm six-nine and I did not play basketball in college."

Now I understood the stares from Suliman and Wilson. So much for quietly skulking. Might as well make the best of it.

"Nice to meet you too. Your wife and son are charming."

Half the team left with Suliman and the rest with Wilson as Cartwright and I joined McManus in his office on the fourth floor. The room was spacious with walls of glass looking out to the northeast and northwest. Like his home, the other walls were covered in African and African-American art. There was a round conference table with eight chairs and a sitting area with two couches and four armchairs. McManus' desk was a counter-level stand-up one with two computers on it looking out the northeast wall. In the distance was the city skyline. An assistant brought in a tray with coffee and a plate of assorted baked goodies. McManus sat on one of the couches; Cartwright and I chose armchairs.

"Please, help yourselves." McManus picked up a cinnamon roll. "One of my vices, I'm afraid."

Cartwright took a coffee adding cream and sugar. I didn't have anything. Didn't need the calories and wanted to stay trim for my wedding. Besides, there'd be too much food forced on me at Mom's. I cut to the chase.

"I take it everyone here knows who I am and what I've

been hired to prove or disprove."

McManus shook his head. "Only me, Harold, Ray and Margaret. Doug's death was an accident, Ms. Cord, I assure you. Nasha suggested hiring you for Stephanie's sake. The sooner she's reassured the better. I'll answer any questions I can. Later, if you'd like to wander and speak with anyone, please do. We have nothing to hide."

"Thank you, Mr. McManus."

"Darren, please."

"Your wife told me what you told her about the accident. I'd like to hear your version directly, if I may?"

"Darren," Cartwright cut in. "Please understand you don't have to tell us anything. I'm sure your lawyer would advise against it, especially as he's not here."

"I'm sure he would, but Doug was my friend as well as partner. We knew each other and worked together for more than 20 years. Our families were close. His death is hard to accept. I admit feeling guilt. That I helped pressure him into the current company situation. That I didn't stop him from drinking so much. That I drank too much as a result and didn't stop him from leaving. So, please, ask anything."

"Mr. McManus—Darren—everyone I've talked with says Grimes didn't drink much and would never drive drunk. Why this time?"

"The offer. It ate at him the whole time. He started drinking that first night. That, in itself, was unusual. I should have seen how it was affecting him. Nasha told you how he was after his divorce."

"I understand the offer was much greater than the company's current value. Why didn't he want to accept such a lucrative deal?"

His lips curled ironically. "How much would you sell your child for, Ms. Cord? That's what Gimmicks meant to Doug."

"Then how did the three of you convince him?"

McManus sat back and stared out the windows. Finally, his eyes turned back to me.

"I'm not at liberty to discuss the particulars of the deal, or even reveal there is a deal. Let me say this. The offer included a great deal more than any cash you've been quoted. We're a growing company with a lot of potential. We want to expand. This deal makes it possible to reach our goals years quicker than if we go it alone. Doug recognized that and finally agreed. He wasn't comfortable with it, but he saw the potential for all of us. For Gimmicks. He wasn't exactly a control freak, but he didn't want others butting in as he put it. We didn't realize the toll agreeing had taken on him. As his friend, I should have seen it. Should have stopped him."

"Grimes wasn't really a drinker, but you say he started drinking right away. How much alcohol do you usually take with you on these trips?"

"Neither Doug nor I drink a lot usually. Primarily social drinking. A beer or glass of wine with dinner. Maybe two at a party. So three cases of beer and a couple bottles of wine is normal for our week away. A case for Doug and me; the other two for Harold and Ray. Harold's the heavy drinker among us. He always brings a bottle or two of bourbon as well."

"How about this time?"

"The usual, but when Doug arrived at the cabin the first thing he did was grab a beer and sat on the porch watching the sunset. That wasn't normal."

"You didn't all arrive at the same time?"

"No. He arrived a little after the rest of us. Which should have been a red flag."

"How so?"

"Usually we all travel there together Sunday afternoon in Ray's Expedition. This time, Doug said he wanted to drive down alone and think."

"What did the rest of you do when he started drinking right away?"

"Left him alone. Harold said to let him think it through. Harold's a pretty good judge of people. I can't recall if Doug ate anything or not that night. He'd just come in every once in awhile for another beer. He may have grabbed a sandwich too. I'm not sure. If we tried to speak to him, he shook his head and went back outside."

"So, right away, he was drinking more than usual?"

"That's right. I wasn't counting, but he must have had at least four beers the first night. Hell, I had three myself worrying about him."

"What happened after that?"

"You should understand these trips were to get away from decision making, away from the grind. To relax. The main reason we picked that area was its remoteness. No cell towers for phone or Internet. We had a landline but kept it unplugged except for emergencies. The offer changed this trip."

"In what way?"

"We got the offer a few days before the trip. Ray, Harold and I recognized the benefits immediately. Doug wasn't so sure. We left it with our lawyers to dissect. Thought we'd discuss it thoroughly when we got back."

"But it didn't happen that way?"

"No. At first, everything seemed normal except for Doug drinking that first night. The next morning we went out and fished the stream as usual. Each of us looking for a prime spot. A private space to clear the head. Just enjoy being alive. Later, Doug would walk over with a couple of cold beers and want to discuss particulars. He did that with each of us. Not a lot of fishing got done. It went on like that every day, and the evenings were worse with all of us together. Made it feel like the three of us were ganging up on him then. Maybe we were. There was lots of drinking. As the beer dwindled, Doug started on the bourbon."

"Did you argue?"

"Not like you're suggesting. No one got angry. There was no yelling or anything. These were serious discussions of the pros and cons. But it was three-on-one. After three days of that, Doug seemed to come around. He had Harold plug in the phone and make some calls to see if the other side was amenable to changes to the offer. While we waited for replies, we went back to fishing."

"Everything was okay at that point?"

"I thought so. I didn't realize it then, but Doug sent Ray off for more liquor. He came back with three cases of beer, a bottle of Bacardi and a case of Coke. Maybe a bottle of bourbon too for Harold. I'm not sure."

"That didn't worry you?"

"Honestly? No. It should have. I should have remembered Doug got wasted on rum and Coke during his divorce. But at the time, regrettably, no."

"What happened that last night?"

"We got a call Saturday afternoon saying they agreed to our amendments. It just needed to be written up and signed when we got back. We also had a great day catching trout. We grilled a ton of fish and drank. Celebrated our asses off. At least three of us did. I thought Doug did too, but he didn't say much all evening. He seemed nervous and agitated to me, but he'd just smile and nod whenever I looked at him. Ray was playing bartender. Doug kept going back for another rum and Coke."

"And then?"

"Must have been after midnight. Said he was leaving. Said he'd see us Monday. Ray and I were nearly passed out by then. Don't know why Doug wasn't. Harold was doing his best to get him to stay. Couldn't convince him. Wished he had."

"Your wife said Cochran left with Grimes. Is that correct?"

"Thought I saw them go out together. Can't be sure I was so drunk. Harold told us about it the next morning, as we packed to leave. So it must be true. It's what I told Nasha. Later, a sheriff's deputy came, told us of the accident and Doug's death. We went to the county morgue, identified him and gave statements. That may be in my statement too. I really don't recall for certain. I called Nasha to have her get a hold of

Stephanie."

"I don't wish to appear accusatory, Mr. McManus—"

"Yes, you do." He gave me his Cheshire grin. "It's your job. You think Doug dying before this deal is signed, makes Harold, Ray and me suspects. That it's only our word Doug agreed to the deal. That each of us will be a whole lot richer."

"True. You must admit a third of a fortune is more appealing than a quarter. Many would consider it a strong motive."

"It would be if it were true."

"It's not? My understanding is—"

"That our partnership agreement gives the surviving partners sole ownership. That the dead partner's family is entitled to only 15 percent of the company's value at time of death."

"I thought I heard 25 percent?"

"No. When we wrote our partnership agreement we decided a 25 percent payout could compromise the company's stability. We agreed that 40 percent must remain with the company and settled on 15 percent to a partner if one of us left or to the family in the event of a death. That's why this audit."

"I see."

"What you don't know is that after Doug spoke in a conference call between our lawyers, the other company's CEO and lawyers, making his amendments part of the final negotiations, that the four of us signed an agreement to the deal at the cabin *before* Doug died. No, there was no one there to notarize it, but because of that, if the deal goes through, we—Ray, Harold and I—agreed to give what would have been Doug's share to Stephanie, Jason and Penelope."

"I . . . see. Do they know?"

"Not yet. We want to wait until after the deal is signed."

"When did the three of you make this agreement?"

"Last week. Signed and notarized. I'll show you copies of both agreements."

McManus went to his desk, brought back a folder and

handed me two papers. I read the copies of the agreement made in the cabin and the notarized one signed Thursday the 25th by the surviving partners. John read them also.

"That's very generous of you and your partners," he said, giving them back to McManus.

"It wasn't generosity. This deal wouldn't be without Doug's approval. Any other questions, Ms. Cord?"

"Who wrote the agreement that was signed at the cabin?"

"Ray. I think we did two drafts—which we didn't keep—and we signed this one. The originals of both are with our lawyers."

"How important is the continued use of Mr. Grimes' copyrights to this deal?"

"Very important. Possibly crucial. We have plans to discuss it with Stephanie, Jason and Penelope as soon as the audit is complete. Anything else?"

"Not at the moment. Where can I find Mr. Suliman?"

"In Finance on the second floor with the audit team. Would you like an escort?"

"I'll find it, thank you."

The three of us rose.

"John," McManus said, "would you like a tour while your team works?"

"Yes, thank you, but let me speak with Rachel for a moment."

Cartwright and I went to the door.

"That blows my profit theory," I said.

"Not really. Once the deal goes through they'll still profit enormously. In that stratosphere, what's a few hundred million one way or another? We still don't know what happened when Grimes and Cochran left the cabin. And there's the blood on the steps to explain. Keep digging."

Fifteen

Before heading for Finance, I asked McManus' assistant where I'd find Cochran's office. He gave me directions to the west corner of the building. Cochran's assistant, a Ms. Davies according to her nameplate, was a handsome woman in her late fifties with silver hair. Cochran wasn't in.

"I don't know when he'll arrive, Ms. Cord, but he left a message he wanted to see you. If I could have your cell number, I'll let you know as soon as he's here."

"Thank you. Have you worked for him long?"

"Nearly twenty years."

"That long? You must have known his former wife; the one who died."

"If it's *pertinent*, you should discuss that with him. *Not* me. Will there be anything else?"

"Not now, thank you."

Was she the lioness at the gate? Her sudden iciness clearly said I'd get nothing *pertinent* from her.

I found Rashid Suliman. The audit was going smoothly. He said he had time to answer questions. He left his assistant in charge, and we went down to the food court, got coffees and found a quiet space by the windows looking out across the broad lawn to the lake. On the lawn were a dozen people doing t'ai chi.

From my research I knew Suliman was 39, single, with degrees from The University of Pennsylvania and its Wharton

Business School; his family emigrated from Persia in the early 1900s; and he lived in Old Town. He had smooth, olive-complexioned skin, and dark trusting eyes with long lashes. His story of the fishing trip was much the same as McManus' without sounding like they had been rehearsed.

"Whose idea was it to get more alcohol?"

"Doug's. The beer was getting low already and he didn't particularly care for bourbon, though he'd had quite a lot of it."

"Did he explicitly request the rum and Coke?"

"Yes. It was his preferred drink—when he chose to drink, that is."

"As you were tending the drinks that last night, do you recall how many he had?"

Suliman looked down at his hands in thought. "Not exactly. He was drinking steadily, not eating much. I tried to get him to eat more, but he kept saying he wasn't hungry. He was still irritated about the deal. Kept rubbing his stomach but kept drinking. I'd say he had five or six at least. I wasn't counting. Not sure how much I had. I know it was a lot. I remember him fixing at least two for himself. So he could have had more."

"And you weren't concerned?"

"It was a celebration. Why not get wasted? We weren't going anywhere. Thought it would relax him. He kept pacing like a caged animal. I mean . . . I figured the worst that could happen would be a massive hangover. Which I certainly had the next morning."

"Mr. McManus showed me an agreement the four of you signed at the cabin. When was it written?"

"Saturday afternoon after the phone call agreeing to our terms."

"You wrote it out?"

"Yes. We drafted it and made changes. I wrote a final copy and we all signed it."

"So after you all agreed, there was no further hostility or

badgering?"

"Not at all. And I wouldn't phrase our discussions as badgering. We were trying to be persuasive and defend our perspective."

"I see. When he said he was leaving, were you surprised?"

"Of course. We all were. None of us should be driving in the condition we were in. We told him so. We tried to convince him to stay."

"Did it get physical?"

"You mean like a fight? No. Darren and I were too drunk to stand much less grab him. We pleaded with him, but he wouldn't listen. Harold tried to hold him, but Doug pushed him away. That's as physical as it got."

"When he left, Cochran followed him outside, is that correct?"

"Yes. Harold was still trying to get him to stay. I'm sorry we couldn't do more."

"I'm sure. So what happens to the company when this sale goes through?"

"'Sale' is a misnomer. This is difficult to explain until the deal is finalized. It's more of an expanded partnership, or merger, where we maintain control. You see, Douglas feared losing control; feared losing the idea everyone here is family and has a stake in our success. He harped on that most during the fishing trip. I think it worried him right up to the end. I think that had a lot to do with his nervousness. Even though we had verbal agreements, he wouldn't be satisfied until it was in writing and he'd dissected every possible meaning. Everyone here stands to profit from this deal, not just the partners."

"How so?"

"We're a profit sharing company, Ms. Cord. Beyond salary, everyone here receives a percentage of profit."

"Everyone?"

"Yes, everyone. In our view, everyone at Gimmicks contributes to our success. We have no outside contractors.

The dishwashers in the kitchens, the people who clean, our groundskeepers, all fulfill a needed role as important as our programmers. Therefore, we believe everyone should share in the profits."

"That's a very magnanimous position."

"Not really. It's only fair. I'm sure there are other companies with a similar philosophy. It was Doug's idea originally. His father was a high school janitor. He understood how every cog was necessary in an efficiently run machine, as he put it. It was his major worry about the merger."

"So, when this deal goes through, everyone here gets a share of the proceeds?"

"A portion, yes. Most of what comes in is for expansion, but what comes to the partners will also be shared with everyone here."

"That's . . . that's mindboggling. Do you need a staff detective, by chance?"

He laughed and relaxed. "Not at the moment."

"Does everyone know?"

"No, only our lawyers until it's done. We don't want to cause anxiety. Please don't discuss it with anyone."

"No, of course not." My phone rang. "Excuse me, a moment. This is Rachel Cord."

"Ms. Cord, Mr. Cochran can see you when you're ready."

"Thank you. I'll be up shortly." I put my phone away. "Mr. Suliman, when Grimes and Cochran left the cabin, do you remember how long it was before Cochran came back in?"

"No. Darren passed out. I covered him with a blanket. There was no way I could have gotten him to bed. I started to clean up but was too wasted. I crashed in bed. Don't really remember. Didn't see Harry until breakfast."

"If I have other questions, may I speak with you again?"

"Of course."

Sixteen

The two glass walls of Cochran's office faced southwest and northwest. Four comfortable chairs sat in a group in the corner. A rectangular conference table with 11 chairs was along one glass wall. Harold Cochran sat behind an imposing ebony desk where he could see the views across the room. Two club chairs were in front of the desk.

Cochran was in his early fifties and balding. On the wall behind him were plaques, diplomas, and many photographs of Cochran alone and with different people. One showed a young Cochran in an Air Force uniform receiving a medal. In another, he posed grinning with a huge marlin hanging beside him. There was a photo of him, Grimes, McManus and Suliman with hardhats and shovels breaking ground for Gimmicks. The only other person I immediately recognized was Arnold Schwarzenegger. He and Cochran looked to be laughing and sharing a joke. Behind them was the Great Seal of California. He rose to greet me.

"Please have a seat, Miss Cord. Sorry I wasn't here to meet you earlier."

His tone was neutral; he clasped his hands together on top of a folder on his desk after he sat back down.

"Quite all right, Mr. Cochran. I've been busy speaking with your partners."

"Yes, I know. I'm certain Ray and Darren have been candid with you. I know all about you, by the way, and what you're trying to prove."

"Or unprove, Mr. Cochran."

"Correct. Doug's death was an accident, Miss Cord, as I'm sure Ray and Darren have told you. And none of us is trying to cheat Stephanie or Doug's children. Ask anything you'd like. But before you do, tell me why you're following my wife?"

"Excuse, me?"

"You heard me. My wife has nothing to do with the company other than being married to me. She has nothing to do with Doug's death, either. So why are you following her?"

"Mr. Cochran—"

He glared and slid the folder across the desk. I stopped it from falling on the floor. He didn't say anything. I opened the folder. Inside was a photograph of Amanda Cochran entering the Comfort Inn. In one corner was the date and time the photo was taken. The next photo showed me entering the motel a minute later. Another caught me exiting. Another showed me in Hardees waiting. A final photo was of my license plate. Busted!

"My apologies. It wasn't intentional. I'm not following her." How to explain it? "It was . . . a spur of the moment lark. I was returning home when your wife passed me. I recognized her and, out of sheer curiosity, decided to follow."

Damn, what a mess. He had the upper hand, and I had nowhere to stand. He was still glaring.

"Did you photograph her or anyone?"

"No, I didn't. It was just curiosity, nothing more."

"Then you better forget anything you saw or think you saw. And I better never hear anything from you about it. Clear?"

"Absolutely. You're right. What she does is none of my business or my client's. Again, I apologize."

He sat back. "All right, then. What can I tell you that you don't already know?"

"What happened when you and Grimes left the cabin?"

"Right to the point. I like that. As you know, we were all pretty drunk that night. I'm a heavy drinker, always have been. And I like the hard stuff. I can handle it better than the others, but I knew I was too drunk to drive. I thought Doug was too far gone, so I tried to stop him. Didn't work."

"How'd you try to stop him?"

"Told him again he'd won. They'd agreed to all our conditions. They needed us more than we them. Told him he could stop worrying. Stop obsessing. There were times he was the worst worrywart I'd ever met. Anyway, I then told him he was too drunk to drive. He needed to sleep. We all did. He said he couldn't sleep. Too worked up. Needed to get away. He couldn't stand still. I told him we should walk it off. He said, 'No,' he was going home. We stepped off the porch, he pulled his keys out, and I grabbed them from him. He slugged me. I fell and hit my head. Before I could get back up, he was pulling away. Nothing else I could do."

"You didn't try to go after him?"

"Hell, no. Didn't need two drunks out on the road. I sat awhile on the steps then went back in. Darren was snoring in a chair. Ray was asleep in his bed. I poured a bourbon for a nightcap and went to bed. The next morning we were told of Doug's accident. That's it."

"Do you recall what time you started celebrating?"

"It was after the conference call. Let's see. We were expecting the call around 2:30. It came in a bit late. Say 2:45 or so. Lasted about an hour. Doug did most of the talking. The rest of us got on the line only to confirm our agreement with Doug's. A second call came in shortly after, about 4:30, saying it was a go for their side. We celebrated with a beer. No, wait. That's not right. We had a bottle of wine. Then Darren fired up the grill."

"And you kept celebrating until after midnight, about seven-and-a-half or eight hours, is that right?"

"Sounds about right, yes."

"What did everyone eat?"

"Mostly grilled fish tacos with salsa and lime. We caught a lot of fish that morning. Best day of the whole trip. There was also grilled sausage and munchies. Pot of baked beans. Nothing you'd call a balanced meal. Sort of picked and drank as we felt like it."

"About the drinking, do you recall what everyone had?"

"Good Lord, no. We all had beer or wine at first with the fish, I think. Then I switched to bourbon. I think Ray and Darren stuck mostly with beer. Doug switched early to rum and Coke. Seemed to have a fresh glass every time I looked."

"Would you say eight or more drinks plus beer and wine would be a fair guess for what he had?"

"Sounds reasonable. It was a long night. I drank at least that much."

"Grimes wasn't a drinker. How do you think he managed not to pass out like the others?"

"Don't know. Let me think. He was worked up about the deal. Moving about like a Nervous Nellie. Ray was pouring the drinks. Maybe he made them light. You know, less rum."

"I guess that's possible. When you grabbed his keys outside, did you hit or push him?"

"No, just grabbed the keys, and then he hit me."

"When you fell, what did you hit your head on?"

"Edge of the porch or a step. Not sure which. Hurt like hell." Cochran felt the back of his head. "Still a little tender."

"What's your blood type?"

"O positive. Why?"

"Just checking. Let's back up. McManus showed me a copy of an agreement the four of you signed at the cabin. When did you do that?"

"Right. I forgot about that. Right after the phone call. Ray wrote it out while I opened the wine. We each made suggestions to the wording. Ray wrote out the final copy and we destroyed the drafts to avoid confusion. Then we signed it and Ray put it away. Then we started celebrating."

"I think that's all. Thank you for seeing me." I stood to

leave. "And, I'm truly sorry for that incident with your wife."

"What incident?"

Right. What incident? It never happened.

Seventeen

Flummoxed! **I screwed up** failing to tame my cat. I lost the edge. Had I asked the right questions?

Were they right? Grimes drove off alone? That it was Cochran's blood on the step? It really was an accident? I hadn't taken notes and needed to keep it straight.

I wandered until I found an empty conference room. Sat and tried to recall each interview.

Everyone agreed Grimes wasn't much of a drinker, but McManus and Nasha said Grimes drank to excess over his divorce. Beverly Norton also confirmed how he fell apart then. He loved his company like his child so it wasn't hard to believe he was torn about giving it up. But he wasn't giving it up.

This was going to be a partnership or merger on his terms if the partners were to be believed. So why was he so worked up that last night?

The partners said he was irritated, agitated, kept pacing. How did Cochran put it? "Like a Nervous Nellie." He was drinking heavily but it didn't calm him, make him relaxed. He had to leave. Said he'd see them Monday. The autopsy said his blood alcohol was 0.18. Why was he still walking? Much less driving? He knocked Cochran down. Drove away. There were brake skids on the road but not where he went off the cliff. Drunk? Careless? Suicide? He said he'd see them Monday.

I found Rashid Suliman down in Finance.

"May I ask a couple questions?"

"Certainly. We can use that office. Please sit. Would you like some coffee or anything?"

"No, thank you. I'm fine. Which day was it, Grimes sent you to buy more liquor?"

"Wednesday. Shortly after the conference call. Everyone was feeling better that a decision had been made. Darren and Harry took a couple of beers and headed for the stream to fish. Doug said we were getting low and asked me to go buy more."

"Did he make any special requests?"

"Yes. He poured a shot of bourbon and made a face when he drank it. Asked me to get him a quart of Bacardi and two cases of Coke. Said to bring back another bottle of bourbon for Harry too as he'd been hitting it heavily."

"Do you recall exactly what you bought?"

Suliman looked down at his hands as he'd done earlier for several moments.

"They didn't have the quart size of Bacardi so I bought the one-and-three-quarter liter one and four 12-packs of Coca Cola. Also a bottle of Evan Williams and three 12-packs of Sam Adams."

"When you got back, did Grimes start on the rum and Coke right away?"

"Yes. He was in the cabin. It looked like he'd had a couple beers while I was gone. There were two empties on the table. While I stored everything, he filled a glass with ice and poured the rum in without measuring and topped it off with Coke."

"Is that the way he made his drinks after that? Not measuring the rum, I mean."

"Yes. That's what I recall."

"When you mixed the drinks Saturday night, did you measure them?"

"Yes. The first two I gave him had full shots, but I cut back to an ounce after that. Figured he wouldn't notice. Not that it did him any good."

"Did you and he talk much that night?"

"What about?"

"Anything. How he was feeling about the deal? Future plans? Anything at all."

"Not really. If I tried to bring up the deal, he shook it off. Said to wait for the lawyers. Didn't want to discuss anything to do with business. Treated Darren and Harry the same way. I didn't—we didn't—really understand how drunk he was getting until he said he was leaving. We tried talking him out of it."

"How long before he left did that occur?"

"I don't know. I was pretty well wiped out. Maybe an hour? Maybe less."

"Was he still drinking at that point?"

"I thought he'd stopped, but while we were arguing over his leaving he had at least one more drink."

I shook my head. "It seems so hard to believe. The drinking was so out of character."

"True, but that's the way it was."

"Thank you. I appreciate your answering my questions."

"That's quite all right. We want you and Stephanie to be assured Doug's death was an accident."

"Yes, thank you. Oh, one more thing. Grimes drove his car to the cabin and left in it. Did he drive it at all in between?"

"No. We had everything we needed for the trip. The liquor run was the only time either car was used."

"Did he mention any problems with his car?"

Suliman looked at me quizzically. "Ah, not that I recall. Why do you ask?"

"Just curious. Not really important. Thank you, again. I'll let you get back to work."

In the hall, I stopped to add what Suliman told me to my notes then went looking for Grimes' office.

The office was in the south corner on the same floor as the other partners' offices. I was sure that—like the others—it had a magnificent view. The doors were closed. The two people sitting at desks in the anteroom stopped their conversation as I entered. Their deep tans implied they spent a lot of time outdoors. A nameplate said the young man to my left was probably Jon Stevens. The nameplate on my right identified the woman as Linda Woodruff, Senior Assistant to the CEO. Her dark hair was short and sun-bleached. Age was difficult to determine, but I guessed late forties to mid-fifties. She looked at me and smiled.

"Good afternoon. May we help you?"

"I hope so. I'm Rachel Cord." I handed her my card. "I work for Stephanie Grimes."

"How is she doing? I haven't seen her since the funeral."

"She's holding up well though still disoriented by what happened."

"I'm sure. It surprised all of us. Doug was a lovely man. Dedicated. Caring. His death is such a tragedy. A great loss to everyone who knew him."

"Were you with him long?"

"Seven years. Before Gimmicks."

"What was he like back then?"

"Why are you asking if you know Steffi?"

"She wonders why a man who doesn't drink much and who abhors drunk drivers would suddenly binge and drive. I'm seeking answers for her. Knowing more about him helps me complete the picture, maybe explain his recent behavior."

She looked at the man. "Jon, why don't you go to lunch?"

"We still sailing later?"

"Of course. I'll meet you at the dock." As Jon left, she stood. "Why don't we go in the office? Less likelihood of being disturbed."

As I suspected, the view was great. A few boats were on the lake; most were pulled ashore. Like McManus, Grimes preferred a stand-up desk for working. But instead of facing the view, this desk faced a wall mounted with four, very large, flat-screened monitors. On the desktop was only a wireless keyboard and mouse. Grimes did not have a conference table. There was a large circular seating area where the two walls of glass met. I didn't see any paperwork or files lying around. Woodruff led me to the sitting area.

"Would you like something to drink?"

"No, thank you. As you were with Mr. Grimes for so long, his death must have been devastating."

"It was. And how he died was not only unexpected, but also confusing. I'm having trouble accepting it."

"Before that final trip, how was he acting?"

"Doug was uptight all that week." Her eye glistened. She seemed to be thinking. Then she looked straight at me. "I don't want you getting a wrong impression of my relationship with Doug. You see, he insisted everyone call him 'Doug.' Not just his partners or senior staff. Everyone. That's the kind of man he was."

She glanced out at the lake before continuing. "I knew he and the others received a huge offer. A real game changer he said. He didn't go into details but said it would affect everyone here. He was worried about those effects. If Steffi had been here—by the way, I introduced them—I'm sure he would have discussed it with her. She was good for him in that way. But she was in rural Mexico on an archeological dig. Darren, Harry and Rashid were all for taking the deal apparently. Doug wasn't convinced. They decided to let it lie until after their trip. Because he died Doug didn't fill me in on what was agreed to, but I understand the deal is going through."

"You introduced Stephanie and Grimes?"

"Yes. I was working with Doug at Grimoire Cybernetics, the game software company he founded. There were only six of us. Doug, four other programmers and me. I felt Doug was lonely. Steffi and I were long time friends. I thought they'd get along. They did."

"How did you come to work for him?"

"I first met Doug at a charity event. I don't recall which one. I was attending with my boss, as his wife wasn't available. In passing, Doug mentioned he was starting a software company and gave us each his card. A month later, my position became untenable. I'm an excellent executive assistant, but I made the neophyte mistake of sleeping with my boss and the relationship fizzled. I remembered Doug's card. I went to see him, we got along, he hired me, and that was that."

"What happened to Grimoire when he created Gimmicks?"

"It became a subdivision of Gimmicks. Jeff Allbright and Charles Stocks stayed and run it. Mike Storm and Eric North decided to strike out on their own. They own Star System Gaming."

"Was there any animosity when they left?"

"None whatsoever. Doug ran Grimoire—like Gimmicks—on a profit-sharing model. When Mike and Eric said they wanted to go independent, he provided financial backing."

"How did the Gimmicks partnership come about?"

"Doug developed some original applications for the burgeoning cellphone market. They didn't fit within Grimoire's master plan. He wanted to exploit their potential and wanted a new company to develop them, but at the same time he didn't want to close out Grimoire entirely. Harry was already marketing Grimoire products through his marketing firm, Cochran International, and Rashid had been contracted to do Grimoire's books. Doug and Darren were old friends and decided to go in together. They both recognized their limitations, and they wanted to keep everything in-house, so they offered Harry and Rashid to come in as partners."

"They were all equal partners?"

"Yes, but Doug and Darren loaned the company a large portion of the start-up costs to be paid back through a percentage of profits. The last installment of the payback was completed in October."

"How would you describe Grimes overall?"

"Everyone's favorite uncle. Everyone was family to him. He wanted everyone to succeed. He was excited by new projects. His excitement excited others. However, he could be obsessive and single-minded. I've seen it a few times. I think that side of him ruined his first marriage. This new deal brought it out in him too."

"What about the partners?"

"Harry's a wheeler-dealer. Not an extreme risk-taker, but he'll go for the long odds. He likes winning big. I've played poker with him, so I know. Darren is as bright as Doug, maybe more so. But where Doug was intuitive, Darren's methodical. They made a great programming team. Rashid is the ultimate bean counter. But in a good way. He can explain all that financial data so it's actually understandable."

"I know they're all well-off financially, but would it be fair to say this deal means more to Cochran and Suliman?"

"I'm not sure about that. Darren and Doug were at Microsoft a long time. They were there when it went public and benefited from it. I think by most people's standards they're quite wealthy. Harry is a wheeler-dealer, as I said. He's been up and he's been down. I know he's had at least one bankruptcy. As for Rashid, his accounting business was doing well. Before joining Gimmicks, I believe he was making more than a million dollars a year. But how many hours he had to work to get it, and how much of it he cleared, I couldn't say. I do know Gimmicks has allowed him more of a personal life. I'd like to think each of them cares more about the survival and continued growth of Gimmicks than whatever personal payout they'll each receive on this deal."

"Were any of the partners particularly aggressive about the offer?"

"They all pushed for it. Maybe Rashid more than the others. He was constantly cornering Doug with financial projections, profit potential. Sometimes Rashid goes on too long without noticing. Which is a shame because his explanations are so clear the first go-round. I've seen meetings where as soon as he's made his point, Doug or Darren has said, "Thank you Ray," and moved on before he could repeat. Doug went sailing with me twice that week just to get away from him."

"What happens with your job now?"

"Good question. Yet to be determined." She smiled. "We haven't discussed it. Everyone seems to be holding their breath until this deal is finalized. In the meantime, I'll keep coordinating with the project teams Doug was directly involved with. That and spending more time on the water." She glanced at her watch. "Which is where I'm headed right now."

"Thank you for talking with me."

"Not a problem. Anything to help Steffi. Drop by again if you have a question."

"Thanks. Oh, one last thing. Do you know where Grimes had his car serviced?"

"I do. I scheduled them for him. All their vehicles, actually, as Steffi was often away on a dig. Why?"

"I was wondering if the car possibly malfunctioned. When was it last serviced?"

"It'd be in my calendar. One moment."

I followed Woodruff to her desk. She called up a calendar on her computer and did a find. She clicked on a date and then a link. A file opened.

"We use Bleeker's Auto Service in Southside for our company vehicles. Doug uses them also for his personal ones. The Subaru was serviced January 20th. All systems were in working order. No problems noted."

I found John Cartwright in the food court. He was talking to someone on his cellphone. I waited until he finished then filled him in on what I had found.

"I'm going to Bleeker's to get more info on the last service of Grimes' car."

"You think the car was sabotaged?"

"Possibly. It looked like Grimes used the brakes several times but not when he went off the bluff. Why? Did the brakes fail? Again, why?"

"Maybe the liquor caught up to him and he passed out."

"That's possible too. It bothers me he didn't pass out at the cabin with all he'd had to drink. They described him as nervous, agitated and irritated. Wouldn't sit still. Antsy. Makes me think he was high on something. But no one has mentioned any drug use."

"We're doing new tox screens on the available blood samples. That should tell what was in his system, and the DNA test will determine whose blood was on the steps. Of course we're totally rechecking the car. I'm sure Bill plans to particularly check the brakes, but I'll mention it."

"How's the audit going?"

"Just getting started but organized. Should be complete Wednesday or Thursday."

"Okay. I'll let you know what I find."

A wall in the customer area of Bleeker's Auto Service displayed large photographs and artifacts of the company's history. Three brothers started the company in 1893 as a blacksmith and wagon repair shop. They soon expanded to anything with wheels and by 1922 exclusively worked on automobiles and trucks. The young woman behind the counter had long dark hair tied up in a French braid and brown eyes. Her nametag read "J. Bleeker."

"Hi. What can we do for you today?"

I handed her my card. "Hi. I'm Rachel Cord. I'm working for the Grimes family. Douglas Grimes died in a car accident two weeks ago. His car was serviced here in January. I'd like to speak with the person who worked on it if I may."

The woman's eyes went wide, her mouth opened and she turned slightly pale. She stood frozen for a moment like a deer caught in the headlights.

"I'm sorry. I think you need to speak with my mother. Just a moment, please."

She stepped away and went into an office with a large window looking out into the customer area. She talked with an older woman sitting behind a desk and gave her my card. She then pointed to me. She returned to the counter.

"My mother will see you. This way please."

I walked in the office. The door closed behind me and the young woman returned to the counter. The woman standing behind the desk was mid-forties, with short dark hair and the same brown eyes as her daughter. There was little doubt of the family resemblance. She was holding my card.

"I'm Martha Bleeker. I think you startled Johanna." She looked at my card again. "Exactly what are you looking for, Ms. Cord?"

"Rachel, please. As I told your daughter, I'm working for the Grimes family and Douglas Grimes had his car serviced here in January. He recently died in an accident while driving that car."

"Are you suggesting our service had anything to do with his accident? Because if you are—"

"Not at all. That's not my intent. I'm looking for information. Were you aware of the accident?"

"Yes. It was on the news. My husband and I attended his funeral. Mr. Grimes and his company have been long-time customers."

"If you read the news reports, then you know the accident was ruled as being alcohol-related. There's no doubt of that. However, evidence showed he used his brakes several times after leaving the cabin but not where the accident occurred. I'm wondering if the brakes could have failed for some reason. What did they look like when the car was serviced? Was a future brake job recommended?

Bleeker pursed her lips as she stared at my card. "Just a moment. Have a seat, please."

She sat and studied some information on her computer. She looked at several different pages. Then she picked up her phone.

"Gilly. Please come to the office." She turned to me. "According to our records, we replaced the brake fluid last year on the Subaru when it had 29,850 miles. That's in keeping with Subaru recommendations. That's the only brake work we've performed. There were no problems with the braking system when we serviced the car in January. The mileage then was 41,695."

She pushed a button on her computer and the printer behind her started. There was a knock at the door. Bleeker made a hand motion. A man about 50 came in drying his hands on a towel.

"You wanted to see me, Martha?"

"Yes, Gilly. Have a seat. This is Ms. Cord."

He held out his hand. "Pleased to meet you."

"Same here."

"Ms. Cord is asking about the service we did on Douglas Grimes' 2008 Subaru Legacy." She handed him a paper from the printer. "Your evaluation didn't indicate any problems with the braking system. Do you recall what you saw?"

He looked over the paper and nodded. "Nice, clean car. Grimes is an easy driver with a soft foot. Pads and rotors barely worn even with 40,000 miles on them. No problems at all. No leaks anywhere. Fluid right at level." He looked at me. "Was something wrong?"

"That's what I'm trying to determine. Douglas Grimes died in a car accident. Evidence showed he used the brakes a lot, but there were no braking skids where he went off the road. I'm wondering if there's a reason the brakes could have failed at that moment."

"As I said, he was real easy on the brakes. Had the kind of wear you'd expect to see with half that mileage. There shouldn't have been a problem with them. I remember reading about the accident. He was on a fishing trip or something. Did he go off-road much? Maybe something tore a brake line."

"As I understand, the cabin where he stayed was on a good gravel road less than a quarter mile from the main road. He didn't drive anywhere else until he left the night he died."

"He was drinking a lot that night, right?"

"Yes."

"Was he weaving on and off the road?"

"From what I know, yes. He used the brakes several times leaving skids, but not at that final curve."

"Well, if he hit something and it tore a lining, he'd lose fluid pretty quickly every time he hit the brakes. Then he'd have no brakes."

"If he didn't lose fluid, would anything else cause the brakes to fail?"

He massaged his jaw as he thought. "Could be fluid fade, I suppose."

"What's that?"

"You said he was using the brakes a lot?"

"Yes."

"Well, when you step on the brakes, friction causes a lot of heat when the brake pistons compress and clamp the rotors. If this heat gets too hot—like when you're using the brakes too much—it could cause the brake fluid to boil and vaporize or evaporate. That would create air bubbles that would keep the brake fluid from compressing the pistons."

"How?"

"Brake fluid doesn't compress, air does. So the air would be compressed instead of the pistons. Have you ever felt mushy brakes?"

"Yes. I'd have to pump my brakes several times to get enough pressure in the pedal."

"Meant your old fluid probably had some moisture in it that boiled causing air bubbles and you needed to replace the fluid. It can do that over time. Of course, brake fluid shouldn't boil. It takes a lot of heat. Typically around 401 degrees

Fahrenheit to boil. And the fluid in the Subaru was relatively new. So that shouldn't have happened unless the fluid somehow got contaminated. If he was using the brakes more than usual because of his condition, they might have overheated. And that would cause the fluid to boil."

"I see. Is there any way to tell if the brake fluid was contaminated?"

"An analysis of the fluid should show if there were water or other contaminate in it. But I'd lean more to his running over something and tearing a line."

"Thank you for your explanation. You're probably right. Ms. Bleeker, thank you. I'll get out of your hair."

When I reached my car, I wrote out my notes and called Cartwright.

"The mechanic *may* be right that Grimes either hit something or overheated the brakes."

"But your tone says you're still dubious, Rachel. I'll pass the information to Bill. He's thorough. He could have thought of it himself. Will you be going back to Gimmicks tomorrow."

"Probably, but I'm not sure what time. You?"

"No, I've appointments all day. The audit team doesn't need handholding. I'll let you know if Bill discovers anything."

Eighteen

A pint of Cherry Garcia and a spoon plopped on the desk.

"Here. As long as you're pigging out, you might as well have this too."

I looked up at Wendy. "What?"

She didn't say anything. Just looked around. I followed her gaze to the half-jar of peanuts, the three fun-size Snickers wrappers, the empty popcorn bag, the banana peel, the hard candy wrappers, the open bag of potato chips, and the tumbler with still a half-inch of Glenfiddich.

Dang! And I thought I was doing so well. A habit I've never conquered is the desire to eat when I'm concentrating or frustrated. That's why I keep only coffee and diet soda at the office. At home is another story. Anything that's easy or simple to grab finds its way to my mouth. At least I had a banana. That's nutritious.

I gathered the debris into a wastebasket and finished the swallow of Scotch. Left on the desk was my home laptop I'd been entering data into, my notepad, and a layout of 3x5 index cards. The cards help me think. They highlight individual pieces of information or hold questions still to be answered. I can spread them out, shuffle them; see patterns I may not have noticed. They're a work in progress.

I stood and picked up the carton of ice cream. "You're right. Too much junk food." I put the ice cream in the freezer and poured two fingers of Scotch in my glass. "Want some?"

"Sure."

I poured her drink and we went and sat by the glass doors to the balcony. We dimmed the lights. It was too cool to sit outside despite a tempting and beautiful full moon. Moonlight and the lights from the city across the river sparkled on the water. We watched a line of barges being pushed upriver. Their dark silhouettes outlined by the lights.

"What is it, Rachel? Are you still frustrated by why Grimes was so hyper that night?"

"Yes, it bothers me. I've learned there were times when he did drink a lot, but that night he should have been comatose, not bouncing around. I still think he was high on something."

"You said he was drinking rum and Coke all night. Coke has caffeine in it."

"I thought of that, but it's only about a third of what's in a cup of coffee. He'd have to have been downing espresso Coke."

"What were his symptoms again?"

"Cochran called him a Nervous Nellie. They all said he was irritable and agitated. Completely stressed."

"Any mention of headache or upset stomach?"

"I'd have to check my notes. Why?"

"They're all side effects of too much caffeine. I remember one of my co-workers was acting strangely. Highly irritable, restless. He took a lot of antacids. I talked to him about it and found he was working another full-time job as well as taking night college courses. He was popping NoDoz pills like candy."

"Let me check something."

I went to my laptop and did a find on "stomach." It came up in my interview with Suliman. He said Grimes "kept rubbing his stomach." I did a find for "headache." No one mentioned it. And no one mentioned him taking any kind of pills. I wrote "upset stomach" on an index card and "NoDoz?" on another. Added those to my arrangement. I was still left with a card with a big "?" on it. I went back to sit with Wendy.

"No one said anything about Grimes taking pills of any kind, much less caffeine ones. It's too late now, but I'll check with Stephanie in the morning if he was in the habit of taking pills."

Wendy reached over and gripped the top of my shoulder in a tight caress. Her hand moved to the nape of my neck and began a soothing massage.

"Have you worked enough for one night?"

My eyes were closed with pleasure. "Oh, yeah."

"Good. Then we should talk about confirming Easter with your family."

I tensed and stared at her. "I know it's the best time, but this case is getting hot and it's—"

"Going to be resolved on its own schedule. If you don't finish it this week, there's next week or however long it takes. Easter is this coming Sunday. I want to meet your family. It's the perfect time. They'll all be there. The sooner it's over, the sooner we schedule the wedding. And Ed's already making our rings. Remember that. This is what you want, isn't it?"

I felt a huge sigh. "Yes."

"Good. Call your mother tomorrow and tell her we're definitely coming. Mother's coming too. We'll drive up Friday."

"But there won't be enough room at my parents'."

"I already reserved two rooms at a B and B in Laman for Friday through Sunday."

"That's sneaky."

"I know. Now turn around so I can give you a massage. You're really tense."

I called Mom first thing in the morning to get it out of the way. I needed to talk to Stephanie and get back to Gimmicks.

"Hi, Pumpkin. You're still coming for Easter, aren't you? I'm looking forward to meeting Wendy and Clare. She and I have been talking quite a bit. Gave me some simple vegan recipes too. The others here won't know the difference 'less we tell them. I like her."

Clare and Mom are in cahoots? Great. "Yes, Mom. We're coming. The plan is to drive up Friday unless something unforeseen happens. I think Clare's wonderful too."

"She says you're staying in Laman. Are you sure you don't want to stay here? We can always find room, you know."

"I'm sure you'll have a houseful already. We can't be the only ones coming from out of state."

"True. Walter will be here with his fiancé. And my sister, Libby, is driving over from Chicago."

"Wally's getting married? I thought he was in Iraq."

"No. He's still at Ft. Hood. Everyone else will be staying with your brothers so we have space."

"Even so, I think we'll stick with the B and B Wendy reserved. Oh, how's Dad doing? Is he out of the hospital?"

"Oh, yes. He's home and his usual ornery self. A woman comes out and helps with his physical therapy. Makes him angry he can't get out and work like he wants to. But he's improving. Uses a cane mostly. Won't use the walker. I had to rescue it out of the dumpster."

"Sounds like Dad."

"Yes, he's back to normal. Be glad when he's out from under my feet. By the way, just between you and me, he's happy you're coming home."

"Thanks, Mom. See you this weekend. Love you."

"Love you too, Pumpkin."

Wally being there is one on my side. Maybe two, if his fiancé knows about me. Wow. My brother's getting married again at last. After losing Cathy, I wasn't sure it would ever happen. Then again—wow—so am I. Back to work. I called Stephanie Grimes.

"There's not much to report. There's no clear proof as yet it wasn't an accident. The forensics team John Cartwright sent are retesting blood and tissue samples, reexamining your husband's car and reevaluating the crash. That will take some time to complete. And I have a couple issues I'm trying to resolve. Which is why I called."

"What's that?"

"When your husband worked long hours, did he ever feel a need for stimulants?"

"You mean like amphetamines? Never. He rarely took anything besides aspirin for pain. He was more likely to have a beer or glass of wine or a cocktail to relax than take something to get him high."

"What about caffeine? Did he use caffeine pills? Or energy drinks?"

"Not that I'm aware of. He'd have coffee with a meal. He did drink a lot of Coke. He used to say he preferred his caffeine 'cold and bubbly.' And he was very against so-called energy drinks. Thought they were unhealthy."

"Okay, thanks. I'm going back out to speak with his partners again and a few others. Oh, has any of the partners called you about the pending deal with this other company?"

"No. Why?"

"Apparently the afternoon before your husband's death, the four of them—your husband included—agreed to it. I don't know the particulars, but I was shown a hand-written agreement with your husband's signature. The agreement included the continued use of his copyrights. McManus said he was planning to talk with you about it."

"Darren called me last night and asked if he and Nasha could come over today. We're having lunch together. Maybe that's what he wants to talk about. I'd very much like to see that agreement. Are you sure it was my husband's signature?"

"I don't know. I'm not a handwriting expert. It's a clear signature, though. An expert should be able to determine its authenticity."

"I'll ask Darren about it if he doesn't bring it up. Thank you for telling me."

"That's part of the job. I'll speak with you soon."

When I reached Gimmicks, I went looking for Linda Woodruff. I was told she was out on the lake but had her cellphone with her. I called and we agreed to meet at the dock in an hour. McManus wasn't in, but I knew he was meeting Stephanie. I found Suliman in Finance overseeing the audit. He said everything seemed to be going well. I asked if he had time to answer a few more questions. We went up to his office.

I thoroughly enjoy the view from the large windows in my office and love watching the river from my condo, but I admit the views the partners have make me jealous. From Suliman's glass walls low rolling hills spread out north and south to the east. Beyond them somewhere was the river. White, puffy clouds raced across the sky. To stand here at dawn and watch as the sun rose would be awesome.

"What did you want to ask, Ms. Cord?"

"Just trying to clear up a few points. Do you recall if Grimes complained of having a headache?"

"I don't think so. I think, except for his obsessions over the deal, he was fine overall. Pretty drunk, like we all were, but fine."

"You mentioned he was rubbing his stomach a lot. Did you see him take any antacids for it?"

"Not that I noticed. What are you looking for?"

"I remember you saying he kept pacing. That he was irritated."

"Yes, of course. He was really bothered by the pending deal."

"Have you ever known him to use high levels of caffeine? You know, energy drinks. Or caffeine pills? Like NoDoz, for instance?"

"Why? Why are you asking that?"

"I was thinking an overuse of caffeine could explain some of how he was acting. The irritability, restlessness, agitation, a bothersome stomach. I suppose it could delay some of the effects of all the alcohol he'd had too. Just a thought. I've another appointment. Thank you for your time."

Suliman wasn't exactly taken aback by my questions, but I had the impression he was a bit worried. He fixed most of the drinks Grimes had. He could have added something to them. Could he have done something to the brakes on the Subaru? Why would he? Did I miss something on his background check? I'd have to look again. I went to meet Linda Woodruff.

She and Jon Stevens were pulling a small skiff from the water. The sail was furled and mast lowered. There was a steady breeze coming off the lake. I felt chilled and wondered if the temperature were above 60 yet.

"Hi, Rachel. Jon, can you finish here?" Woodruff walked toward me. "Let's get into the warm. It's a bit early, but would you like to have lunch? I'm starved."

Before I could answer, she strode for the building and I had to quicken my pace to keep up.

"Woo! That was fun!"

She ruffled her hair into place and took off her coat. After finding us a table that took advantage of the sun on the windows, she proceeded to the salad bar. When we settled back at the table, she had a large mixed salad, a cup of yogurt, a toasted bagel with cream cheese and lox, and coffee. I had hot chocolate, a grilled ham and cheese panini, and a small bowl of grape tomatoes. I would have preferred fries, but remembered where I was going this weekend.

"So, what you want to talk about?"

"Douglas Grimes' drinking habits?"

"You already know Doug usually didn't drink alcohol. That's why that fishing trip was so out of character. I've never seen him drunk. Like at an event or a party, if he had a glass of wine or a bottle of beer you could practically guarantee an hour later that same glass of wine or bottle of beer would still be half full."

"What about energy drinks? If he were working long hours for instance."

"You mean like Red Bull? One of those?" She shook her

head. "No. He tried one and said he didn't like it. Gave him the jitters. Said he'd stick to regular Coke. That was his drink of choice at work. Even early in the morning. Often said he preferred his caffeine 'cold and bubbly.'"

"How about caffeine pills? Or something stronger?"

"No. Never." She set her coffee down. Her index finger began tapping the table next to her cup. She had a faraway look as she gazed through her salad.

"What are you thinking?"

"We have a very strict drug policy here. Everyone—including the partners—is subject to random testing at any time while here. It's in the contracts we all sign. Uppers and such aren't a problem. Caffeine isn't tested for because it's everywhere. The coffee, sodas, energy drinks. Even in chocolate and other food I think. I know a lot of the staff use the energy drinks. So I wouldn't be surprised if they use caffeine pills too. I even saw Rashid once with a box of Vivarin on his desk."

"But it wouldn't be something Grimes used normally?"

"No, not at all. Why the interest in his using caffeine? He was drunk when he died, right?"

"Yes. But as basically a casual drinker, he was still fully functioning after hours of heavy drinking. The disparity bothers me. I wonder why. A high caffeine level would help explain it."

Woodruff pursed her lips in thought. "What was he drinking that night? I'm not sure I heard."

"Mostly rum and Coke."

"Coke. That's Doug. He loves his Coke. Wouldn't that explain it?"

"Some, but you'd have to drink an awful lot of it."

The conversation lapsed and we finished eating. The sun's warmth through the polarized glass felt nice. I enjoyed the lake view. I turned back to take in the food court and saw Rashid Suliman on an upper balcony staring down. I felt he was staring at me. It seemed we stayed that way for several moments when he turned and walked quickly away.

I thanked Woodruff for meeting with me and said I hoped to see her again. I decided not to do any more interviews and headed for my car to write up my notes.

A light wind blew chill but the car was warm from the sun. There were still a few sailboats out on the lake, and a group of six runners came around the side of the building and headed over a rise. I looked up at the top level.

Was Suliman watching me? Did he spike the drinks with caffeine? Did he add more rum than he claimed? Why was Grimes still upset over the deal that had been agreed on? His partners claimed they were trying to make him relax. Trying to calm him. But was it true?

What if they — or at least one of them — were playing to his anxieties? Subtly suggesting things could still go wrong? Would the alcohol, and maybe extra caffeine, be enough to spur him to leave? To drive in a state of intoxication he would never do normally? Was it hoped he'd have an accident? Were the brakes fiddled with to ensure it?

I added my notes and conjectures to my pad. Would the forensics team find any evidence to support my thoughts? Cartwright said he'd be busy all day. I checked to see if I had Bill Roberts' cell number. My phone rang.

"Rachel, this is Linda Woodruff. I just had a strange talk with Rashid and I'm not sure what to make of it."

"What was that?"

"He was asking what you and I talked about in the food court? I didn't realize he even knew we were there. He kept asking for details like he was grilling me. Kept going over and over about you wanting to know about caffeine. I don't understand."

"Did you tell him you told me about seeing him with a box of Vivarin?"

"I'm not sure. He hardly gave me time to answer him."

"Where is he now?"

"I don't know. Maybe back to his office or down to

Finance. The thing is he seemed angry and I don't know why."

"It does sound strange. I can't explain it either." This could be bad. I needed her not to excite him. Get him suspicious. "Look, Linda. Maybe he was worried or still worked up over Grimes death and wasn't himself. He'll probably come back later and apologize. I suggest leaving him alone for now."

"Maybe you're right. There's been a lot of tension since Doug's accident. Rashid's not the only one to snap at someone."

"There you go. It'll work out, I'm sure. If you need to talk again, please call."

"Thanks. I will."

I added the conversation to my notes, then found Roberts' cell number and called him. I gave him my concerns.

"John told me about the brakes yesterday, Rachel. We didn't find any indication of broken lines or fluid leaks, so we plan to have the brake fluid analyzed. I'll also have the tox screens check on caffeine levels in the blood samples. But it's going to be days before we get results. Anything else?"

"No one mentioned which type of Bacardi Grimes was drinking. There's a big difference between 80 proof and 151. It would be good to know exactly what Rashid Suliman bought."

"We'll check that too. I expect to be through here by tomorrow. So far, everything's inconclusive. It's going to come down to the lab results. Later."

Time for a relook at Suliman.

Nineteen

Doris Garrity was at the reception desk on the second floor of Mann Avenue Plaza.

"Hi, Doris. Anything new?"

"Just Sal Rizelli wants you to call him."

"Didn't you refer him to Fields & Cook?"

"Yes, but he insists on talking to you."

"Okay. I'll call him. Do you know how Ray Carlson is doing?"

"I saw him out walking yesterday evening. He's using canes, and he's slow, but it looks like he's making progress."

"Good for him."

"Any word on your wedding date?"

"We're leaving Friday to spend Easter with my family. If we survive that, hopefully not long after."

"Well, keep us informed."

"Will do."

In my office I laid my notepad on Table Two with the Grimes file and got out my laptop. While it was booting I called Salvatore Rizelli.

"Rizelli Brothers Pizza. Sal speaking."

"Sal, it's Rachel Cord."

"Rachel, what's happening? You going outta business or something? You gotta fob us off onto some gumshoes we don't know from Adam?"

"Sal, I'm really slammed at the moment and then I'm

taking some personal time off. Don't know when I'll be back. Norm Fields and Dan Cook know their business. They'll do a good job for you."

"Maybe so, but we trust you. We know you're discreet."

"So are Dan and Norm, Sal. Believe me."

"But you always come through, and . . . and . . . well . . ."

"And I'm patient about getting paid."

"Hey, that's not nice. We had a cash flow problem. Could happen to anyone."

"You're right. Sal, I'm sorry, but I don't have the time."

"When you coming back?"

"I don't know. Could be two weeks. Could be two months. It's family business. You understand 'family business' don't you?"

"Yeah, I do. This is family business too we needed you for. But I get where you're coming from. You say these guys are good people?"

"The best, Sal. The best."

"All right. We'll give'em a call. Good luck with your family matter, Rachel. Maybe next time, okay?"

"Maybe next time. Best regards to your family."

That done, I went back through my file on Rashid Suliman. Again, I found no red flags. In my original research, I found three additional spellings of Suliman. Suleiman, Suleyman and Sulaiman. None of the hits fit the profile of the one I wanted. But I did find the occasional misplaced item in Rashid's file that didn't belong to him. Could something derogatory about Rashid be in someone else's file instead and not in his where it belonged?

I did a whole new search following every variation on his name that came up. My cellphone rang. It was Wendy. It was also 7:35. The sun had set and the western sky was darkening.

"Rachel, where are you? I haven't heard from you."

"I'm lost and at a dead end. Sorry. I'm at the office. I've been doing online searches all day and getting nowhere. Lost track of time. I'll be home in twenty. As soon as I shut down.

What's for dinner?"

"Nothing's made and you don't sound like going out. I'll have something delivered. It'll get here about the same time you do."

"Sounds good to me. Love you."

"Love you too."

I'd found nothing in my searches to discredit Rashid Suliman in any way. He appeared to be everything his names implied. A *person of integrity* and a *man of peace*. And yet he was upset about my queries. If anyone was in a position to harm Grimes, it could be him. That is, if the lab results came back the way I feared. But there was no timeline when that would be. I'd concentrated my investigation around Grimes. Time to circle in a new direction.

Unlike his partners' McMansions, Rashid Suliman owned a loft apartment in Old Town's art district. The burst housing bubble had slowed the area's revitalization, but there were signs of renewed progress. Workers were active at a renovation project three blocks away; a new, Greek restaurant not far from Suliman's building announced its grand opening; and several galleries had signs for the upcoming Spring Art Fair in April.

The day promised an unseasonable 84 degree high and was already a pleasant 70 at 10:00 a.m. Nice enough for me to sit outside at The Daily Grind with a latté and croissant and contemplate my chances of nosing around The Galleria Lofts where Suliman lived. He was already at Gimmicks, which I'd verified with the audit team.

There was a doorman as gatekeeper, and I'd seen security cameras in the lobby as I'd passed earlier. Deliveries were left with the doorman or someone came down to sign for them. There was a loading dock in the alley behind the building, but it was protected with security cameras also. There were no empty or "for sale or lease" apartments to look at to get me into the building.

Breaking into Suliman's apartment wouldn't be legal, but I didn't plan to steal anything. I just wanted to get an idea of his personal life. His online existence was too sterile. He wasn't into social media, and, except for the recent stories on Douglas Grimes, he wasn't mentioned in the news. As I dunked my croissant, a painting in a gallery window next to the Lofts entrance caught my eye. It reminded me of Mondrian. It also reminded me of a similar painting I'd seen in Suliman's office. I finished my croissant and went across the street.

On closer examination, the painting was a poster. The illustration was mostly vertical and horizontal black lines. Down the right side was a wide, vertical line in blue. Off-center to the left was a pale yellow vertical rectangle. Below that a small black square. The artist was Marlow Moss, an artist I didn't know. The bottom of the poster read, *Painting Like Mondrian at Chartreuse, March 7-April 11.*

Next to the poster was a hardcover copy of *The Burglar Who Painted Like Mondrian* by Lawrence Block. I don't read mysteries—I have enough of my own—but I knew the author and series because Wendy liked him. A small note said it was author signed. The dust jacket looked pristine. I went in the gallery.

The gallery's name, Chartreuse, was painted on the glass doors in yellow green. The walls of the entryway were the same color, but I was glad to see the separate gallery walls were a pleasing off-white. I saw another *Painting Like Mondrian* poster beside a gallery to my right. A security guard stood by the opening. We nodded. I picked up a brochure as I entered.

It included more artists I didn't know and short biographies. I discovered that English artist Marlow Moss was a famous lesbian of her time and a follower of Mondrian. Others represented were Dutch artists Bart van der Leck and Theo van Doesburg, Belgian Georges Vantongerloo, American Mary Heilmann, German Gerhard Richter, and Venezuelan Alejandro Otero.

I walked around the room. There were three posters of Mondrian works to complement the other artists. Their paintings were colorful and shared the gridded rigidness of Mondrian yet different in ways I couldn't explain. Karen could have told me. None had price tags. Three had "Sold" signs.

"Good morning. May I be of assistance?"

The woman, in her mid-thirties, was slim and very tall. Much of the tallness was an illusion because of her platform shoes and the long line of her thigh-length, open jacket. The lightweight, camel jacket and slacks were fitted yet gave a sense of loose comfort. Her scoop-necked top was a soft peach. She had a pixie face and hairstyle. Her makeup was nicely muted. Her eyes a rich, exciting brown that scanned me quickly from flats to hat.

"Yes. I'm admiring the paintings but fear they're way beyond my budget. The book in the window, is it for sale?"

"The signed Lawrence Block? Yes. It's $25. I have three. They're all in excellent condition. Would you like one?"

"Yes, thank you. It's a gift. Can you wrap it?"

"Certainly. Right this way. If you *are* interested in any of the paintings, we have posters of all of them and giclée prints of many."

"What are giclée prints?"

"Fine art quality prints produced on 12-color ink-jet printers. Most in our catalogue are under $800 framed."

"And the posters?"

"Twenty dollars unframed."

"I'd like the Marlow Moss poster and a poster with the Mary Heilmann painting."

"I'll get them."

She came back with two poster tubes and a box and began wrapping my book.

"When I saw the poster in the window, it reminded me of a painting I saw yesterday. That's why I came in."

"Oh, really? What painting was that?"

"I don't know the artist. My first impression was Mondrian. I didn't realize so many others did similar work. I saw it in an office at Gimmicks, the software company."

"Rashid Suliman's office?"

"Yes. Do you know him?"

"Yes. Rashid has bought several works from us. Originals as well as giclées. If I recall correctly, I believe the one you saw is a giclée by van Doesburg. Rashid lives in this building, you know."

"Really? Have you seen his place?"

"Many times. Quite modern. Lots of glass and steel. Geometric patterns. A wonderful showcase for these artists and others he has. He even has four of Heilmann's chairs."

"Chairs?"

"Yes. Did you see those square, brightly colored chairs in the gallery? Mary Heilmann designed those."

"Wow. Sounds like his place is a gallery too. Wish I could see it."

"Oh, you can."

"Really?"

"Yes. In conjunction with our current show, Rashid is hosting a soirée this evening to display his collection. He's very gracious. There'll be wine and snacks. Would you like to come?"

There was a hint of a smile and emphasis on the last word. A warmth in her eyes.

"Yes, I would. Thank you."

She took an invitation card from a drawer and handed it to me.

"Just show this to the doorman. It's from seven to nine. Your total for the posters and book is $69.62. I hope to see you this evening. I'm Morgan."

Her fingers slid along the back of my hand when she gave me my packages.

"I'm Rachel. It's been a pleasure meeting you. I look forward to this evening too."

Morgan was a luscious temptation it would have been hard to resist years earlier but no longer. Still, her obvious interest left me pleasantly charged and tingly. Would that cause problems if Wendy came with me? I very much wanted to see Suliman's apartment, to get a feeling for his lifestyle, his character. To snoop if possible. This was a chance too good to miss.

The invitation did not specify it was for an individual only. I presumed others would arrive as couples. And having Wendy with me could provide a screen, a distraction, to my activities if Suliman didn't notice me too quickly. But would Morgan cause a scene and make me the center of attention? I'd discuss the risk assessment with Wendy later. Meanwhile, I'd see how well known Suliman was in the neighborhood.

Chartreuse was open and busy when Wendy and I arrived at the Galleria Lofts at 7:45. It was too hard to tell if Morgan were there or upstairs. Several people left the gallery and went to the Lofts entrance. We followed and I showed our invitation to the doorman then waited for an elevator.

My earlier walkabout hadn't produced much. Suliman was known in several of the galleries and bought artwork from most of them. He ate often at local restaurants like the Omelet where he always ordered an egg white omelet with mixed, grilled vegetables. A waitress there thought he was "sweet." Then again, so did the male barista at The Daily Grind. He also frequented a local bakery and green grocer. All in all, no one had anything bad to say about him.

It was easy to find 4A. Several people were standing in the hall with drinks. There were framed posters of Mondrian paintings on the walls. The door to the apartment was open. There was a pretty good-sized crowd inside. The woman at the door took the invitation, our coats and gave us claim checks. She handed the coats to another woman.

"Welcome. So nice of you to come. Mr. Suliman's

collection contains many original works as well as a few giclée prints. If you have questions, any of us wearing nametags will be honored to assist you. Please enjoy yourselves, but please don't take or post any pictures. This is a private home. Thank you."

The room was huge with 12-foot ceilings. It's living, dining and kitchen areas separated only by the furniture arrangements. Outer walls were mostly window much like his office at Gimmicks. The inner walls were a soft gray, as was the carpet. As Morgan had said, the furnishings were modern, primarily geometric, with liberal use of steel and glass. Fortunately, I didn't see Morgan anywhere.

A server offered us white wine. It was chilled with a crisp clean taste that reminded me of my Army days in Germany. A man in front of me moved and I saw the four, brightly colored chairs by Mary Heilmann in the middle of the room. I also saw Rashid Suliman sitting there. I moved behind Wendy and tapped her shoulder. She turned.

"Yes?"

"Rashid Suliman is behind you sitting in a yellow chair. Let's move where he's less likely to notice me."

Wendy turned and looked as we moved. "Handsome fellow. Doesn't look like a killer. Are you sure?"

"Not as yet. Same with the others, really. Still waiting for information and test results."

I admit bias. Grimes' death was strange, but was it murder? Did I want it to be murder to satisfy my client? Was I forcing evidence or following it? It's a fine line of perception and interpretation. Much like looking at a M. C. Escher print or those illusionary blocks that flip direction.

We wandered to a place that kept a crowd as cover. Wendy studied a painting as I scanned the room.

"Would you ladies like a refill?"

A man behind Suliman's bar held up a bottle of wine. I could see many bottles of liquor displayed behind him. I took Wendy's glass and stepped closer for a better look.

"Yes, thank you."

As he filled our glasses, I spotted a rare, 23-year-old, Duncan Taylor Blair Athol single malt. My mouth watered but didn't expect to be offered a taste. I scanned the bottles. On a lower shelf I saw a bottle of Bacardi 151, and on the bottom shelf a bottle of Everclear. I gave Wendy her glass.

"What do you think of this painting?"

"What?"

"I asked what you think of this painting?"

"Sorry. My mind was elsewhere."

I looked at the painting. It was vertical, about 3 feet x 2 feet of muted-colored, overlapping rectangles. A Chartreuse card on the wall simply read, "Oil, Ralph Balson, NSW 1890-1964."

"I like it. I wonder what NSW means?"

"New South Wales," said the bartender. "Balson helped pioneer Australian abstraction. The painting's original but not from Chartreuse as the card implies. I sold it to Ray two years ago. I do have another Balson available, if you're interested. My apologies if I'm intruding."

I glanced at his nametag: "Gregg, The Madsen Gallery." Wendy walked over to him.

"No apology needed. Thank you for the information."

"Excuse me," I stepped forward. "Is there a ladies room?"

"Yes. Down that hall. Second door on the left."

"Thank you." I set my glass down and looked at Wendy. "Be back shortly."

As I walked away, I heard Wendy asking, "Could you tell me about the painting you have?"

The bathroom was unoccupied. It was a full bathroom with separate shower and Jacuzzi tub. There were doors left and right. I locked the door to the hall and tried the others. The left one was locked from the other side. The right one opened on a darkened room. I flipped the switch. It was obviously a guest bedroom. I looked in the closet. Obviously unoccupied and not telling me anything.

I opened the hallway door and looked out. No one was

waiting for the bathroom or looking this way. I stepped out and tried the door at the end. It was locked. I tried another door across the hall. Also locked. Not my night. I went back into the guest room, through to the bathroom and out to rejoin Wendy who had finished her discussion with Gregg and was standing to guard the hall. She handed me my glass of wine.

"Find what you were looking for?"

"No. I crapped out. No pun intended. Not going to get a chance to look at Suliman's personal stuff. Sorry I've wasted your evening."

"Not wasted at all. I've seen some lovely paintings and learned about Ralph Balson. I'm going to see the other painting tomorrow."

"Seriously?"

"Of course seriously. Didn't you like this one?"

"Yes. It's very nice, but I'd hate to see the price tag."

"Price doesn't matter. This one belongs to Suliman and I doubt he's selling. However, the one tomorrow *is* available *and* within my budget."

"Really?"

"Really. So what do we do now?"

"We could go get something to eat."

"We ate before . . . Oh. I get it. You're frustrated, so you want food. Preferably hot and greasy, I presume."

"Now that you mention it. Sounds like a good idea."

As it was on the way home, we stopped at Belle's Diner, a 50s-styled eatery that brought pleasurable memories of the diners of my youth. Lisa, our favorite waitress, was working. Tonight her nametag was "Margie." I ordered a double chocolate shake, cheeseburger deluxe and a basket of fries. Wendy had coffee and a slice of vegan apple pie. I poured enough ketchup on a saucer to count as a veggie. Wendy just smiled and snagged a hot fry when my order came.

One of the countless things I've loved about Wendy is she's not preachy. Nor does she put others down. She'd been vegan the last few years and vegetarian long before that for ethical reasons. I'm more of a work in progress — your basic omnivore. If it tastes good, I'll eat it.

As I ate, and she nibbled, we weren't talking. My head was spinning trying to line up thoughts and facts sensibly. The Bacardi 151 and Everclear kept coming to mind. They could be instruments of disaster at the best of times. Add in high levels of caffeine and the disaster potential climbs quickly. Then there were the failing brakes screeching for attention. What had the mechanic at Bleeker's said?

"Could be fluid fade." Brake fluid shouldn't boil, but a bit of moisture or water could make it happen. Lower the boiling point. Create air bubbles. "Brake fluid doesn't compress, air does." Brake fluid boils around 400 degrees. Water 212. What about alcohol? Say 151 or 190 proof? How soon would brakes fail with a couple ounces of that added?

"Lisa? Do you have a piece of paper I could have and a pen to use?"

"Here you go. Wendy, you want more coffee?"

"Yes, thank you." Wendy took another fry. "You think of something?"

"Yes." I wrote out my thoughts. "If what I *think* happened, did happen. It's murder. If not, it remains an open question. I'll discuss it with Cartwright and Roberts tomorrow."

I put the paper in my pocket and sat back. I glanced down at my food. My burger was two-thirds eaten, my shake half gone. I couldn't recall tasting them. I took a big sip of the shake, added more ketchup to the saucer and dipped a fry. It wasn't as hot as when it first arrived, but it was still crisp and satisfying.

Twenty

Thursday morning—April Fools' Day, Maundy
Thursday, however you want to name it—I called John
Cartwright. The forensics team was done out in Washaw
County. The audit was complete with no red flags or
inconsistencies. There was no apparent reason for Rashid
Suliman, or the others, to have wanted or benefited from
Douglas Grimes death. We agreed it was a waiting game at
this point. We also agreed to speak with Stephanie Grimes
together. John called back to say we were meeting Stephanie
at her home at 1:00 p.m. I said I'd meet them there.

I spent the morning organizing my notes and writing an
interim report. I hated that I didn't have a definitive answer. It
was a beautiful, warm day. I arrived at the Grimes home five
minutes early. John's car was already there. Yvonne met me at
the door and led me to the living room. Stephanie and John
rose to greet me. She and I hugged.

"Would you like something to drink, Ms. Cord?"

"No, thank you, Yvonne. I'm fine."

Yvonne left the room and the three of us sat. I went
through my report with her.

"Finally, until the test results come back next week, there's
nothing further for me to investigate."

"So, all we can do is wait?"

"I'm afraid so."

"What happens if the results show it wasn't an accident?"

"Then," John said, "Rachel's and my firm's investigation results will be turned over to the Washaw County District Attorney. That's where your husband died. It will be the District Attorney's responsibility to determine charges and whom to charge."

"I pray it doesn't come to that. The idea that a friend or friends are the cause of Doug's death makes me ill. Thank you both for what you've done."

John handed Stephanie his audit report. "At this moment, without counting any proceeds from the pending company merger, you and Jason and Penelope Grimes will be splitting a little more than one hundred million dollars before any tax liabilities. From my reading of what the partners signed among themselves, once the merger is complete you and your stepchildren should receive another hundred to two hundred and fifty million."

"Yes, Darren explained that to me. In your opinion—both of your opinions—how significant are Doug's copyrights to this merger?"

"Highly significant," John said.

"I agree, Stephanie. I believe McManus said, 'possibly crucial.'"

Stephanie nodded. "Do you think if I withheld the use of the copyrights, Gimmicks would collapse?"

I shrugged, as I had no idea. John said, "The company is quite strong. It could survive. It would definitely be weakened. The merger would most likely fail. Are you considering that?"

"If Doug were murdered, yes. If I thought they were culpable, even if they're not found responsible, yes, again."

I took her hand. "Stephanie. Your husband built Gimmicks. The people who work there he treated like family. Would you want to hurt them as well?"

"Of course not, but I need to consider doing it regardless."

"Ms. Grimes, once we have the test results and a completed investigation may be a better time to consider your options."

"You're right, John. And please, please, call me Stephanie. Can you both stay for lunch?"

We agreed.

"And Rachel, do you have plans for Easter dinner?"

"I'm visiting my family in Iowa, but I'll be back for the results."

"Nervous about this weekend?"

"As a cat on a hot tin roof. I know you and Clare are excited, and my mother promises peace, but I'm not sure my family will comply."

"It'll be over soon. And, remember, my love, what doesn't kill us makes us stronger."

"Right."

Wendy held me and kissed me. I felt safe and loved in her arms. It was the *killing* part that worried me.

Twenty-One

Wendy and I split the driving stopping once to snack at a wayside picnic table before hitting the interstate north. The trip was pleasant but the weather cooled the nearer we got to Iowa. Crossing the state line we exited the interstate and headed north toward the small city of Laman, home to Grace University.

The first road sign I noticed was a yellow diamond with a black, silhouetted horse and buggy. I'd forgotten there were Amish in Decatur County. We soon passed such a rig headed south. The view was of open fields, ponds, gently rolling countryside, and isolated farmhouses and barns until we neared the city. When we entered the city limits, I started seeing election signs. The only names I recognized were Chuck Grassley for reelection to the Senate and Terry Bransford for Governor. That threw me because I thought he was governor when I left nearly 21 years ago. Maybe some things never change.

We turned east on Main Street and went past the high school and public library. At the corner of East Main and North Dogwood was our destination, a charming, brick B&B.

"Welcome to the Dogwood Street Inn. I'm Janet. You're the Devlins?"

"Yes. I'm Wendy Devlin. This is my mother Clare and my fiancé Rachel Cord. You have a beautiful place."

"Why, thank you. We certainly hope you enjoy your stay

with us. Let me see we have everything right. You reserved two rooms for the three of you — you'll be staying in the Traveler and Peace rooms. They're on the first floor and have private baths. You're leaving Monday. Checkout is 11:00 a.m. And let's see, you've requested vegetarian breakfasts. Is that correct?"

Wendy hesitated a moment, so I said, "Yes. We thought it would be more convenient for you."

"Oh, it's no problem at all. Though we certainly appreciate your letting us know. Makes ordering supplies easier. Are there any other dietary restrictions?"

"No," I added. "No meat. No dairy. That's it. We'll be fine."

Wendy rolled her eyes as I smiled at her.

"That's fine, then. Breakfast is from seven to nine in the dining room. We can adjust that if you let us know the night before. We can also provide a 'to go' breakfast if needed. Will you be having breakfast Easter morning?"

Wendy glanced at me and I shrugged and nodded. "Probably," she said. "I'll let you know if our plans change."

"That's fine. Our kitchen is state licensed, so I'm afraid it's off-limits to guests. There is a microwave and refrigerator in the dining area you may use. If you would like to use the dining table for other than breakfast time, please let us know so we can remove our antique items. Some are quite delicate."

"I don't think we'll be needing it. Can you suggest somewhere for dinner tonight?"

"Su Casa, the Mexican restaurant on Laurel, is very good. It's family owned and they don't use lard. Veggies and vegans who've stayed with us recommend it. It's just a block away. The two pizza places will make to order, but The Shack has a more complete, Italian menu. It's very popular with the students. It's two blocks east. They open at five."

"Thank you. One of those should work."

"My pleasure. Laman is simple, quiet country living with a highly rated university. There are many unique shops and galleries and the Laman Theater right across the street. You should stop at the Amish store out by the Interstate too. They're well known here for their quilts and baskets. Are you visiting anyone at the university?"

"No. Rachel's from the area. We're visiting her family for Easter."

"Really? Would I know them?"

"Joe Senior and Mary Cord over by Terryville. They're my parents."

"I know Nancy Cord. She lives out that way. We quilt together. One of hers is on the bed in the Peace Room. But I think her husband's name is Frank. Are you related to them?"

"Nancy's my sister-in-law. Frank's my oldest brother's middle name. He never liked being called Joe Junior."

"Isn't that nice. I expect they're all excited about seeing you."

"I'm sure they are. Thank you."

"Well, I'll let you get settled. If you need anything let me know."

Wendy set her suitcase down. "The room's beautiful."

The quilt on the bed was a Fractured Star in muted colors. I bounced on the bed to test its firmness.

"What are you grinning about?"

"I was just thinking how much pleasure it'll be making love to you under this quilt."

"Why is that?"

"Because Frank and Nancy hated me the most." I waggled my eyebrows. "Want to try right now?"

She laughed. "Later. You better let your mother know we made it. Then unpack so we can go eat."

Mom was happy to hear from me. Most likely glad I hadn't chickened out. She was waiting to hear from Wally. Wasn't sure how late he was getting in. Her sister had arrived and Sarah Ruth, my brother Al's youngest and born after I left, would be staying at the house also with a college friend. Mom asked if we would like to come out Saturday afternoon and stay for supper. It would be a smaller crowd than at Easter dinner, and she wanted time to get to know Wendy and Clare. Sounded like a good idea to me.

We walked around the block to Su Casa. It looked small and had an outside eating area. It was too cool for that and luckily the restaurant was larger inside. It was busy. The food was great. Large portions flavorfully spiced without killing your taste buds and chilled Dos Equis to wash it down. By the time we finished, the wind had died down, and though the air was chilled, we had a leisurely walk back.

Clare stopped at the Hy-Vee on the corner for a couple of items while Wendy and I looked in the windows of the Antique store next door. I saw another like it across the street in the window's reflection. Clare rejoined us and we talked about antiquing in the morning. I was feeling good about the trip and stopped fretting over unfinished work or meeting the family trolls.

We passed a few more storefronts, one was for rent, and stopped next to Pastry Heaven. Below the store name on the window was the slogan "Our Tarts Are Puckery Good." A small sign in the corner read, "Vegan-friendly." The lights were on and the shop looked open.

"Anyone for dessert?"

A bell above the door jingled as we entered. The woman behind the glass-fronted counter was at a worktable decorating cupcakes, her back to us. "Be with you in just a moment. I've got to get this order finished. There are free samples on the center table. Help yourselves."

Behind the glass were shelves of delicious looking pastries. The shelves were about half empty. Another glass-fronted counter had a "Half-Off Sale" sign. There were still a few brownies, cupcakes and turnovers available. I joined Clare and Wendy at the center table.

The table was round and high like those in a stand-up bar and covered with a blue tablecloth. There were four trays with clear plastic, dome lids. Two were marked vegan. The trays held bite-sized samples of cupcakes and fruit turnovers; tiny lemon, cherry and strawberry tarts; doughnut holes and mini mince and pecan pies. Clare took one of the two-bite pies, Wendy a cherry tart, and I chose the lemon. The taste was sweet and tart at the same time with a pleasing pucker. The pastry was flaky and perfect. Judging from their smiles, they were as pleased as I with the result. Visions of an evening of carb heaven filled my mind.

I walked back over to the main counter and watched the woman reach into a bag of multi-colored sprinkles and toss them over the cupcakes. Then she loaded the cupcakes into two large pastry boxes and set them on the counter. She went to a sink, washed her hands and came back to the counter with a radiant smile.

"So, how can I help you ladies? Everything in that display over there is day-old and half price. Everything here was made fresh today."

Looking straight at me her smile suddenly slipped, the sparkle in her eyes faded. Her left eyebrow rose quizzically. Her beautiful and large, doe-like, brown eyes widened, her mouth opened in a gaping O.

"Oh my Gosh. Rachel? Is that really you?"

She darted around the counter and her arms enclosed me tightly before I realized Betty Jean Cooper—my first love— was hugging and kissing me. The kiss lingered becoming as puckery tasteful as the tart I'd just eaten. I felt her tongue pushing between my lips before I came to my senses. Wow! Betty Jean Cooper. And Wendy right behind me. Oh, yeah.

I pulled away. "Ah. Well. Betty Jean. Long time no see." Did I *really* say that? How lame.

"Tell me about it. You run off to the Army and—"

"You were supposed to go with me."

"That's true, but we both knew it wasn't going to happen. But you stopped writing and you never came back and it's been, what? Twenty years? No, closer to 21. And *now* you're back." She stepped away. "Gosh, you look good." She hugged me again.

I disentangled us again. "Betty Jean—"

"Rachel, I heard about your father being in the hospital. Is that why you're back?"

"No. Dad's going to be fine. That's not why. I came back because I'm getting married. Betty Jean I'd like you to meet Wendy Devlin, my fiancé, and her mother and my friend, Clare Devlin. Clare, Wendy, this is Betty Jean Cooper. The first girl I ever kissed."

"Or went down on. Though I'm sure I wasn't the last. Ladies, my apologies for being crude, but I've been wondering and worrying about this deserter for a generation." She shook their hands. "I'm very pleased to meet you. By the way, Rachel, I'm now Betty Jean McComber."

"Like in Mrs. McComber where we hung out?" She nodded. "I thought they only had sons."

"They did. Remember Terrance, the oldest?"

"Wasn't he four years ahead of us? Played fullback on the high school football team?"

"That's the one. Like you, Terry joined the Army right after graduation. He was wounded and medically discharged during the first Gulf War. We had a couple classes together here at Grace after he came back. He bugged me for a date for nearly a year before we started going out. I discovered I was a switch hitter and I wanted kids. We married in '93. I have two beautiful daughters, but lost Terry four years ago to cancer."

"I'm sorry for your loss."

"Thanks. He was a good man and I miss him, but I'm finally moving on. I started dating an associate professor at Christmas. I think you'd like her."

"Her?"

Betty Jean shrugged. "Said I was a switch hitter. It's not just for my baking some in town call me the 'Queen of Tarts.'"

"How's that go over with your girls?"

"They're teens. I get the 'Oh, Mom!' and the 'You're embarrassing me!' but they love me anyway. And they like

Kelly and know I'm happy. Besides, I am who I am and they're stuck with it." She turned to Clare and Wendy. "Taste anything you like?"

"It's the best mince I've had since I don't know when," Clare said. "Reminds me of my mother's pies at Thanksgiving."

Wendy held another tart. "These are addicting, but I'm having trouble believing they're vegan."

Betty Jean smiled. "Let you in on a little secret. Nearly all my pastries are vegan. I just don't tell that to the sweet-toothed carnivores who turn up their noses at the very mention of the word. So, where are you staying? With Rachel's mom and dad?"

"We're across the street at the Dogwood Street Inn. Would you like to join us there after you close? I'm sure you and Rachel have a lot to catch up on, and I'd like some disclosure of her scandalous past."

Wendy's amused expression made me blush, and I wasn't sure I wanted my Alpha and Omega trading notes, but—

"Please, Betty Jean. We're only here this weekend for Wendy to face my family. A couple hours with you will strengthen my fortitude."

"I'd like that. Normally I close at nine on Friday nights, but as soon as my customer picks up her cupcakes I'll close and join you. Would you mind if Kelly joins us?"

"Not at all. We'd love to meet her."

"Good. Now what sweets can I interest you in?"

Betty Jean and her friend, Kelly Richards, arrived later with wine and what smelled like freshly baked goodies. I guessed Kelly a couple years older than Betty Jean or me. Not that that mattered. She was an inch taller than me, but that may have been from the low heels she was wearing with her slacks and jacket as I'd changed to slippers. Her dark hair fell naturally to her shoulders and her makeup was understated. I could see her fitting in nicely with the femmes at Phil's. She had a lovely smile that brightened whenever she looked at Betty Jean. However, I thought I saw a hint of anxiety in her eyes when we were introduced.

I gave her a sisterly hug and whispered, "I'm not competition. Just ancient history." I felt her relax and she whispered back, "Thank you. I hoped so." We settled in the inn's comfortable sitting room.

Betty Jean passed a pastry box to Clare. "Mrs. Devlin—"

"Please call me Clare."

"Okay, Clare. I baked these mince turnovers just for you."

"Why, thank you. That was very kind."

"Hey, no fair," I teased opening another box filled with triangle pastries that were still warm. "What are these?"

"Savories. Thought they'd go better with the wine than sweets."

Betty Jean passed out paper plates and napkins as Kelly opened the wine. They even brought wineglasses. From its light red color and fresh fruity flavor, I was pretty sure the wine was Beaujolais, but a far better one than the Beaujolais nouveau I've usually been served at Thanksgiving. This one went well with the pastries.

Betty Jean told how she and Kelly first met years ago at Grace when it was still only a college.

"Kelly was a senior working on her B.A. in Art. She had a minor in English. It was my freshman year. She tutored on the side and I was having problems because I was still mourning your leaving."

Kelly squeezed her hand. "We had a brief, discreet affair. I wasn't expecting it. I mean, who picks rural Iowa to look for gay love? Definitely not back then."

"True." I smiled. "One reason I left. Not that the Army was any more understanding, mind you. But there were a lot of us cozying between the sheets the Brass weren't aware of."

Kelly nodded. "Understandable for the times. Anyway, I graduated and moved to San Francisco where I got my MFA with an emphasis in Sculpture at the Academy of Art University. I was doing all right. I liked San Francisco, but my social life was dragging from too many years of short-time lovers. I wanted something quieter. I applied to Ohio University for their Ph.D. program in Interdisciplinary Arts, and started looking for a home. I remembered the good times I had at Grace. It had become a university, so I began inquiries for openings while working on my doctoral thesis. I didn't know Jean still lived here."

Betty Jean leaned over and kissed her cheek. Wendy and I traded looks and she took my hand. Kelly took a sip of wine.

"I'm well into my second year here and last October a colleague asked me to pick up the pastry order for a staff meeting. I'd been enjoying these great turnovers but had never been to the bakery. Imagine my surprise when I discovered Jean behind the counter."

"Probably as great as mine earlier this evening."

There was gentle laughter from all of us. Clare stood up.

"Ladies, I think I'll turn in. Betty Jean, thank you for the mince turnovers. They're delicious. Kelly, it was a pleasure meeting you. I hope to see you both again. Rachel, I'm going to call your mom. Any messages?"

"No. Just give her my love and say we'll see her tomorrow."

"Okay. Good night, everyone. Enjoy yourselves."

We all said, "Goodnight," and I opened the second bottle of wine. It was a 2007 Domaine des Marrans Chiroubles from Beaujolais, France. I filled our glasses.

Betty Jean leaned toward Wendy. "I think your mother's great." Kelly agreed.

"Thank you. We think so too."

Kelly was looking at me. I glanced down at my blouse.

"Did I spill something?"

She shook her head. "No. I was just remembering what Jean told me about you years ago. I always thought she exaggerated, and now—"

"That's right," Betty Jean said. "I noticed earlier but forgot to ask. I know my memory's not perfect," she held up her hands about a foot in front of her breasts, "but I certainly remember a whole lot more of you." She got a worried look. "I'm sorry, you didn't get breast cancer, did you?"

"No. I just got tired of hauling the heavy things around and having them enter rooms before I did." I looked at Kelly. "Betty Jean wasn't exaggerating. My breasts were huge. Double-H huge. I had reduction surgery a few years ago and wish I'd done it ten years earlier."

"Well, you look great."

"I feel great." I raised my glass. "Here's to greatness."

"So now that you know about Kelly and me, how did you two meet?"

I looked at Wendy. She nodded for me to tell my tale.

"Let me top up your glasses. This is a long story. I met Clare first. She introduced me to Wendy. But my story starts back when I left here and joined the Army. I became an MP, and like your Terry, I was in Saudi Arabia and Kuwait for the first Gulf War. When my enlistment was up, I thought of law enforcement but didn't want bosses anymore. So I became an independent professional investigator."

"You mean like a private eye?"

"Exactly."

Betty Jean and Kelly traded glances, and Kelly made a nearly imperceptible shake of her head. Neither said anything, so I went on with my story.

I told them of catching a killer who raped and murdered five women at a nearby college. About other cases and how I began to specialize in finding runaway teens because "in a way, I was a runaway too." I talked about falling in love with Karen Tanaka, and how I thought she ran out on me. About the gay bashing at Miss Kitty's Kathouse Kabaret and losing a possible love when Sarah Hastings was killed. About searching for teenage runaway Linda Miller and finding her held prisoner. About my torture and rape and its aftermath.

"Rachel that's horrible."

"Yes, but I came out of it partly with Clare's help. I joined a rape survivors group. Clare was one of them. She was raped three years before me at age 67 and left to die in a field. But Clare's a tough lady. She and the others became my sisters. My helpmates. We're there for each other. It's a bond so tight it can't be broken. Then Clare introduced me to Wendy. That was five-and-a-half years ago."

I told Betty Jean and Kelly how Wendy and I started hot and steamy only to go blizzard cold then hot again. "We're still hot." I talked about the ghost of Karen returning and finding out she hadn't run out on me, but had been murdered too. How we discovered the killer and I almost lost Wendy to him. How three years later, someone was gunning for me, and it was Wendy who saved us that time.

I don't know how long I talked, but I also included the good times and the good people in my life, like watching 25 couples dance in a fountain pledging love and faithfulness as 300 of us helped them celebrate; of Philadelphia Long and her lesbian tearoom; Margo Lane and his *Voice*; PJs, her daughter and granddaughters who took in runaways and throwaways; good cops like Frank Taylor, Ed Montero, Dean Lockhart, and, especially, Kerri Trujillo who ran the Sex Crimes Division.

"And as I face down my family this weekend so this wonderful, sexy woman here will marry me, I've an open case waiting at home. Waiting for lab results as to whether a man's death was accidental or if someone influenced his dying."

It was late. The wine and pastries were finished. Betty Jean needed to get up early to start her Saturday baking. "Gotta make dough while the oven's hot." The four of us hugged and kissed. Said we'd try to get together again before Wendy and I needed to leave. Wendy headed for our room as I told her I'd be right in as soon as I saw Betty Jean and Kelly to their car.

Outside, I asked, "Is anything wrong? I thought I saw something when I said I was an investigator."

That same, quick, worried look passed between them

again. The same, barely perceptible, negative reply.

"No. Nothing. Why don't you stop by before going to your mom's tomorrow? I'll fix a basket of goodies you can take with you. Your brothers may hate who we are, but I know for a fact they love my pies."

Wendy was waiting for me in bed. I undressed and crawled in beside her. Her body was warm and I held her tightly. She kissed me.

"I like them."

"Me too."

"Think Betty Jean would bake for our wedding?"

'I'm sure she would. I'll ask her tomorrow."

"Something wrong?"

"I'm not sure. Thought I sensed something. Might be nothing."

"Want to talk about it?"

"No. I'd rather do this."

I kissed her lips; softly kissed her eyelids; kissed the middle of her forehead. Kissed the spot on her neck that always brought a contented sigh. Gently massaged her back as I moved down to her breasts, lingering for a moment, then continued down beneath the covers. She reached out grabbing my leg behind the knee and pulled it toward her. Forcing me to turn to continue my descent. As I breathed her in and my tongue sought her sweet wetness, I felt her lips along my inner thighs seeking their own pleasures.

Twenty-Two

The alarm got us up, and the walk-in shower large enough for two woke us completely as we shampooed, lathered, tickled, teased, caressed, satisfied our desire and calmed in a cooling rinse.

There was the smell of freshly baked biscuits when we came to the dining room. An older man was sitting having coffee and talking with Clare. Of course, *older* is a relative term. His hair was gray, but he could have been only a few years older than Wendy. In front of Clare was a half biscuit covered in a dark jam. The man stood.

"Good morning. Hope you slept well. I'm Carl Nielsen, Janet's husband."

We said, "Good morning," and Wendy added, "Quite well, thank you. The bed was great."

"And I *love* your shower."

"That's the type of comments we like to hear. Would you like fresh, orange juice as well as coffee?"

We said, "Yes, thank you."

He pulled out chairs and seated us. "I'll get it and then help Janet finish breakfast."

On the table were chilled plates with sliced fruits and figs; chilled bowls with what looked like cinnamon-laced balls of butter; a covered basket of biscuits; three glass pots with jams and marmalade; a warming plate with two, white, ceramic pitchers: one marked "Maple," the other "Sugar-free."

"The cinnamon *butter* is Earth Balance," Clare said before taking a bite of her biscuit. "How late did you stay up talking?"

"Close to midnight. Betty Jean said she needed an early start on her baking. She's also making up a basket to take to Mom. I'll pick it up before we leave."

Carl returned with a tray holding a pitcher of orange juice and glasses and a carafe of coffee. He poured the juice, filled our coffee cups and refilled Clare's. Janet came out with three plates and set Belgian waffles before us.

"Good morning. Hope you had a good night."

I could feel a broad smile. "We did, thank you. This looks delicious."

"Thank you. I'm sorry it's going to be a cold day for sightseeing. You'll need to bundle up. It's barely 40 out there right now. I just hope we hit 60 this afternoon like the weather report predicts. At least there's no snow. I didn't know whether or not to put out honey. It's not animal, but I've been told it's not vegan either."

Wendy was buttering her waffle. "No one agrees. Some feel gathering honey exploits the bees and kills many of them. Others believe it's a symbiotic relationship and all right to eat. Those that would like some will ask if there is any. Those that don't won't ask."

Janet and Carl returned to the kitchen. The waffles were crisp on the outside and melt-in-your-mouth centers teeming with chunks of pecan and every bit as tasteful as they looked. At just the right moment, Carl returned to clear the plates as Janet arrived with the next course: scrambled tofu with green and red bell pepper, mushrooms and onion, a large half biscuit covered in a peppery, soysage gravy, and a broiled, half tomato. Carl asked if anyone wanted hot sauce. Clare and I said "No," but Wendy said she would.

I looked at her. "We're going to have to exercise more." My eyebrows did a lecherous waggle.

She had to put her hand over her mouth to stifle her laugh

and keep from spewing the bite she'd just taken. Her face was turning beet red but she nodded enthusiastically. It took several moments before her face returned to normal and she could drink some water.

"That's mean when I have food in my mouth."

"You can punish me later."

"You should be so lucky. Mother, do you still want to go antiquing?"

"Yes, but not too soon after we eat. This is more than I have all week. Rachel, what time does your mother expect us?"

"She just said in the afternoon. I was thinking between three and four. It's a short drive. She used to serve supper on Saturdays around six. Of course, we can go earlier if you'd like."

"I think your mother and I would like a nice, long visit. How does this sound? We go to the antique stores at noon. Hopefully it will have warmed up some by then. When we finish, you pick up the things from Betty Jean and we leave."

"Sounds good." I looked at Wendy, winked and silently mouthed "noon."

Breakfast finished with warmed, peach compote and faux crème.

"Would anyone like more coffee?"

We all had another cup. Carl cleared dirty plates but left the fruit, the basket of biscuits, the cinnamon spread and jams.

"Take your time. Relax. No need to rush. Enjoy. Oh, there's a family coming in this afternoon. They'll be taking the two upstairs rooms and will be here for breakfast. Just to let you know."

We took our coffee into the sitting room to allow Carl to finish clearing. Clare said she was just going to sit and read until time to leave. Wendy and I finished our coffee and headed for our room. Two wanton hours before we needed to get dressed.

Oh, well. As much as our minds wanted unbounded

lechery, our bodies were saying "slow down." It really was too much breakfast, but it tasted too good not to eat it all. Sometimes it's just nice to cuddle. I must have nearly fallen asleep when Wendy's finger lightly traced a line along my hairline, down the side of my face and along the edge of my chin.

I turned my face to her. "That feels nice."

She kissed me softly. "I was thinking about last night. There were times I thought Kelly seemed uncomfortable. I wondered if she were worried about your being back in Betty Jean's life."

"I thought that too. So when I first hugged her I told her Betty Jean and I were ancient history. She relaxed after that."

"Then I thought she was worried someone would suggest a foursome."

"Wouldn't have been me. Why would she think that? Did *you* think that might happen?"

"I'm afraid it crossed my mind. Why wouldn't it have been you? From stories you've told of your past—"

"Because, my one and only, five-and-a-half years ago you told me you wanted no part of anything other than being 'an only' in my life. And that's the way it's been, and the way it will remain. Unless, of course, *you* decide to dump *me* sometime in the future. Then all bets are off."

"Never gonna happen."

She held me tight. Kissed me hard and long.

"But you're right," I said when I could breathe again. "There were moments when Kelly seemed nervous. I swear a couple times I caught them in silent conversation. It's as if Betty Jean asked her 'Should we tell?' and Kelly replied 'No.' I'm definitely finding out later. Meanwhile, how much time do we have before we need to dress?"

"About twenty minutes."

I put my hand behind her head so she wouldn't pull away. As I kissed her, I pressed my tongue between her lips and ran it along her teeth until they let me in. My other hand slid down to part her other lips and knead her clitoris. Her tongue pressed back. I sucked it in. Her fingers slid down to knead me in return.

Betty Jean was at the cash register giving a customer change when I entered Pastry Heaven. Two others were in line to pay for their selections. Another was being waited on, as two others tasted the free samples.

"Thank you, Mr. B. Say hi to your wife and have a Happy Easter." Betty Jean waved and took the next in line. "Afternoon, Mrs. Newcomb. Did you find everything you wanted?"

I picked up a lemon tart from the sample table—I couldn't resist—and ate it as I stood in the checkout line.

"Hi, Rachel. Your basket's ready. I'll get it."

"Do you have a minute to answer a couple questions?"

"Sure, I guess. Susan? Take the register for a minute. I'll be right back. Come on, we can talk back here."

Two teen girls were working in the back. One was piping icing onto turnovers and the other was putting trays into a large oven.

"My girls. They like to help out on Saturdays. Jenna? Jordan? This is Rachel. She and I went to high school together."

Both sang out, "Pleased to meet you, ma'am."

"Nice meeting you too."

"Jenna, would you help the lady at the Day-Old counter? Susan's busy at the register. Thanks. We can talk in the office."

"You know, I'm not sure I like being old enough to be called 'ma'am.'"

She closed the door. "They are polite, if nothing else. So, what do you need?"

"I'd like to know what was bothering you two last night. It was right after I said I was an investigator. And don't say 'Nothing,' because that's not what your body language was screaming."

"Kelly doesn't want to talk about it."

"That part I already know. What is it?"

"I shouldn't tell —"

"But you want to."

"She's going to be *so* mad if I tell."

"Only if she finds out. Look, I'm only here for the weekend with the family. Then it's back to work and arranging our wedding. Oh, by the way, Wendy wants to know if you'll bake for our wedding reception. The date's not set yet, but it'll be soon."

"I'd love to. Just give me the date when you decide." Betty Jean sighed and stared at the ceiling. "She's gonna kill me. We went round and round about it after we left last night."

"And *it* is?"

"Kelly's being harassed. She doesn't know who."

"Threats?"

"Kinda sorta. More implied than direct. Text messages, notes in her inbox. That sort of thing. She's even been sent pictures of herself on campus and leaving my house."

"That's stalking. Has she told campus security or the police?"

"No."

"Why not?"

"She doesn't want to make a big deal of it."

"It is a big deal. Stalkers don't go away, and they can become dangerous. Talk to her. Let me talk to her. I've dealt with this before. I don't have time now. I have the number you gave me. I don't know how late it'll be, but I'll call when we leave Mom's. *Convince* her to see me."

"Rachel, you're scaring me."

"Good. It's scary stuff.

"All right. I'll talk to her. How soon are you going to your mom's?"

"As soon as I leave here. Wendy and Clare are waiting at the inn."

"Okay. I'll get your basket."

"Thanks. How much do I owe you?"

"Nothing. Consider it my Easter present to soothe the savages. Among other things there are spiced apple and sour cherry pies. Joe Junior and Al's favorites. Everything's marked. Be careful. It's heavy."

"Thanks." We hugged. "Don't forget to talk to Kelly."

Twenty-Three

We headed toward Terryville on highway 69 and the
memories flooded back with each passing mile. When I made
the turn leading to Nine Eagles State Park, there was a distinct
lump in my throat. This is where I grew up. This was my
beginning. I slowed on the bridge crossing Jeffers Creek but
didn't stop. A quarter mile upstream where Deckers Branch
met Jeffers was a waterhole favored by swimmers and catfish
and where Betty Jean and I first made love. I needed no
directions to find my way home. Just gumption.

I turned at the first left then took the left fork north. The
east fork led to Frank and Nancy's farm. There was open
farmland to our left and wooded hills on the right. By the time
we reached the drive to my parent's farm, my eyes were
burning and filling with tears.

The yellow house was two-story with a wraparound porch
and looked overdue for repainting. My room had been the
middle one upstairs facing the road and woods. I remembered
watching deer at dawn cross to eat the grass out front or go
into the fields in search of grain. And foxes sneaking for the
henhouse. Not that Duke, our black lab, ever let them succeed.

The huge oak, where Frank and Al built a tree fort that
years later Wally and I restored and expanded, had suffered.
One of the four major branches that supported the fort was
gone. You could see the scorched wood from an old lightning
strike. The fort was gone too. The old one-car garage was still

there, but beside it was a wide building with two oversized roll-up doors. Out back were the sheds and barns and grain silos. Several cars and pickups were parked in the turnout. I parked next to a new Toyota sedan with Kansas plates.

The kitchen-side of the porch was shrouded in several layers of plastic sheeting. Three people on ladders secured the sheeting along the porch beam and two others attached it to the post supports. Wendy helped me carry the basket to the front steps. Betty Jean wasn't kidding when she said it was heavy.

"Pumpkin!"

My mother came down the steps with more energy than I could have imagined. I didn't have time to set the basket down before she engulfed me. I was overcome by how much I missed her hugs. Over her shoulder I saw Aunt Libby standing with a serene smile and tears in her eyes. I could feel my own sliding down my cheeks.

"I've missed you, Mom."

"You're home now. That's all that counts."

"Mom, this is Wendy."

Wendy put out her free hand to shake Mom's, but Mom ignored it as she hugged her.

"Thank you. Thank you, for bringing my girl home. You are most welcome here."

"Thank you, Mrs. Cord."

"Posh! You call me 'Mom' or 'Mary Ella.' Whichever you're comfortable with."

"Okay. May I present my mother, Clare Devlin?"

"Clare! I've *so* wanted to meet you."

"And I you, Mary. How are you?"

"Right this minute, the happiest woman on Earth."

As Mom and Clare hugged and nattered mysteriously, Aunt Libby came down the steps.

"Aunt Libby, you're looking well."

"As compared to what? You haven't seen me in 22 years. Give me a hug, you rascal."

"And this is my fiancé, Wendy Devlin. Wendy, this is Elizabeth Fisher, my mother's younger sister."

"As opposed to her older sister, which we've never had. There being just the two of us. Call me 'Aunt Libby' like everyone else. You're part of the family now. At least today you get to meet the Good'ns."

"Good'ns?"

"The good ones. It'll help prepare you for the 'Bad'ns' and 'Sours' tomorrow. Land of tarnation! What are you two carrying? I swear. That's the biggest picnic basket I've ever seen."

"It's baked goods from Pastry Heaven in Laman."

"Looks like enough to feed an army. Think I'll give up any thoughts of dieting until I get home. Bring it inside before your arms start looking like an orangutan's."

"What's with all the plastic sheeting?"

"For Easter dinner. Not enough room inside for a sit-down with the horde that's coming. And too cool outside to be comfortable. We're closing off that end of the porch. Got two gas patio heaters for warmth. But I doubt we'll need 'em once everyone's seated. You know how hot a barn can get in winter when all the animals are contained. Let's see what goodies you brought."

We carried the basket to the kitchen and laid it on the table. Aunt Libby opened it and started taking out boxes.

"'Pastry Heaven. *Our Tarts Are Puckery Good.*' Catchy. Spiced apple pie. Says it's for JJ. Who's that?"

"Joe Junior. Betty Jean won't call him Frank. She says it's his favorite pie."

"Betty Jean? Isn't she the one you started the so-called scandal with back in high school?"

"One and the same. She owns Pastry Heaven."

"And sour cherry for Al. She trying to get you on their good side?"

"She says it's to soothe the savages."

"Stranger things have happened. 'Hope springs eternal' as

they say. Can't hurt. What else we got? Blackberry turnovers. Where did she find blackberries this time a year? Your dad'll like those. Why don't you take one to him now with a cup of coffee? He's in the parlor."

My father, looking every day of his 79 years, sat in a rocker using the afternoon light through the window to read his *Des Moines Register*. The sweet smell of his pipe tobacco filled the room. There was a cane within easy reach. A red and white springer spaniel lay at his feet. She raised her head, wagged her tail and came to greet us. Wendy kneeled down and petted her behind the ears.

"Hi, Dad."

He looked up, laying his paper down and removed his reading glasses.

"Hi, yourself." His tone was his usual sarcastic, but I caught the hint of a smile behind it that always mellowed it. "Seen your mother yet?"

"Yes, sir."

"Good. She's been on pins and needles ever since you called two weeks ago."

There was a long pause. "Dad—" "Rachel—" we said at the same time. Another pause.

"How are you doing, Dad?"

"Been better."

Another long pause. Another "Dad" "Rachel" at the same time. "Sorry, sir."

He reached up and removed a speck of something beneath his eye.

"Me too. So. You going to introduce this handsome woman or just leave her standing there?"

"Dad, this is my fiancé, Wendy Devlin. Wendy, please meet my father, Joseph Franklin Cord, Sr."

"I'm pleased to meet you, sir."

"Likewise. What kind of name is Wendy for a grown woman?"

"My mother was partial to Peter Pan."

He nodded. "Good story. Enjoyed it as a kid. Sit down. Pull up a chair. What are you holding, Rachel?"

"Hot coffee and a blackberry turnover."

"Trying to bribe me, I suppose. Is it warm?"

"No, sir, but I can go warm it for you."

"That's okay. Will you please sit? Hurts my neck looking up at you two."

The dog nuzzled Wendy's hand. "What's the dog's name?"

"June." Dad looked at me. "April died a few years after you . . . anyway, she died. May died four years ago. This is June. What do you do for a living Wendy?"

"I'm a bank vice president. Been one about eight years now."

"Why aren't you president by now?"

"Waiting for the current one to retire."

"Or die of old age more likely. Probably hates to leave all that money."

"Probably."

"Devlin. A good, old, Irish name. Means . . . 'fierce' I believe.

"Yes, sir. It does. Also translates as 'raging valor.'"

My father nodded. "Root is 'dubh' meaning dark or black-haired. Do you know when your people came over?"

"During the Potato Famine. First New England, then Pennsylvania coalmines, and finally farther west building tunnels for the railroads. There were miners on my mother's side too. From Cornwall. There's a family saying, 'a mine is a hole anywhere in the world with at least one Cornishman at the bottom of it.' The first of her family here being Paul Helston in 1883, though that may not have been his true name. One family tale says Paul was his surname, and he took the name Helston after a town in South Cornwall because he was wanted for murder."

"Happens in the best of families. Thomas Cord came from County Tyrone in Northern Ireland and settled in what would become Maine in the 1760s. Like your family, my great grandfather came west with the railroads and settled in Council Bluffs. Still have distant cousins over there. My grandfather, Duncan Cord, settled here in Decatur County and began farming in 1896. My father, Andrew, was born two years later. He and I were born in the original house my grandfather built not two miles from here. It burned down in 1935 and the new house went up the following spring. My oldest, Frank, lives there now."

I sat there fascinated as Wendy and Dad talked, learning things I never knew about each of them. Dad turned to me.

"Rachel, this turnover is really good. Did you bake it?"

"No, sir. It's from Pastry Heaven. There are five more if you want one."

"Not right now, but will you make sure one is saved for my breakfast?"

"Certainly."

He turned back to Wendy. "I met Mary Ella, Rachel's mother, at Letterman Army Hospital out in San Francisco in 1953. I was wounded in Korea at the Kumsong River and evacuated. Nearly lost my leg to shrapnel and gangrene. She was a nurse's aide. Only 17. Helped with the debriding. Never shirked. Took nearly a year to recover. Got a scar from here to here. Mary Ella was a Dame from Massachusetts. Dame was the family name. I wasn't being disparaging. Her father was an MP Colonel at the Presidio nearing retirement. Didn't think much of me at the time, but that didn't stop us from courting. We married in March '55."

I stood. "Excuse me, Dad. I need to see Mom. Would you like more coffee?"

"No. I'm good. Would you like something, Wendy?"

"No, thank you, sir. I'm fine." She looked up at me and winked. "You said you married in San Francisco?"

"That's right. At the Presidio. Her father walked her down the aisle."

I left them and went to the kitchen. Mom, Clare and Aunt Libby were there. They looked at me expectantly.

I shrugged. "Dad and Wendy are trading family histories. I wasn't needed. Oh, Dad asked to save him a blackberry turnover for breakfast."

"We'll set the box aside for him," Aunt Libby said. "One may not be enough for breakfast, and he'll probably want one tonight for dessert." Mom nodded her agreement. "Anyway, I don't see any blood. Looks like you survived."

"Looks that way. Mom, I was thinking. Frank was born in September 1955, right?"

"Yes. Why?"

"Well, Dad says you were married in March 1955. That can't be right. Shouldn't it have been '54?"

Aunt Libby was suppressing a laugh and Mom was blushing. Clare turned away and flipped through Mom's Betty Crocker Cookbook.

"Would you believe your brother was an early baby?"

"Three months? Is that even possible? Especially back then?"

Libby burst out laughing and I could see Clare shaking, her hand over her mouth. Mom just sighed.

"Why don't you go out and help Walter?"

As the kitchen door closed behind me, I heard Mom mutter "kids" and more laughter. The plastic sheeting was complete. It looked like bubble wrap sandwiched between flat sheets of plastic. I saw two silhouettes through the translucent sheeting. They were nailing wooden strips along the base of the plastic. They stopped a moment and kissed, then continued working. I turned toward a noise. Wally and two others were setting out folding banquet tables.

"Hey, big brother."

"Hey, little sister." We came together in a huge hug.

"I'm sure glad you're here."

"Happy to see you too." He stepped back and inspected me. Turning me this way and that. "Heard you were in with Dad. Looks like no harm done. Wait a sec. Did he do that?"

He pointed at my breasts. "No, you goose. I had reduction

surgery three years ago."

"Good for you. Come meet my Becca."

Wally is six foot and the lithe woman waiting for us was just as tall. She wore jeans and a tucked-in, work shirt with the sleeves rolled back to the elbows despite the chill. Around her neck was a beaded choker with a geometric pattern. Her black hair was cut super short and brushed back. She had dark, captivating eyes, high cheekbones, warm brown skin and an easy smile. In a word: drop-dead gorgeous. Also, distinctly Native American.

"Rachel, I'd like you to meet the love of my life—and, confidentially, one really badass combat Apache pilot—Rebecca BrightStar. Becca, this is my kid sister—and private eye extraordinaire—Rachel Cord."

"The preferred term is 'professional investigator.' Pleased to meet you."

"Drew's told me so much about you, I feel I know you already."

Her handshake was firm and dry, her voice a pleasing contralto, and gorgeous besides. No wonder Wally loved her. I'd love her too. I hugged her.

"Welcome to the chaotic Cord clan."

"No more so than my family on the rez. You should have seen the first time I took Drew home with me."

"And you fly helicopters too?"

"I fly *Apaches*. Which is appropriate being Jicarilla."

It sounded like she said, "heek-ah-REE-ah," which I'd never heard of. My confusion was apparent.

"We're an Apache tribe. Northern New Mexico. Jicarilla is Mex-Spanish for 'little basket.' We call ourselves 'the people who came from below.' The sole descendants of the first people to come from the underworld after Ancestral Man and Ancestral Woman created the first people."

"I'd like to learn more. Especially how you two met."

"We can do that. I know there must be things you can tell me about this guy no one else will. But first we need to get these tables together."

"Right. How many are coming?"

"Thirty-plus, I was told. So we're setting up for 40, just in case."

"Not sure I can handle 30 at one time, much less 40. Wally, when we get a chance I need to ask you something."

"Okay."

"Hi, Aunt Rachel. Remember me."

A young man who'd been standing there the whole time came forward. He looked a lot like my brother Al who I hadn't seen since I left, but taller. I tried to think of his name.

"You used to babysit me."

"Joey? You used to be just . . ." I held my hand below my waist, "and now you're—"

"All grown up. That can happen over 20 years, you know."

"So it seems, but how'd you get . . . how tall are you?"

"Six-four. Comes from clean living and Mom's genes."

"That's right. All the McCombers are tall. You look great."

"Thanks. Just want you to know *I'm* glad to see you."

"Thanks."

We set up the five banquet tables end-to-end nearly filling the length of the porch. We started placing chairs when the two silhouettes I'd seen kissing came round the corner. They were two girls no more than 20 wearing red and gold plaid work shirts, bibs and boots. The taller one's face looked like Joey, but the cut and color of her hair reminded me of soccer star Abby Wambach. The other girl was a foot shorter with a sweet face and honey blonde hair tied back in a ponytail.

"Sis," Joey said, "Come meet your Aunt Rachel."

I like to think at five-nine I'm considered tall, but I didn't feel that way with most of the people around me at the moment. Joey's sister had me by two inches, but I hoped that was partly the fault of her work boots. Her hand was callused and strong from hard work and her stare was direct.

"Pleased to meet you, Aunt Rachel. I'm Sarah, Joey's sister. This is my girlfriend, Elsa Lindstrom. We're Aggies at State."

"Thought you might be from the colors of your shirts. It's a pleasure to meet both of you."

"Hope you don't mind, but Grandma's put us in your old room for the weekend."

"Don't mind at all. I seriously doubt Mom's been holding it for me all these years. Besides, Wendy and I are staying in Laman."

"Okay. I was worried because there's still some of your old stuff up there."

"You're kidding."

"No, seriously. You should take a look."

"Think I will. Thanks."

"No problem. Uncle Drew, you guys need any help? Otherwise, we're going over to the barn Grandpa says we can use and do some cleaning."

"Go ahead. We're about finished here. Just remember your grandma wants you here for supper."

"We will. It really is nice meeting you, Aunt Rachel."

"Same here, but please, how about just Rachel? I'm not ready for all the 'Aunt this or that' I'm going to hear this weekend."

"Okay. Bye"

The girls headed quickly for an old F150 and drove off. I turned to Joey.

"How long have they been together?"

"Since they first became roommates at State. Mom and Dad blame your influence."

"Why? Your sister never met me."

"Still your fault. They even sent her to a gay re-education camp after she came out at her high school graduation."

"Really?"

"As Elsa would say, 'Yah sure you betcha.' She's from Minnesota."

"Your parents coming tomorrow?"

"Grandma will skin 'em alive if they don't."

"Great. Just great."

"Well, guess I better head to Mom and Dad's. I know they're itching to interrogate me over what's happening here."

"Good luck with that."

"It's okay. I doubt they'll resort to waterboarding. See you tomorrow, Ah . . . Rachel."

"Bye, Joey."

I turned around and saw Wally and Rebecca had finished with the chairs. I tried to picture where everyone might be seated the next day. Would I be honored like the Prodigal Son and treated to the "fatted calf" or set among the wolves and *be* the "fatted calf"? And where would Wendy be placed? I felt reassuring hands on my shoulders.

"Worried about tomorrow, little sister?"

"Big time. And not just for me."

"Look at this way. It'll only last two, three hours at most before the haters feel they've fulfilled their filial duties and slink away. Before that, and after that, you'll be with people who like you and want to know the person you love. Speaking of which, where is your wonderful Wendy? Becca hasn't met her yet."

"She was with Dad the last I saw her."

"Well it's time we rescued her. Oh. What was it you wanted to ask me?"

"Did you know Mom was pregnant when they got married?"

"Yes. Didn't you?"

"Not until today I didn't. How long have you known?"

"I don't know. Since I was 10 or 11, I guess."

"Really? How'd you find out?"

"Are you sure you're a detective?"

"Answer the question."

"Do you remember the family albums?"

"Yes. We used to look at them all the time."

"Do you remember how Mom carefully captioned and dated every photo and kept copies of important events?"

"Yes."

"Well, Mom and Dad's wedding picture is in there. And so was a copy of Frank's birth complete with the certificate the hospital gives out with his footprints on it. Even back then I knew how long pregnancies last. And I never had a problem counting to nine. How could I not know?"

"Point taken."

"Does knowing make you think less of her?"

"Not less. Just . . . a bit surprised, maybe . . . and it makes me realize she and Dad are as human as the rest of us . . . which makes them somehow better—not less—to me. I'm not making any sense. Forget it."

"You're overthinking it. Let's go find Wendy."

Opening the kitchen door I was surprised by the mouth-watering flavors of Clare's, vegan, Six O'Clock Chili when I half-expected smelling Mom's roast chicken, our traditional Saturday supper before Easter. I sniffed again and couldn't detect even a hint of roasting chicken. The old kitchen wall clock said 4:00, so it was too early to put the chicken in anyway. Wally went straight to the huge stockpot I hadn't noticed earlier simmering on a back burner.

"What's cooking?"

Libby was grating cabbage into a large bowl. "Six O'Clock Chili. Clare's recipe. Stay out of it. Won't be ready until six like the name says. Have you met Clare yet?"

"No I haven't. Pleased to meet you, Mrs. Devlin, I'm Rachel's brother Drew."

Clare stopped stirring a bowl of dressing. I saw grated carrots and diced onions and green and red peppers. A pile of cucumber peelings made me certain they were making coleslaw for Easter based on Charlie's secret dressing recipe. Charlie's Chicago Hot Dog Stand had the best tasting coleslaw ever, and Charlie shared his dressing recipe with very few people. Clare being one. Best of all, it was vegan.

"Nice meeting you, Drew, but please call me Clare."

"Sure I can't have an early taste? It smells great."

Clare smiled and shook her head. "Won't be ready till six.

Waiting's good for the appetite."

And well worth the wait. It should be called "12-Hour Chili" because it goes on the stove at six in the morning and slow-cooks until it's ready at six in the evening. It's a jackpot blend of six different beans, onions, garlic, peppers, celery, spices and bulgar wheat for a "meaty" texture. I haven't met anyone who didn't believe they could taste the beef or didn't want seconds. Mom must have soaked the beans overnight and started the chili this morning following Clare's recipe. And the cabbage and carrots for the slaw probably came from the root cellar. I felt a lump in my throat.

"Where's Mom?" I asked Libby.

"Upstairs with Wendy and Rebecca. Your dad's napping. He's still recovering from his fall. Where are the girls?"

"Said they were going over to some barn Dad's letting them use. What's with that?"

"Goat farm. A project for their senior year. Got a business plan all worked out. Your Dad's letting them use the Old Houzer Place and 20 acres of its pasture. They've been coming down from Ames every weekend they can to work on getting the place ready. This summer they'll work on it full time. Elsa says her family will be providing the goats, which if everything goes to plan will be the end of July."

"A goat farm."

"Dairy goats. Their goal is to make artisan cheeses to sell at farmers markets and to fancy restaurants in Des Moines, Omaha and Kansas City."

"Good luck to them. Wally, you want to go upstairs and see what's going on?"

Wally turned from the counter where the Pastry Heaven boxes were stacked. He held a half-eaten turnover and licked his lips.

"Sure. I've only seen Wendy that one time I visited on leave four years ago. If we're quiet, we might hear what they're saying about us." He wore a Tom Selleck grin.

We stopped when we heard voices coming from my old

room across from the stairway.

"This is Rachel's and Betty Jean's junior year pictures," Mom said.

"It looks like they're posing as a couple," Wendy said.

"It does, doesn't it?"

"It's the same in their senior yearbook," Rebecca said.

"I never noticed that."

I remembered the photo sessions. We were allowed to pose with whichever side we liked best facing forward. As my last name immediately followed Betty Jean's, our pictures were always together. So Betty Jean posed with her right side forward and I posed with my left forward. It was our subtle announcement to the world of our love.

"Tenth grade too," Wendy said. She and Rebecca laughed.

"Those sneaky, little imps," Mom said.

Wally goosed me. We continued up the stairs and stopped in the doorway.

"Hi, what's going on?"

"Your mom's filling us in on some of your scandalous past." Wendy turned the yearbook around and showed us the pictures.

"Nice looking couple."

Rebecca flipped through the yearbook she was holding and held it up. It was a picture of Wally as a senior holding a football as if ready to pass."

"You were a good-looking guy back then."

"What do you mean 'back then'? How about now?"

She held out a hand and waggled it slowly back and forth.

Wally pointed at her. "I'll get you later."

"Promises, promises. Always promises."

We all laughed. Mom stood.

"I should see if Libby and Clare need any help. It'll be a light supper. Mainly chili and cornbread. Perhaps a side. Need to leave room for tomorrow. Enjoy yourselves."

I followed her to the stairs. "Mom?"

"Yes, dear?"

"Thank you."

"For what?"

"For being you. I love you."

"I've never doubted that, Rachel. Not for a single moment." She lightly ran her hand along my cheek and pressed a finger to my lips. "Not one single nanosecond." She took a deep breath. "Mm, the chili smells good even up here. Can't wait to taste it. See you downstairs."

Wally and Rebecca sat on the bed looking at pictures of him in the yearbook. There were several of him playing football and baseball and at dances. Wendy was on a chair with my senior yearbook using a finger as a bookmark. I moved a chair over and sat beside her. She opened the book to a collage of pictures of my senior prom and pointed to one of Betty Jean and me with our dates, Dennis Kiley and John Lott.

"Thought you didn't date boys."

"We were each other's beards."

Rebecca looked over. "What are beards?"

Wally said nothing but rolled his eyes and casually covered his mouth. Wendy turned the yearbook and showed Rebecca the picture as I explained.

"A beard is someone who pretends to have a romantic relationship with someone to hide *that* someone's true sexual bent. After Betty Jean's and my sophomore year scandal we decided to be more low-key. During our junior and senior years we dated Dennis and John who were on the basketball and football teams. What no one knew was they were every bit as gay as we were. Each of us was the other's beard and had a *gay* ole time on double dates at the river deciding which real couple got the back seat."

Rebecca nodded. "Clever."

My brother was surprised Dennis and John were gay as he'd played on the same team with them. He said John got a football scholarship to UCLA but lost track because the Lott family moved away. He knew Dennis at West Point. An Infantry captain, Dennis was killed by an IED in Iraq in 2004. I said I'd try to see his family, as he had been my high school "boyfriend."

Then Wally told how he went from being Wally to Andy to Drew. "Rachel used to tag after me and I was always getting into fights whenever someone said, 'Here comes Wally and the Beav.' Rachel was too young to understand the sexual meaning, but I wasn't. So I became Andy in Junior High. When I went to the Point, I settled on Drew because I thought it sounded mature. Been Drew ever since except for Mom and Little Sis here."

"I'll try to remember big brother."

Rebecca talked about growing up on the reservation in northern New Mexico. "Our clans are matrilineal. Daughters' families staying with or near their mothers. As a result, my uncles were more important in helping raise me than my father. Whereas, he was more significant in his sisters' children's lives. It all works out.

"We're one of few reservations that have grown larger. Because of oil and gas, timber and ranching income, we've added tens of thousands of acres buying adjacent ranches. No one's making more land, so you should get some for the people while it's available. Which is funny because a federal agent once wrote 'the Jicarilla Apache has no home.' Still, unemployment remains high, over 14 percent, and the standard of living low. There's a lot of crime and drug use, particularly meth.

"I went to the Air Force Academy but chose an Army commission because I wanted to fly aircraft named for Indian tribes. Though these aren't names we would use. 'Indian,' 'Native American,' 'Jicarilla' are other people's words to identify us. Even 'Apache' comes from the Zuni and means 'enemy.' The easiest word for us is 'Tinde' or 'Dinde' which simple means 'the People.'"

She then entertained us with the misadventures of Trickster Fox and a creation myth of the beginning of the world.

She had two tours in Iraq and one in Afghanistan and got her "badass" rep for her aggressive, low-level flying providing cover fire to ground forces. If the ROEs, rules of engagement, were too strict to allow firing, she'd streak in at treetop level and drop flares and chaff. "Scared the shit out of the enemy and made them run."

When she was transferred to Ft. Hood, she was assigned to the public affairs office and flying only enough to maintain her flight status. She met my brother while arranging flying time. Then they talked about the mass shooting at the fort last November.

"That was a nightmare. Thirteen dead. More than 30 wounded or hurt. Having to rein in your emotions while putting all the info together, making sure the media got timely reports and the facts were accurate. Squelching misinformation. Setting up interviews and photo ops. Have no idea when Major Hasan's court-martial will be. He's still hospitalized at Brooke in San Antonio, hasn't had a competency eval, and his Article 32 is pending. I know JAG will seek the death penalty, but no one's been executed since 1961."

Sarah stuck her head in. "Supper's ready."

Wendy and Clare sat with Dad at one end of the dining table while Rebecca and I joined Mom at the other end. Wally—*Drew*, have to remember it's Drew now—Libby, Sarah and Elsa filled in the center.

"Why didn't Joey stay?" Mom asked.

"He was ordered to return and be debriefed by his parents on enemy status."

Even Dad chuckled. Clare's chili and cornbread were a hit. Everyone had two servings. No one told Dad there was no meat in it. Wall—*Drew*—and Rebecca heated theirs hotter with some of Clare's homemade hot sauce. Much of the conversation came from Sarah and Elsa as they laid out their extensive business plan including projected costs and revenue. Elsa's enthusiasm was liberally punctuated with "Yah sure" and "You betcha."

After supper, I sat quietly with Dad in the parlor. We did little talking. Neither of us wanted to cause any upset or repeat the past. At one point he caught himself nodding off.

"Guess I better call it a night." He patted my knee. "Think you found a good woman. Hang onto her. That's what I did with mine."

"I love you, Dad."

He wiped his eye and nodded. We stood and hugged.

"Me too, Rachel. Me too," he whispered in my ear.

I watched him lean on his cane and shuffle to their downstairs bedroom. I dried my tears and went to the kitchen. Drew and Rebecca were drying and putting away the cleaned dishes. Mom, Clare and Libby were at the kitchen table with coffee, a list and a drawing.

Mom looked over. "Everything okay?"

I nodded. "Dad's tired. Said he's going to bed."

"I'll go check on him."

She stood and pointed to the drawing. "Don't put Frank and Albert too close together. They'll just egg each other on." She patted my shoulder as she left.

"What are you making?"

Libby smiled. "Seating arrangements. Divide and conquer. Keep the enemy dispersed and outflanked. We'll scatter the children to keep any off-color comments PG-rated. Rebecca?"

"Yes, ma'am?"

"You have any objections sitting across from one of the ringleaders?"

"Put me anywhere you think I'll be most effective. I'm a highly decorated Apache warrior. Says so right in my official military record."

"Drew? How about you?"

"Same here, Aunt Libby. We'll blaze in across the treetops, the sun at our backs, with guns and missiles firing. They won't know what hit them."

They had me laughing. This was a good day. These

people—my family—cared. Wendy was welcome and I wasn't a total outcast. The others no longer mattered.

"You know," Libby said, making tick marks on the list. "Once we neutralize your brothers and their wives, and Al Junior—who's as bigoted as his father—the others aren't that bad to be around."

Rebecca came over drying her hands on a towel. "Libby, of the children, who's the oldest girl?"

"Let's see. That would be Ella Grace, Anne and Nat Worthington's daughter. She just turned 10."

"Would you sit her next to me, please? The next generation will need tough women to lead in every avenue of life. I may as well start influencing some of them now."

Drew came over. "Too bad Jessica can't be here. She'd keep her brother in line."

I thought a moment. "Jessica? She and Al Junior are twins, right? I used to babysit them. Where's she?"

"Kunsan Air Base, Korea. She's an F-16 fighter pilot."

"Little Jessica? How cool."

"Rachel?"

"Yes, Clare?"

"I called the Nielsens at the B&B to let them know I won't be having breakfast tomorrow. Your mother invited me to stay tonight. I'm going with her and Libby to sunrise services, and then we'll be fixing the last of the food for tomorrow's dinner."

"Okay. Do you need anything tonight?"

"No. Just bring the garment bag hanging in my room with you tomorrow, please."

"Not a problem. Do you know where Wendy is?"

"She went with Sarah and Elsa. They may be upstairs."

"I'll look."

I heard Wendy's voice as I went up the stairs. It was coming from my room. I stopped near the top to listen.

"What defines you is you. Not someone else's idea of you. You're not going to be turned down because of the way you dress. Approval depends on the solidness of your plan and your experience. You're from families with long, dairy experience. If your plan is as detailed as what you described at supper, I see no problems. But loans should be way down on your list of priorities. Something to consider for future expansion. You should be looking for grants you won't need to repay. There's a lot of money out there. Talk to your families about it, your professors and advisors, the local farm bureau."

"Am I interrupting a business meeting?"

Sarah was leaning against the headboard. Elsa was curled up beside her, her head on Sarah's shoulder. Wendy was on a chair. Sarah shook her head.

"Just a couple questions."

Wendy held up a magazine. "Is this another secret I should know about?"

It was the October 1983 issue of Playboy. There were several on the end of the bed, and should be a couple dozen more in the box on the floor. Sarah and Elsa were quietly snickering.

"It was a gift from Wally. I mean Drew. It was his secret collection. I found them on my bed wrapped and with a bow when we got back from driving him to the airport when he left for West Point. A card simply said, 'For You.' Years later he said it was his way of letting me know he knew which way I was leaning. Had no idea they were still here. You girls can have them if you want. You could probably sell them on eBay."

"What about this?" Wendy held up my old diary.

"That *is* secret. Hang on to it."

We relaxed and talked for a while and invited the girls to visit if they had a few days free this summer. I glanced at my watch. It was nearly nine o'clock.

"I told Betty Jean I wanted to see her and Kelly tonight. We should be going."

220

Twenty-Four

The four us were seated around Kelly's dining table. Wendy had insisted on coming along. We had wine and some of Betty Jean's savories. On the table were six notes that had been left for Kelly on campus or in her mailbox. I was scrolling through the messages and pictures she received on her smartphone. These were the only ones she'd kept. She'd thrown away or deleted earlier ones. She was nervously twisting a wineglass back and forth between her hands. I was sure she'd been drinking before we arrived.

"I told Betty Jean she shouldn't have bothered you with this. It's really no big deal."

I picked up one of the notes. "'Repent harlot! The clock is ticking!'" I swiped back through the messages, "'God may forgive you. I won't!' This is personal. Sounds like a threat." I swiped to a photo of a lighted, curtained window. "And what about this? Do you recognize the window?"

"It's my bedroom window."

"Your bedroom window. Taken in your backyard. And someone sent you its picture. This is a big deal, Kelly. Seriously big. Are you sure you don't know who's doing it?"

"No. I can't think of anyone."

"How long has the harassing been going on?"

Her gaze went above my head. Her brow furrowed. Her lips pursed. She looked at me.

"Between Christmas and New Year. I found a note on my

office floor when I stopped by to pick up a box of Thank You cards I'd made."

"Do you remember what it said?"

"'Stop what you're doing' in big block letters."

"Did you know what it meant?"

"Hadn't a clue. I threw it away."

"When were you contacted again?"

"The Monday after New Year's. It was left in my mailbox here. It said, 'Stop now.' It was underlined several times. I still thought it was a joke. I tossed it."

"After that?"

"Not for several weeks. I think the week before Valentine's Day I got another at the office. I don't remember the message. More of the same, I'm sure. Then just after Valentine's Day I received a card in the mail. There was no return address. Inside was a ripped in half, heart-shaped Valentine. No message."

"Do you remember if it was postmarked?"

"I'm not sure. It was stamped though. Is that important?"

"Being stamped, it was most likely mailed. A postmark would tell us if it were mailed locally or not. It may or may not help discover who's doing this. Did you happen to keep it?"

"No. I'm sorry."

"You remembered it was stamped. Was there something special about the stamp?"

"I remember it having two stamps. Both the same. I remember thinking it didn't need that much postage."

"Do you remember the picture on the stamps?"

"They were Love stamps. Two blue doves and a red heart."

"I liked those stamps," Wendy said. "They looked like Amish artwork. But they came out years ago. They aren't current. Maybe that's why the mailer used two."

I nodded. "When did you get the first text message?"

"The next day. The day after the valentine came."

"Is it here?"

"No. I deleted it."

"Do you remember it?"

She thought for a moment. "Something about ashes and 'Pray for forgiveness.'"

"Do you have a notepad and calendar I can use?"

"I'll get them."

"What are you thinking, Rachel?"

"A picture's forming, but I need to write it down. Betty Jean, you said you and Kelly started dating around Christmas. Exactly when?"

"Our first *real* date—and *you* know what I mean by that—was December 19th. We had dinner at The Shack, went to the movie, and I stayed most of the night here. The girls knew I'd be home late. Just not how late. I got home about five and slept in because the shop's closed on Sundays."

Kelly came back with a pad, calendar and pen."

"Anyone want more wine while I'm up?"

Wendy and Betty Jean raised their glasses.

"Do you have any Scotch?"

"A bottle of Chivas."

"Two fingers, please. No ice."

"Her brain's percolating, ladies. The game's afoot."

"Really, Wendy? *'The game's afoot'*?"

She just smiled. Kelly came back with my Scotch and the bottle of wine. They watched as I made entries on a page. I wished I had my blackboard. I sat back, picked up the tumbler of Scotch and held it close to my face. I covered my mouth, nose and the glass with my hands. I blew on the golden liquor to warm it then slowly breathed in the essence of Scotland as I stared at the sheet of paper for several moments. I took a small sip, rolled it in my mouth, tasted its sweet and astringent flavors, swallowed, breathed deeply again. Set the glass aside.

The calendar was only the current year. I took out my smartphone and scrolled my calendar back to the previous October.

"Do either of you remember what day in October you met at Pastry Heaven?"

"It was our bimonthly department meeting. So it would have been the third Friday."

I looked at my calendar and wrote down "Oct. 16" on the paper. "When did you see each other again?"

"We didn't have time to talk, so I came back the next day. We went to the Roasted Bean for coffee around noon I think."

I wrote "Oct. 17 — Coffee." "But you didn't have a *real* date, as Betty Jean put it, until December 19th. Correct?" They nodded. "How many times do you think you got together between October 17th and December 19th? You know, just to talk, have coffee, maybe lunch; drop by the store?"

They looked at each other. "Four or five?"

Betty Jean shook her head. "More like six or seven. I wanted to have Thanksgiving together, but I was already committed to take the kids to my mother-in-law's. We're still close. It could have been eight times."

I wrote "Met 6 to 8 times Oct. 17 — Dec. 19." "These were primarily public meetings? Nothing clandestine?"

They nodded and Betty Jean said, "That's correct. Where are you going with this? What's it have to do with Kelly being harassed now?"

"I'll get to that, but I need these questions answered first. And if my questions get too personal, please understand I need to know. It's not prurient curiosity."

"If you'd feel more comfortable if I left," Wendy said, "I won't be insulted."

"Oh, no. Please stay. You're welcome here."

"Besides," Betty Jean said, "We've nothing to hide. Our relationship is pretty much out in the open."

I scrolled my calendar forward to December 19. "Betty Jean, before your first intimate date, did your daughters know Kelly?"

"Let me think. They caught me sneaking in after our third date. So I had Kelly over that evening to tell them about us.

But before that? Probably. As I told you, the girls often help out on Saturdays, and the holidays were coming up, and they wanted to earn extra money, so they were working every Saturday before Christmas, and Kelly and I must have gotten together for lunch two, three or four of those Saturdays, and at the very least I would have introduced them to each other, it would have been rude not to, and they probably said 'hi' whenever she came in and they were there. So to answer your question, yes."

"Thank you. Their names are Jenna and . . ."

"Jordan. Jenna's the oldest. She's 16. Jordan's 13."

I wrote "J&J met K 3—4 times before Dec. 19." "All right, your daughters caught you on your third date. When was that?"

"We went out on the 26th, but I overslept and didn't get home until nearly nine the next morning. The girls were already up and eating breakfast. Kelly came over that evening so we could tell them about us. And before you ask, our second date was an intimate nooner on the 23rd here."

I added all of that to my paper. "Kelly, you found the first note with the message 'Stop what you're doing' in your office between Christmas and New Year. Could you be more specific?"

"Most likely the 28th or 29th."

"Did you spend New Year's Eve together?"

"Yes," said Betty Jean. "At my house with Jenna and Jordan and they each had a friend over for the night. We celebrated at midnight with noisemakers and champagne. The girls had sparkling apple juice. Kelly and I made breakfast for everyone the next morning."

"And the 'Stop now' note was in Kelly's mailbox Monday?"

"That's where I found it. On top of my mail."

And so it went. Asking questions. Getting answers. Writing them down. Filling pages. Establishing the timeline. Filling blanks. Going back. More questions. Getting personal.

"Kelly when did you start to teach at Grace?"

"Fall 2008."

"Any relationships?"

"No. I wasn't looking for any."

"Flings? One-nighters?"

"Not here. If I got the urge I'd drive up to Des Moines or Ames on a weekend. Nothing serious. A casual hook-up to feed the yen, tame the beast."

"How about back in Ohio? Anyone serious there?"

"No. I was burned out from San Francisco. Strictly one-time things. 'Slam, bam, Thank you, ma'am' and move on."

I nodded. "And you didn't meet Betty Jean again until October?"

"Correct."

"Okay. Betty Jean? In '89, I left for the Army and you went to Grace. When did you and Kelly have your brief affair?"

"My first semester. I was missing you and failing English. Kelly got me through both difficulties."

"And Kelly, you graduated the next spring and went to San Francisco. Any relationships there end badly?"

"A few. Especially at the end, but we're talking several years ago now."

"Still, you never know. Do you stay in touch with anyone?"

"Some friends. Talk on the phone. Exchange cards. Make promises to visit. That sort of thing. Think it's someone in my past?"

"Possibly. Or Betty Jean's. Betty Jean, anyone special between Kelly and Terry?"

"Not really. Nothing to write home about. Like Kelly, if I felt the need to party I'd head out of town. But I preferred Kansas City. I was sure you weren't being celibate either."

"Very true. When I joined the Army I didn't expect to find many like us. I was lustily surprised, and for a while, I wanted to lick my way through every hot, sopping slit in uniform or die trying. When did you and Terry meet?"

"Beginning of our junior year. He transferred in under the GI Bill. He lost his lower left leg in a missile attack on his barracks in Saudi Arabia in February that year. He was discharged in July and came home and started school. He didn't talk about it, but said he lost friends that day."

"We all did. Dhahran, Saudi Arabia, February 25th. I was there. A Scud missile hit the barracks. Twenty-seven of our soldiers were killed and another 98 wounded. Most were reservists but not all. An intimate friend of mine took my place on MP patrol that night. Her Humvee — my Humvee — was hit by shrapnel in the explosion, and she was wounded. It could have been me — should have been me. But where was I? I was in a supply closet on a makeshift bed, my face buried between another soldier's thighs."

I finished the Scotch and handed the empty glass to Kelly. She went and refilled it and brought it back.

"That's when I lost my appetite for conquest. I went dry for a long while before seeking intimacy again. Guilt will do that. Anyway, that was then and your problem is now. Betty Jean, did you have any affairs while married to Terry?"

"No. I never cheated on him."

"After he died, any relationships before Kelly?"

"None. Maybe a trip or two to Kansas City to scratch an itch, but mostly I raised my girls and ran my bakery and let people think whatever they wanted."

"Then it's your relationship that's key to the harassment. You spent three nights together in December and Kelly gets a note on the 28th or 29th. You're together New Year's Eve and through the weekend. There's another note Monday. A week before Valentine's there's another note, and I'll be surprised if there wasn't another tryst a few days before that. Then came the ripped valentine. You were together Valentine's Day, right?"

"We went away for the weekend."

I consulted my notes and the calendar on the table.

"Did the valentine arrive Monday or Tuesday?"

229

"What difference does it make?"

"Because if it arrived Monday, it had to have been mailed Saturday or before. If it arrived Tuesday, it could have been mailed locally Monday. And you got the first text Wednesday so I'm betting Tuesday."

"How do you know that? I don't remember."

"Because you said the text was about ashes and praying for forgiveness. February 17th was Ash Wednesday, the beginning of Lent. Do you own a gun?"

"A gun? No. Why would I want a gun?"

"For protection. This note: 'Repent, harlot! The clock is ticking.' The last message: 'God may forgive you. I won't.' The last picture sent is of your bedroom window. But you haven't repented, haven't sought forgiveness. Your relationship continues, blossoms even. These are threats. Believe me. And they're local. This person knows you. Knows you both. Knows when you've been together. And, for whatever reason, hates you for it. Lent is over. The time for forgiveness is over. I don't think this person is waiting any longer. I think you're in danger. Both of you. I think it's time you talk to the police."

"Rachel, have you seen our police department? It's very small, and the county sheriff is over in Leon. What do we tell them? Does any of this tell us who is doing it?"

"There are clues. It's someone who knows Kelly's number and can text her. It's someone who's been in her yard and took the picture of her window. It's someone who has access to old unused stamps. It's someone—and I admit this is a stretch—who reads science fiction."

"Science fiction?"

"As I say, it's a stretch, but I've always liked it, and I remember a distinctive story title by Harlan Ellison, *Repent, Harlequin! Said the Ticktockman*. That's awfully close to the 'Repent, harlot' note. Too close for me to dismiss an influence. And then there's the torn valentine. Someone with a broken heart. A lost love? Very personal."

"Rachel, you've convinced us, but tomorrow's Easter, and

I don't think Chief Carnes — as nice a man as he is — would appreciate having his day ruined anymore than the rest of us. Especially as we can't give him a definite suspect or crime."

"Stalking is a crime."

"You're right. It is. Kelly and I will go in Monday morning and talk to him or Assistant Chief Zimmer. I promise."

"Okay. I can go with you if you'd like. We don't check out until eleven, and we don't need to leave immediately."

"That would be nice. Gives us another chance to see you. You've been gone too long."

"We'll be back soon. You going to your mother-in-law's tomorrow?"

"The girls are. They love being spoiled by their grandmother on any holiday, as much as she enjoys spoiling them. They keep Terry alive for her, she says. And she hasn't reconciled losing her husband Sean two years ago from a heart attack. They were married 43 years. I love her and want her to be happy, but Kelly and I want the day for us too. A joyful Easter to you, Rachel. And to you, Wendy."

We said our good-byes and well wishes and headed for bed. It was 1:00 a.m. before we were cocooned beneath the covers.

"Still thinking of Betty Jean and Kelly?"

"Yes. I think the danger is real. I think it could explode any moment. I'm worried my thoughts are more conjecture than conclusion. That they're going to be hurt badly, whether physically or only emotionally, I can't say. Especially Betty Jean."

"You think you know who it is?"

"Maybe. I think it being someone from either of their pasts is remote. I think it's someone in their here and now. Someone very close. I'm afraid I suspect Jenna and Jordan."

"Betty Jean's daughters? I thought they liked Kelly. That they were happy for their mother."

"I believe on one level they are. But I believe they miss their father too. That they could resent someone taking his place. That they may not approve of their mother's lifestyle. And if it is one or both of them . . . I don't know. I hope I'm wrong. It's the stamps that bother me."

"The stamps?"

"The Love stamps on the valentine envelope. While you were in the bathroom I did an online search. They were issued in 1990. Twenty-five cents. So you were right about needing two for postage. But where did they come from? A stamp collection? Found in a drawer? Were they saved because they meant something special? I think, like the torn heart, they were used purposely. As a message. And I'd have a better idea of what the message is, and who it's from, if I knew where the stamps came from."

"Well, we're not going to find that out tonight."

"True."

"So think of something pleasanter."

"Like what?"

Wendy shifted and did something beneath the covers. Her hand appeared and she pressed a wet finger against my lips.

"Earlier you said you had a taste for something hot and wet."

I licked her finger. "The word I used was 'sopping.'"

Twenty-Five

We were up early and bundled against the cold. When we came out of our room at 6:30, there was hot coffee waiting. We poured two cups and went outside. Janet and Carl Nielsen were sitting in folding lawn chairs on the corner facing east down Main Street.

"Happy Easter," they said. "Happy Easter," we returned.

"Pull up a chair," Janet said. "We were hoping someone would join us for sunrise."

The sky had already lightened. Dark clouds were showing a soft glow along their undersides. Trees, hills and buildings were sharply silhouetted. Minutes later a bit of glowing, red arc appeared on the horizon. I sipped my coffee and watched it grow larger. A new day. A new beginning.

When the sun fully appeared and had changed from red to orange to gold, Janet and Carl stood and folded their chairs.

"Guess I better get breakfast ready," she said. "Come in when you're ready."

"Would you like fresh juice?" Carl asked as he folded two other chairs.

"Yes, thank you," we said.

We sat a few more minutes enjoying the peace then folded our chairs and set them with the others by the porch railing. It was another marvelous, filling breakfast. It'd been a short night, so we set the alarm and went back to sleep.

I came out of the bathroom drying my hair and was

surprised to see my Phillip Marlowe-inspired, powder blue, pinstriped suit hanging on a hook. I hadn't packed it.

"What's that doing here?"

"Orders."

"Orders? From whom and why?"

"From High Command for Operation Homecoming." Wendy was absolutely smirking.

"Our mothers planned this?"

"My thought too but I discovered yesterday this is the brainchild of my future sister-in-law, Major Rebecca BrightStar. She calls this a PsyOps and Recruitment action to confuse and neutralize the current enemy — meaning your brothers and their wives — and inspire the next generations of Cord women and men to boldly seek their own destinies."

"Why wasn't I told of this maneuver?"

"You've fretted so much about just being here, it was deemed in your best interest not to add to your anxieties."

"Why this suit?"

"I was instructed to provide the outfit that best epitomizes Rachel Cord, PI."

Everything was there. The suit; the dark blue shirt, tie and display hankie; the shined black oxfords.

"It is a nice suit for Easter. Just needs the snap-brim."

"Hat box on the chair."

"What are you wearing?"

"My camel and coral I save for executive meetings. Conservative and understated as befits a banker, yet exudes my confident and independent nature. Now get dressed. We're supposed to be there no later than thirteen-thirty hours, or 1:30 in civilianspeak."

The tradition in my family — at least as it existed 20 years ago — was an Easter egg hunt and outdoor activities to run off excess energy so the children were calm enough — if not exhausted — to sit quietly at the family table. Before I left, I was in charge of running my nieces and nephews ragged at such events. As we drove in, I was happy to see others had that responsibility. Sarah and Elsa, in fresh jeans and pressed, plaid shirts, were running about the yard with their arms stretched out like airplanes followed by half-a-dozen children. The youngest looked to be no more than three or four years old. All of the children seemed to be holding some kind of aircraft and making airplane noises.

Rebecca was watching with her arms folded. She was wearing a combat flight suit and aviator sunglasses. Running circles around her was a girl wearing a flowered Easter dress and Rebecca's flight helmet. She also was holding up an aircraft and making flying noises.

Wendy headed for the house with Clare's garment bag while I walked up to Rebecca, stopped and saluted.

"Reporting as ordered, Major, ma'am."

She inspected me up and down and side to side before returning my salute.

"Lookin' good." She smiled. "So this is what a PI wears?"

"Just this one."

Rebecca reached out and stopped the girl with a hand to the helmet. The girl was holding a model of an AH-64 Apache helicopter. Rebecca removed the helmet and turned the girl to face me. She had curly blonde hair and blue eyes.

"Ella, this is your Great Aunt Rachel. Rachel, please meet Ella Grace Worthington, age 10."

"Happy Easter, Ella. I'm pleased to meet you."

She curtsied. "Happy Easter. Granddad called you the B-word this morning."

"He did?"

"Yes. Several times. And Grandma says your queer, but you don't look strange to me." She smiled. "I'm old enough to know what she *really* meant. My best friend at school has two mothers."

"Thank you and good for your friend. So what do you want to be when you grow up?"

"A combat pilot like Aunt Becca or my cousin Jessica."

"Ella, why don't you go play with the others?"

"Okay. May I wear your helmet?"

"Sure."

"Thank you." She turned back to me. "May I just call you 'Aunt Rachel'? You don't look old enough to be a great aunt."

"I'd like that."

"Okay, bye."

"I see you're already 'Aunt Becca'. Did you bribe them all with helicopters?"

"Apache gunships. There's a difference. Even little Kirsten there bringing up the rear. She's three. A Christmas baby. Told me her name means '*beliefs* in Christ'."

"Do you know them all, already?"

"I think I've got it straight. This is easy-peasy compared to my extended family on the rez."

"Which of my loving brothers is Ella's granddad?"

"Frank. Wife Nancy. Parents Anne Marie Cord and Nathan Green. Siblings Nathan, Jr., age 11, and Patrick, age 6."

"I'm impressed. Who does Kirsten belong to?"

"Same grandparents. Parents Albert Walter Cord and Anne . . . Petersen with an E. Siblings Karen, 5, born on Thanksgiving Day — that's her there — and Karla due in July. Think they're hoping for the 4th. Who's the youngest you remember?"

"Joey. He was here yesterday. Sarah wasn't born yet. I babysat for Joey and the twins, Albert Junior and Jessica. Hard to believe Jessica's a fighter pilot. They're Al and Debbie's kids. Is Al Junior still called A.J.?"

"Yes, he is. He married Marian Abby and they have a son, Robert, age 10. I don't see him right now."

"I also babysat Frank and Nancy's kids, Anne Marie, Albert Walter known as A.W., and Nancy Drew, the oldest. She resented my babysitting because we're only four years apart."

"She may have gotten over it. She's wearing her go-to-court clothes. She and her husband, Tom Yount, are lawyers. They have a daughter, Thomasina, age 6. I think that's all of them."

"So you've met everybody?"

"No. Only Joey and Sarah, and Nancy Drew and Tom. They brought all the youngsters. Saw them last talking to Drew. The others will be as much a surprise to me as they will be to Wendy."

"I wish us luck."

"Luck has nothing to do with it. Our mission is to win the hearts and minds of those we can and ignore the rest."

"Is this what you're wearing to dinner?"

"No. This was for the children. I'll change to my Class Bs shortly. Need to show the fruit salad to awe the locals. By the way, Ella says Frank calls me 'That damn Injun' or 'Damn savage.' Seems he uses both. Your brother's a real bigot."

"Don't I know it. Al's not much better. When will they be here?"

"Your mother said two o'clock to meet and greet. Sit down, I believe, is 3:30. I better go change. We can talk later."

Sarah and Elsa were still entertaining the kids. I wandered on to the porch and closed off area. No one was there. The two patio heaters were on and the area was warm. With tablecloths and settings in place, it looked like one long, continuous table. There were nametags at each space. I read them as I went down the table.

Dad's tag was at this end, which meant Mom would be closest to the kitchen. Nancy, Frank's wife, would be on Dad's left and across in the place of honor on his right was Wendy. Hope that works out. Next came the little girls, Karen and Kirsten. Who did Rebecca say were their parents? A.W. and . . . I saw the tag. "Anne P." Right. "P" for Petersen or "P" for pregnant? Joey was on this side. Next to Joey was Anne Marie and across was young Robert, A.J.'s son. My brother, Al, Sr., would be next to his grandson. On this side was Aunt Libby. She'd keep Al in line if anyone could. Next was Tom, Nancy Drew's husband and a lawyer. So was she. On the other side was Patrick. I forgot who Patrick was. Someone would remind me later. My place was next to Tom. Right in the middle. Across from me was Nathan. Ah! Ella's dad and Anne Marie's husband. I was doing pretty well remembering what Rebecca told me. Next to me was Elsa and across from her, Nancy Drew. Next was A.W. on my side and Marian, Robert's mother, on the other. Debbie, Al's wife, came next and Drew was on the other side. Then it was Nathan, Jr. across from Sarah. I'm sure she would have preferred sitting with Elsa, but at least they could see each other. Clare was next to Sarah with A.J. on this side. Next to him were Ella and then Rebecca on Mom's right. Across would be Thomasina and Frank on Mom's left. I pictured Rebecca firing missiles across at Frank. All in all, they'd done a good job of dispersing the enemy.

The door behind me opened followed by the sweet smell of roasting ham accented by Clare's chili. Apparently that was on today's menu too. I turned and Nancy Drew came out holding a large tray.

"Rachel!" She set the tray on a side table and hugged me. "I'm glad you're here."

"I don't recall that being your attitude when I left."

"Well that was in a galaxy long ago and far away. Some of us grow up. I think Wendy's wonderful and Tom's dying to meet you."

"I think he's seated next to me."

"Good. I'm really excited for you. Truly. Oh, do you think Clare would give me her chili recipe? Tom's been drooling since the moment he smelled it."

"I'm sure she will. So, you and Tom are lawyers?"

"Yes. We're two thirds of Mitchell, Yount & Cord. Our office is in Des Moines. We specialize in personal injury. Which is what Tom wants to talk to you about. We can discuss it later. I've got to get this stuff laid out."

"Can I help?"

"Sure. It's just the relish bowls. Pickles and olives. They go down the center."

"I'll carry the tray and you can place them where you

want."

When we got to the end of the table, Nancy Drew hugged me again.

"Your mom and dad are really happy you're home."

"I know. I'm happy too. Happy Wendy twisted my arm."

We heard voices on the walk.

"I don't know why that bitch had to come back and ruin Easter."

"Frank, you promised."

"I know, but wasn't it bad enough she ruined our lives 20 years ago?"

"Frank, stop it."

"I'm just sayin'. Best thing she ever done was leave. Bet she even voted for that damn, Muslim Nig—"

"Frank Cord, you say one more word like that and—"

"All right. All right. Don't get your shorts in an uproar. I'll shut-up."

"Thank you. Think of your parents. You know how your mom has always felt, and your dad hasn't fully recovered. So please be nice."

"I'll try Nan. It just riles me. Look at Al's heart attack."

"You can't blame that on Rachel."

"No? Hell's bells! Where do you think Sarah Ruth got the idea of being a dyke? Tell me that!"

Nancy Drew closed her eyes and shook her head. They came up the steps onto the porch.

"Happy Easter, Frank. Nancy. Glad to see you."

"Hi, Mom. Hi, Dad."

Frank glared at me. His face turned beet red, but I was sure it wasn't from embarrassment. Nancy gaped, turned her head to look back down the path, and then back at me. She blushed. Frank stormed off through the front door.

"Rachel. How nice. I know your mother's happy to see you."

"She is. Dad too. By the way, I didn't know you quilted. There's a really beautiful one you did at the B&B where we're staying. Wendy and I love it. It's so warm and cozy and looks great on our bed. Would you consider quilting one in a Double Wedding Ring pattern?"

"I . . . I need to get this in the fridge." She followed after Frank.

"That was nasty, Rachel."

"You really think so?"

"Definitely."

"Not too subtle?"

"Definitely not."

"Good. I feel better already. What did she bring?"

"Her classic Jello mold."

"The lime one with marshmallow creme and walnuts?"

"And pineapple and cherries."

"Think she'll feel too insulted if Wendy doesn't have any? Wendy's vegan."

"Maybe Mom won't notice."

"They're sitting across from each other by Dad."

"That could be a problem."

"I'll speak to Wendy."

"I need to get back to the kitchen. See you later."

I looked back down the length of the table. Two more for our side. The odds of a successful visit were getting better and better. I pinched two black olives from a bowl and went in the front. No one was in the living or dining rooms. I heard voices coming from the parlor. Frank was loudly grousing. I didn't need that.

Rebecca came down the stairs in uniform. Her slacks were blue with an officer's gold stripe down the leg. Her short-sleeved shirt was white with open collar. Her shoulder epaulets bore a Major's gold leaf. Of the three rows of ribbons on the left side I recognized the Distinguished Flying Cross with Oak Leaf Cluster, Purple Heart, Meritorious Service Medal, and Army Commendation Medal with two Oak Leaf Clusters and one "V" for Valor. There were several ribbons I didn't know. Above the ribbons was her Senior Army Aviator

Badge. Above her nametag were two unit citation or commendation awards and on the lower right side of her shirt was a Combat Service Identification Badge.

I smiled. "Fruit salad indeed. That should impress the masses."

She returned my smile. "Has the enemy been sighted?"

"Just my oldest brother Frank and his wife Nancy. Still waiting on the others."

The front door opened and two women and two men entered. The obviously pregnant woman I presumed was Anne Petersen Cord, so the man with her must be my nephew Albert Walter or A.W. I made the guess the others were my niece, Anne Marie and her husband Nathan Worthington. My guesses were right except Nathan's first name was really Nathaniel. He was manager for a large food distributor in Omaha where Anne Marie taught middle school. A.W. was a police officer in Iowa City and Anne P. a stay-at-home mom. Apparently none of Frank and Nancy's kids stayed close to home.

They were all friendly, or at least neutral, as neither Rebecca nor I picked up any negative vibes. Anne Marie did make the comment that she'd heard I'd been "downsized."

"I think you look great."

"I'm glad the word's out. I won't have to see the shock and explain it a dozen times."

"Rebecca, I'm very happy to meet you. Uncle Drew's talked of you and his face lights up every time he says your name. I was worried he'd never get over losing Cathy."

"Thank you. I think he's special."

"Excuse me, Rebecca," A.W. said. "Is that the Purple Heart?"

"Yes it is."

"Where'd you get it?"

"From General Odierno." She laughed. "People always ask and I can't resist saying that. My Apache gunship took enemy fire while supporting a ground unit in Iraq. I was wounded in the thigh. My co-pilot and good friend, Chip Dawson, was also wounded but we managed to fly back to base."

"Well, we certainly appreciate your service."

"And I yours. Police work's hard duty." She turned to Anne P. "And especially on families. Only those of us who serve truly understand your sacrifices. Thank you for being there for him."

Anne's eyes watered. "Thank you. Welcome to the family."

The two Annes went to the kitchen and the men headed toward the parlor.

"No wonder you're in public affairs. Talk about winning hearts and minds. You're a natural. I don't cook and I've no desire to be around Frank. Shall we go outside?"

"Sounds good to me. I'm not much for being in the kitchen either unless it's K.P. duty. I'll be helping with the cleanup later."

Wendy joined us a few minutes later. "There you are. Have you been hiding?"

"No, just staying out from under foot. You?"

"Mashing potatoes. Mother and Libby acted as screens so I don't think anyone saw me using soymilk and Earth Balance. I put enough roasted garlic in no one will ever taste the difference."

"Did you meet Nancy?"

"Yes. I'm sure she was surprised to see I'm closer to her age than yours. Though I seriously doubt we'll be best of friends."

"You're going to be sitting across from her at dinner."

"Yes, I know."

"She's pretty proud of her Jello mold. It's been a part of the Easter feast as long as I remember."

"And you're afraid she'll be insulted if I don't have any. Not a problem. I'll take a few bites for the team to keep the peace. At least for today."

"Did you happen to compliment her on that quilt on our bed?"

"I did, and it seemed it made her angry."

"I told her how much we enjoyed cuddling beneath it and asked if she'd like to make a Double Wedding Ring quilt."

"That's my Rachel, winning friends and influencing people."

"I'm going to take lessons from Rebecca. She has the knack."

Two pickups pulled into the drive. Joey was in one. He came up the steps carrying four bags. My brother Albert and sister-in-law Deborah got out of the Ford Crew Cab followed by A.J. and a redheaded woman. I glimpsed a redheaded boy earlier who must be Robert.

"Hi, all. I'd hug you but my hands are full and not because I'm afraid of my folks."

We gave him a peck on the cheek and Rebecca opened the door for him.

"Happy Easter, everyone. I'd like you to meet my fiancé, Wendy Devlin, and Drew's fiancé, Major Rebecca BrightStar. Ladies, this is my brother Albert, his wife Deborah, my nephew A.J., and . . ."

The redhead elbowed him. "Oh, sorry. Aunt Rachel, ladies, this is my wife Marian."

"I'm pleased to meet you all," she said.

Debbie shook hands with Rebecca and Wendy. "Welcome to the family." Then actually gave me a half-hearted hug. "You've been missed, Rachel. Welcome home."

My brother simply nodded and said, "Rachel, ladies. If you'll excuse me," and went in the house.

"Debbie, I was sorry to hear Al had a heart attack. Hope he's all right."

"Happened a few years ago. Scared the life out of me. He's fine now as long as he remembers his meds and watches his weight. That's part of my job. Thank you for asking. Please don't think he was being rude. On the way over he said he shouldn't have had that third cup of coffee. We're a bit late so we need to get to the kitchen."

Marian nodded. "It was nice meeting you all."

She followed Debbie and as the door closed I heard her comment, "I don't think she's nearly as large in the bosom as all of you were telling me."

We looked at each other and Wendy said, "I thought that went well." We agreed.

A few minutes later Marian appeared. "Do you know where the children are?"

Rebecca said, "With Sarah and Elsa out back."

"Thank you. I need to let them know it's time to wash up. Dinner will be ready shortly." She went down the steps and around the house.

From somewhere in the house, we heard, "Damn it! She doesn't deserve it! It's not right!"

Drew came out and his uniform was as gaily decorated as Rebecca's with the addition of a Legion of Merit but no Purple Heart.

"Dad would like to see us in the parlor."

Dad was sitting in the same rocker as yesterday. He had a frown on his face but smiled when we entered. He looked more rested today.

"Sit down, all of you. I hate looking up. Rachel, I'm told you're partial to single-malt Scotch, but all I've got is Tennessee sour mash. That'll have to do."

"That's fine."

"Drew, would you please?"

Drew passed each of us a shot glass of whiskey and sat next to Rebecca. Dad took a tiny sip of his.

"Rachel, you know the Old Houzer Place."

"Yes, sir. You're letting Sarah and Elsa use it for a dairy goat farm."

"That's right."

"You know, I've always wondered why it's called the Old Houzer Place."

"Named for Cyrus Houzer who settled on a full section there in 1879. For those of you who don't know, a section is a square mile. The Old Houzer Place is where he built his house and raised his family. That house burned down and was replaced. The second one was destroyed in a tornado and replaced with the one there now. Some say the original name was Houser, but that Cyrus was dyslexic and wrote the 'S' backwards like a 'Z.' Don't know that's true, but it's as good a tale as any."

He took another tiny sip of his drink. "Anyway, my grandmother Prudence, my mother's mother, was the last of the Houzers. She left the property and house to my mother, Carrie Belle, who left it to me. All told, there's still 160 acres of it left. As you say, I'm leasing the house and barns and 20 acres to Sarah and Elsa to start their farm. There's another 40 acres also of pasture. Frank leases a hundred acres where he's been rotating crops. Think he's planning on soybeans this year. Now I said, 'lease.' He don't own it like he'd like people to think, and don't let him tell you anything different. I make him sign a lease every year to make that perfectly clear."

Dad stopped for another sip. "Where was I? Oh, yeah. Oh, and another thing. Speaking of my Grandma Prudence, you can thank her for your over-sized development. I remember she suffered terribly in her old age. Glad to see you took care of that problem. Meant to tell you that yesterday. Anyways, as my grandmother left it to her daughter, and I was an only child so it came to me, it's always been my intent to pass it on to my daughter if I had one. For a while I didn't think that was going to happen, but it did, and that's you."

"But Dad—"

"Don't give me no 'But Dads.' The land's yours. I planned to give it to you when you married. Took a bit longer than I expected. So unless you two have changed your minds about getting hitched, consider it a wedding present. It's a done deal, either way. Papers all signed and recorded with the county. Cheers."

Dad finished his drink and we followed though I wasn't feeling particularly cheerful at the moment.

"What am I supposed to do with 160 acres?"

"Anything you want. I know you're not going to farm it, and don't want to live in the middle of nowhere on a permanent basis. Do what I do. Lease it. It's a good moneymaker. You're stuck with the taxes after this year anyway, so you may as well make it pay for itself. Now you won't see much from Sarah and Elsa until they get established, but they're making improvements to the house and facilities and adding value. As for Frank, he's had a sweet deal and won't want to lose it. I've only been charging him 60 percent the going cash rent rate per acre. Serve him right if you raised it. But that's up to you. Drew, pour us another round, then I think it'll be time for dinner."

Twenty-Six

We all stood around the table. I noticed Robert had the same red hair as his mother. A.J. must carry a recessive gene from either our family or the McCombers. A quick glance at Frank made me feel he wanted me dead. Maybe I *should* consider raising his rent. As we came to the table, Dad said there were others willing to lease the land if Frank balked. Dad called for everyone's attention.

"This is a day I've wished for for a long time. To have all my children again at a family gathering. To heal old wounds. And I want to welcome, with all my heart, new members to this growing menagerie. Clare I welcome as sister; Wendy and Rebecca, you are my daughters; Elsa, my granddaughter; and Karla," he looked at Anne P., "I hope to welcome her as soon as she decides to get here. Welcome everyone. Welcome. May our Lord's blessings be upon us, and may we always follow His path and wisdom to treat all others as ourselves. Amen."

Most of us sat as Joey, Sarah, Elsa and Nathan Jr. brought trays and bowls of food around for each of us to choose what we wanted. Nathan looked proud that he was now considered old enough to serve, and the envied stares he got from Robert and Ella attested to their anticipation of next year. Beside me, Tom opened a biscuit on his plate and covered it with Clare's chili when the bowl passed.

"I've been waiting to taste this all afternoon."

I moved a small condiment bowl over. "If you like it *really* hot, add some of Clare's ghost pepper salsa."

"Thanks, I might."

I took a bit of Mom's ham, Wendy's garlicky mash potatoes, Clare's coleslaw, Debbie's glazed, roasted carrots and turnips, and Marian's bean casserole for my first round. I'd be saving room for Libby's shrimp gumbo for round two. I filled Elsa's plate as she was serving. Round two was serve yourself.

Tom was making satisfying sounds over Clare's chili and added a heaping spoonful of the salsa. I heard him moan and quickly reach for his glass of water.

"Eat some potatoes first. It'll soak up the oils. Water makes it worse. Trust me."

When he was able to breathe again, he nodded. "Thanks. That salsa should be considered a dangerous weapon."

"I think it is in three states."

"As an investigator, can you work here?"

"Yes, but I'm not looking for any work at the moment."

"And you're going home tomorrow?"

"Yes. I have a case I need to finish. Wendy and I need to make final plans for our wedding. Mom wants us to have it here at the house. We need to let friends know and arrange accommodations. We're hoping for three weeks from now."

"Would you have time to track a witness for us while you're at home? We've been having trouble locating her. She witnessed an accident. We'll pay your going rate, of course."

"I won't have time. I'm closing shop until after the wedding and—hopefully—a lusty honeymoon. I can recommend another agency. They're very good and our rates are similar."

I took out one of my cards and a pen and gave him the number to Fields & Cook Detectives.

"When I reopen, I'll be happy to take on work you have in my area or if you need me up here. I do most types of investigative work, but I specialize in locating runaway teens."

I heard Frank's slightly raised voice. "Why don't you go back where you came from?"

"Frank!" Mom said under her breath. "Behave!"

Rebecca fired back, "I'd be happy to. Why don't you get off our land so we can? My ancestors were here thousands of years before yours crawled out of their European caves."

Deadly silence drifted down the table. I looked down at the other end. Dad had raised his head but it didn't look like he knew what was happening. Before the awkwardness became unbearable, Marian filled the growing gap.

"Grandma, did you like the Easter card Robbie made for you?"

"I don't think I've seen it, dear. When did he mail it? Maybe it's late."

"He didn't mail it. He was supposed to give it to you today. I know he brought it. One for you and one for Grandpa. Excuse me, please."

Marian got up and walked over to where Robert was seated. All I heard was her say, "Well go get them." Robert left the room and Marian returned to her seat.

"Sorry. He forgot. He's getting them now."

Robert returned and gave an envelope to Dad, who thanked him, and then gave one to Mom.

"Happy Easter, MawMaw."

"Thank you. Happy Easter to you, Robert."

Robert returned to his place. Dad had opened his envelope and was holding up a card. It was hard to see it.

"Look everyone. Isn't this beautiful? Thank you, Robert."

"You're welcome, PawPaw."

Robert was beaming and Dad passed the card to Wendy. I turned to Mom. She pulled her card out and set the envelope aside.

"This is wonderful. Did you draw this, Robert?"

"Yes, MawMaw."

"You're a real artist. I'm going to frame it. Thank you, so much."

"You're welcome, MawMaw. I'm glad you like it."

I could see a drawing of a rabbit on the front. Mom passed it to Rebecca. Marian was feeling very proud of her son. Al, Sr., passed Dad's card to Patrick then patted Robert on the shoulder.

"Good job."

"Thanks, Grandpa."

The cards made their way around the table to "ohs" and "ahs" and other compliments. If Robert's face got any brighter, he'd explode. Mom's card reached me. It was simply worded at the top, "Happy Easter" and at the bottom "MawMaw." The calligraphy was well done and the illustration outstanding. It was a detailed, pen and ink drawing of a sitting, long-eared rabbit. The lines were finely drawn and the shading made the rabbit three-dimensional. I was surprised a ten-year-old was so talented, and it reminded me of something I'd seen. Below the drawing was the year, "2010" and below that were stylized initials, a small "c" set inside a large "R." I realized it was nearly an exact copy of Durer's famous *Hare* etching. I passed the card to Tom.

"Robert, this is great. Would you draw something I could buy?"

"Sure!" His chest puffed out. "What would you like?"

"Artist's choice. Whatever you think I'd like."

"Okay."

Wendy caught my eye. She was holding the envelope Dad's card came in and pointing at the corner. It looked like a stamp. She kept pointing to it. I turned to look at the envelope beside Mom. It lay upside down.

"Mom? Could I see the envelope, please?"

It was passed to me. The envelope was fully addressed from Robert Cord to MawMaw Cord. In the upper right corner was an un-cancelled, US stamp of a box turtle. The postage was 37 cents. Seven cents shy of the current rate. I felt a chill and exchanged looks with Wendy. She nodded.

"Is something wrong, Rachel?" Marian asked.

"No, not at all. I was just admiring that Robert took the time to address and stamp the envelope even though he wasn't mailing it. That kind of attention to detail shows imagination."

"Thank you. I try to encourage him."

"Of course it would have needed more postage if he really mailed it. It's a nice stamp. Where'd he get it?"

"From his grandma's Aunt Alice." She pointed to Debbie a couple seats to my left. Debbie leaned forward to look my way as Marian continued. "Uncle Sean collected stamps. Robbie loved to look at them. After Uncle Sean's death, Aunt Alice gave some to Robbie to start his own collection. I guess he used one of those. I would have given him a stamp if he'd asked."

"He's a fine artist. I won't be surprised to see his work in a museum some day."

"Thank you."

Marian's face glowed almost as brightly as Robert's. Debbie smiled and nodded her approval and sat back. I'd been raised a notch—maybe even a level—in their eyes, but how long would it last. I wanted a source for the Love stamps on Kelly's torn valentine, and now I had one.

Did Jenna and Jordan also have some of their grandfather's stamps? Or was Alice McComber Kelly's stalker? Was she still so deep in mourning for her husband and son? How far would she go to keep someone from taking Terry's place? Especially a woman?

I remembered the McComber home as always welcoming and full of people. A second home to many of us. And Mrs. McComber would always listen to whatever bothered me. I hated to think—

"I'm sorry, Tom. What did you say?"

"I'm going to see if there's any chili left for my dessert. Can I bring you anything?"

"No, thank you. I'm good."

My mind was racing. Jenna and Jordan were having Easter

at Alice's and the McCombers held large family gatherings like we did. I leaned forward so I could see Debbie. I also noticed Frank had left the table.

"Debbie, I meant to ask, how are your parents? Are they having a get together with Alice and everyone?"

"They're doing well, thank you. They are at Aunt Alice's this year. We're going to stop by later for coffee and cake. I'll be sure to let them know you asked about them."

"Please tell Alice I'm thinking of her too. She was like a second mother when I was growing up."

"I will. Would you and Wendy like to join us? I'm sure she would love seeing you again."

"Yes, I think we would. I'll ask Wendy."

I got up. Wendy stood and went to the dessert table. I met her there. She put a very small scoop of Nancy's Jello mold in a dessert bowl. She spread it with a spoon to make the serving appear larger. She looked at me.

"You thinking what I am?"

"That the Love stamps came from the same place Robert got his? Yes. Alice McComber's. The question remains as to who used them on the valentine. It could be Jenna and Jordan or Alice. All three have reasons not to like Kelly. Right now all three of them are together with other family, so Kelly, and Betty Jean, should be safe. Debbie's related and she's going over later. We've been invited and that should give us a chance to find out more. You really going to eat that?"

"Some. It's all a matter of timing."

I got a bowl of Libby's gumbo as Wendy went back to the table licking the spoon and taking the tiniest bit more.

"Nancy? Did you make this?" Wendy licked the spoon again as she sat.

"Yes. Do you like it? I make it every Easter."

"It looked so good, I couldn't resist having some before I sat down."

"Thank you. It always seems to disappear quickly. It looks rich but it's quite light. I've never had garlic mash potatoes, but those you made were quite good. I'm going to have to try that. And your mother's coleslaw is the best I've ever had. Would she share the dressing recipe do you think?"

"She's sworn to secrecy. Won't even let me have it."

"Well I know Frank liked it too. You didn't see where he went, did you?"

"No, I didn't. Sorry."

"I better find him. Excuse me. It was nice talking with you."

As I passed, Wendy licked the spoon one more time and set it in the bowl of Jello she'd hardly touched. All of the kids were gone and several of the others. Libby and Clare had their heads together. Mom was still apologizing to Rebecca and Drew for Frank's behavior. Debbie, Al, Marian and A.J. were together looking at the cards Robert had made. I sat back next to Tom.

"I was lucky. There was some chili left. But I'm passing on the salsa this time. Too bad Frank made such a scene. I know he's volatile and a bigot, but I've never seen him do that around his mother before. I think she's more upset than anyone."

"Finding out Dad gave me the Old Houzer Place didn't help, I'm sure."

"True. I was standing in the hall when he stormed out of the parlor. Said he wanted to hire me to fight it in court. Tried to tell him he'd be wasting his money, but he didn't want to hear it."

"Think I'll try and find him. See if we can work something out."

"You carrying?"

"No, why?"

"Might need it for self-defense."

I thought of my rolled-up magazines. "I usually put my faith in the power of the word. Catch you later."

After looking several places, I heard Nancy's voice in the parlor.

"Frank, please put the bottle down. You've had more than enough."

"Don't tell me when I've had enough."

"You'll just aggravate your ulcer and won't solve anything."

"The hell with my ulcer. I still can't believe he gave that worthless bitch my land."

"Frank, it's not your land. Your father leases it to you. He's always made that perfectly clear."

"I've worked that land for 30 years. I've improved it so it'll grow whatever I plant. I get more yield off that hundred acres than anyone else in the county — in the state — ever could. And he gives it to her? Fuck!"

I opened the door and entered. "Frank, shut the fuck up."

"You can't talk to me like that."

"Somebody needs to, and it looks like I'm elected, like it or not."

"Why I'll bust you —" He raised his fist and started toward me.

"Stop right there, Frank. You're my brother. You may be bigger and stronger and think you can take me, but if you attack me — I swear — I'll put you down for the count. You're not my first, trust me."

I stared him straight in the eye and held a tightly rolled magazine low and close to my leg. He stopped in the middle of the room puffing and blowing like a bull ready to charge. He turned around throwing his hands in the air and walked away.

"Get the fuck outta here."

"No. Listen to me. For once in your narrow-minded life, listen to me. I'm your little sister. Brothers are supposed to listen to their little sisters. To protect their little sisters. It's part of the genetic code. So hear me out."

He put his hands on the window frame and stared out.

"We've never been close. We're too far apart in years. When I was tiny I didn't even realize you were my brother.

Probably thought you were an uncle or friend of Dad's at first. But you are my brother. And I can remember when you thought of me as your little sister and let me ride on your shoulder. Held me in your lap on the tractor as you worked the fields. Took me and Nancy Drew to the Kansas City zoo and let us eat hotdogs and cotton candy till we were sick. And when you worked the county fair and before the rides opened, you let me ride the ponies."

I took a deep breath. "But I grew up and we grew apart. I wasn't that sweet little girl anymore. And when I discovered I was lesbian, you took it personally. Thought I betrayed you. Thought I was anathema. That I had shamed you. But, Frank, it wasn't about you. It was about me. Discovering who and what I was. Life's a bitch, Frank. And there've been times I've had to be a bitch back just to survive. I felt the hate and ridicule from others, but you were an unholy bastard who went out of his way to see to it my life was hell and I was punished for crimes I didn't even know existed much less committed."

I took another breath. Dropped the magazine. Wiped tears from my eyes.

"Frank, I didn't want to come back. I was afraid to come back. I'm not a masochist. Why would I return to a place and to people who rejected me? Hated me for being me? What could possibly make me want to return for more of that? Do you know why I'm here? I'm here because I'm in love. Oh, I love my parents. I love my family. Even you who made my life so miserable I had to run away. But was that enough love to bring me back? To face more crap? It hasn't for more than 20 years."

I closed my eyes, felt my face flush. Tried to keep a sense of control.

"I'm in love, Frank. I think you understand being in love. I dearly hope so. Well, I'm in love. In love with someone who makes me whole. In love with a woman I want to marry, to bond with for all of my life. But guess what? She wouldn't marry me, Frank. Wouldn't have me to love and to hold and to cherish till I brought her here. That's all. If I wanted her badly enough, I had to bring her here. To Hell. And I did. And I'm glad I did. And not only because she'll marry me now. But because coming back I'm no longer afraid of you. Any of you. You're not my demons any more. You're my family. My demons no longer exist. Let go of your demons, Frank. They just eat you alive."

"Some demons are harder to let go than others."

"True. But you have Nancy, Frank. You have her love. You have Nancy Drew, Anne Marie, A.W. You have their husbands and wife and children. All their love. You have Mom and Dad. Your brothers. Me, if you'll let me."

I paused. "I know you've worked hard all your life. Taken whatever Nature threw at you and tamed Her as best you could. Worked the fields to bend to your will. I hardly knew the Houzer property existed. Never desired it. Never dreamed about it. Never asked for it. So I'm as surprised as you to find I own it. Surprised that before either of us was born, that it was decided that piece of dirt was mine. When you were born a piece of Cord land became yours. To be given you when you married. And it was the same for Al and Drew. And now, for me. Tell me, Frank. What makes your birthright more important than mine? Or Al's or Drew's more important?"

Nancy went and put her hand on him. "Listen to her, Frank. I've loved you for more than 40 years. We've been married nearly 36. Your parents and my parents gave us land when we married. Told us it had been set aside for just that purpose. You know it's true for her too."

"Frank. Dad says you and he have had a deal about that land for years. I see no reason we can't continue the same way. Do you hate me so much you'd give up working it and let someone else profit from what you made of it? Really? Dad says I can make more money per acre renting to someone else, but I'd rather keep it in the family. Keep it the way it is. Your choice."

I saw his shoulders heaving. Thought he was shaking. He turned. His grumbling may have been laughter. Hard to tell.

"Now that does sound like a dumb move, doesn't it? Sorta like cutting my nose off to spite my face. I don't understand you, Rachel. Don't understand your lifestyle, your wants or needs. Doubt I ever will or want to. But it's your life, not mine. What'd that guy in the movies say, 'Stupid is as stupid does'? Well, I don't think I'm so stupid to give up the best land in the county just because I don't like the way you live your life. We got a deal on that. My hand on it."

He held out his huge callused paw and I was glad he didn't try to crush mine. It was the first time my brother and I had touched in 23 years. It was a start.

"Frank, understanding my wants and needs should be easy if you'd give it a try. They're exactly the same as yours. The love of a good woman."

"Maybe so. But don't waste any money sending me an invite to the wedding. Don't think this old oak can bend that far in the wind without breaking. I need to go make some apologies. Then I think it's time we went home."

I stared at the empty doorway for several minutes then went and picked up Dad's bottle of sour mash. Frank put a big dent in it. Hoped Nancy would do the driving. I considered having a drink then remembered Betty Jean's tarts on the dessert table.

The desserts had been picked over. Nancy's Jello mold was mostly uneaten. There were a few of Betty Jean's turnovers left. Hoped Dad had gotten another blackberry one. I looked around, but he was gone. The spiced apple and sour cherry pies were gone. There was a pecan pie someone brought that looked tempting. A couple more empty boxes and then I lucked in. One box still had three tarts left. I took the lemon and went and joined Wendy, Mom, Rebecca and Drew at the table.

"Dad leave?"

Mom nodded. "Went to lie down. I'm not surprised. Big

day for him and I understand he had a drink earlier. Frank was here a few minutes ago to apologize to Rebecca and everyone. I think he'd been drinking. Did you see him?"

"In the parlor. He'd had a few drinks from Dad's sour mash. He was angry about the Houzer land. We came to an understanding. We're going to continue the same arrangement he had with Dad." I bit into the tart and enjoyed the flavors and tartness on my tongue. "Where's Debbie and Marian?"

"Locating Robert and getting their things together," Wendy said. "We should get our coats."

We said our good-byes. Rebecca and Drew would be leaving early in the morning to catch their flight back to Dallas. I hugged Mom and said we'd stop to see her and Dad before we headed home. Clare was going to stay awhile. Joey volunteered to drive her to the B&B later.

Twenty-Seven

The sun was low promising a gorgeous sunset when we arrived at Alice McComber's. The old porch swing where I'd spent many hours laughing, or crying and pouring my heart out to a patient and understanding Alice, was still there. I didn't want to believe she was Kelly's stalker; or that it was Jenna or Jordan either. But you have to follow the path you're given, and mine led here.

Inside, Jenna and Jordan were playing Monopoly with two other girls. They looked up and waved. Debbie reminded her parents who I was and introduced Wendy. Their warm welcome cooled quickly to mere politeness when they realized we were a couple.

I interpreted Mrs. McComber's sideways look to Debbie as "How could you bring these—fill in the blank—here?" They were soon distracted by the Easter cards Robert made them. He had one for Alice too, but she wasn't there. Mr. McComber said she was on an errand but should return shortly. Alice's son, Taylor, who I was in school with, introduced us to his wife, Rosemary. They both taught at the high school.

I pulled out my phone to check the time but it was off. I'd turned it off before sitting down to dinner. I turned it on. It was 6:14 p.m. My phone pinged to let me know I missed a call. At that moment Alice McComber came in from the kitchen. She still had her coat on. She was surprised to see me but gave me a welcoming hug. I caught a whiff of something

acrid and familiar but couldn't place it. She shook hands with
Wendy and asked if we were staying for coffee and cake.
Robert gave her her card.

I stepped away to see who called. It was Betty Jean at 5:28.
There was a voicemail message. I checked it. "Rachel! Call me
as soon as you get this." She sounded stressed.

"Excuse me a moment, please."

I stepped out to the porch to return Betty Jean's call. It
barely rang twice before she picked up.

"Rachel? Kelly's been shot! Oh my God. Rachel. Rachel."

"Betty Jean, where are you? What happened?"

"She's been shot, Rachel. Someone shot her."

"Where are you?"

"What?"

"Where are you?"

"I'm . . . They shot her."

"Betty Jean, take a breath. Tell me where you are."

"The . . . the emergency room. In Leon. The county
hospital."

"Has anyone told you her status?"

"No. They took her into the emerge . . . the O.R. Ah . . . Let
me think. Oh God, Rachel. There was so much blood. So much
blood. Kelly. Kelly. Kelly."

"Betty Jean. I need you to try and calm down. Are you
hurt?"

"Me? No, I'm . . . I'm . . . Oh shit! I'm covered in blood. Oh
Kelly. I can't lose her, Rachel. I can't."

"I know. Is anyone with you?"

"No. I'm in a cubicle. I'm waiting — What? No, I'm not
getting off the phone. Fine! I'll go outside. Fucking idiots.
Rachel? You still there?"

"I'm still here."

"What were you asking me?"

"Are you hurt?"

"No. No. A cut on my cheek. Don't know how that
happened. The EMT put a bandage on it. My clothes are

ruined. Oh, Rachel. I'm covered in Kelly's blood. What am I going to do?"

"Betty Jean, we'll be there as quick as we can, but I need you to talk to me. Where was she shot?"

"In the back."

"I mean where were you and Kelly when she was shot?"

"Her bedroom. We'd just come in from a walk and hung up our coats. We were standing in the bedroom. Something hit the window. Kelly screamed and fell. I think I heard a shot. I don't know."

"How long ago did it happen?"

"Um. I don't know. Not that long ago. I held her and called 9-1-1. Then tried to call you but only got voicemail. I'm sorry. I'm not sure."

"That's okay. I have the time you called. I want you to hang up and go inside. Let them make sure you're not hurt. We're on our way. We're coming."

"Thank you, Rachel. God. I'm glad my girls weren't there."

"Me too."

Breathe, Rachel. Breathe. Think. Leon's not that far. We can be there in —

I looked through Alice's living room window at the people inside. I knew what I smelled on her clothing. I called Mom.

"Mom, I need you to do something for me right away."

"What is it? Is something wrong?"

"Betty Jean's friend, Kelly Richards, was seriously injured this evening. They're at the Decatur County Hospital in Leon."

"That's terrible. What happened?"

"I don't have time to explain. Kelly's in the Emergency O.R. and Betty Jean's alone. I need you and Clare to go to her right now. I can't."

"All right, dear. We'll take Libby too. I hope she'll be okay."

"Me too. Oh, and bring something Betty Jean can wear. She wasn't hurt but her clothes are all bloody. Thanks, Mom. I'll talk to you later."

I put my phone away and went in. Wendy was standing near Jenna and Jordan watching the Monopoly game. She gave me a questioning look. I put a finger to my lips and walked up to Alice.

"Sorry for the interruption."

"Quite all right. I've started a fresh pot of coffee. It'll be ready shortly. Aren't the cards Robert made beautiful?"

"They are. I think he's very talented. Alice? Could we talk? Outside, please?"

"Surely. Let me put my coat back on."

We went and sat on the porch swing like long ago. The years disappeared for a moment, and then I was back in the here and now.

"Is something bothering you, Rachel? Can I help?"

"Where's the gun, Alice?"

"Gun? What gun?"

"The gun you used to shoot Kelly Richards. I smelled gunpowder on your coat when we hugged."

"I'm sure I don't know what—"

"Yes you do. Was it your husband's gun? I remember he had a .22 target pistol we used to plink at tin cans in the back yard. Is that the one you used?"

"Rachel—"

Alice pressed her lips tightly together and closed her eyes. She hugged herself as if she were cold. The front door opened and Debbie stepped out.

"Aunt Alice? The coffee's ready. Shall I cut the cake?"

"Yes, dear. Thank you. Don't wait for us. Rachel . . . Rachel and I need to speak privately."

"Okay. Don't stay out too long and catch cold."

"We won't, dear. Thank you."

Debbie went back inside and closed the door. She must have turned the porch light on so we wouldn't be sitting in the dark when the sun set. I looked west over my shoulder. The sun was a red ball barely above the horizon. The clouds were glowing against a deepening azure sky. I turned back to Alice and waited.

"She should have stopped seeing Betty Jean. She should have stopped."

"Is that sufficient reason to try and kill her?"

"She's not dead?"

"I don't think so. She's at the emergency room in Leon."

We sat silent for several minutes.

"I like to think I'm a tolerant person, Rachel. A good person. Years ago, when you and I sat here, and you were crying because everyone was calling you and Betty Jean terrible names, I understood. You were growing up. Going through changes on the inside as well as developing on the out. Perfectly natural. Happens to all of us. And when those changes include sexual feelings, you want to know what it's like to touch and be touched. And who better to experiment with, to explore with, than a best friend?"

She had a faraway look and wistful smile. "For me, it was Amy Prendergast. We were both 14. We never went beyond kissing and light petting. The most daring we ever got was a French kiss. Wanted to know what it was like before doing it with a boy. Didn't want to be embarrassed by gagging or finding it gross. It's a phase. We all go through it."

She looked at me. "Of course, Amy and I were more circumspect than you and Betty Jean. You two were a caution. But I thought it was just a natural phase the two of you were going through. That you'd grow out of. Like Amy and I did. And I was convinced of it when you started dating those boys in high school. So when Terry came home wounded from the war and went to Grace and began dating Betty Jean, I was happy for the both of them. Terry lived here, you know, until they married. She was here so much, I thought of her as the daughter we never had. Still do. I'd watch them together. She was never bothered he'd lost his leg. Or by the burn scars."

Alice took a tissue from her pocket and wiped her eyes and nose.

"She was very patient with him. Helped him with his exercises. Rubbed him with salves and ointments to soften and lessen the scarring. Encouraged him in everything he tried to do. When they told us they were getting married, we were so excited. So were Rob and Lori, Betty Jean's parents. I remember Rob saying he was 'over the moon' about it. I always liked that expression. It was how we all felt. Did you know she lost her parents in a plane accident?"

"No, I didn't."

"They were flying back from a vacation in Mexico. That was . . . January 2000. They were supposed to transfer in San Francisco. I forget what happened, but the plane crashed into the ocean somewhere off California. Everyone on board died. It affected all of us. Maybe not the girls so much. They were still very young. But after that I was the only mother Betty Jean had. And the girls. They were Terry and Betty Jean's whole world. Mine too. Jenna was our first grandchild. March 18th 1994. Jordan was our third. She was born September 2nd 1996. Barbara Ann was our second, August 21st 1995, and Bethany Alice our fourth, May 7th 1998. They're Taylor and Rosemary's daughters. That's them playing games in the living room with Jenna and Jordan. And then we lost Terry."

Alice needed to stop again. Her family losses still too near the surface.

"I'm sorry. Do you have a tissue? This one's used up."

I gave her a clean handkerchief from my inner pocket.

"Thank you. His cancer was very aggressive. He went downhill rapidly. He was gone in less than a year. Betty Jean stuck by him. She was right there to the end. I truly believe they had a good marriage. That she really loved him. Then Sean two years ago. Betty Jean and I shared all those losses. So when Jordan told me that—"

She clasped my handkerchief in a death's grip, holding it close to her face, teeth clenched, eyes tightly closed. She took a deep breath.

"I don't want to insult you, Rachel. I truly don't. I know

you're a good person. I'm sure your Wendy is too. But I won't pretend to understand your lifestyle. The choice you made. I was taught that homo . . . homosexuality is a sin. Against nature and against God. A wickedness not to be tolerated. That must be destroyed as God destroyed Sodom and Gomorrah. Yet I've tried to be tolerant of others. Your choice is your choice. Your life is yours. But as close as you are to me, you're not my family. And when that wickedness threatened to invade my family's life, my son's family's life, his daughters' lives, my daughter's life — *that* I could not tolerate. I warned her, Rachel. Many times. She should have stopped. Do you know if Betty Jean was hurt?"

"She's distraught. Her heart's breaking. Does that count?"

She had no answer, so I asked again, "What did you do with the gun?"

"Threw it away. After I . . . After. I drove around before coming home. No plan. Just drove. I threw it in the creek from the bridge before getting to your parents house. Then I came home. What do we do now?"

"I think it's time we made a phone call. Do you wish to do it or shall I?"

Alice took out her smartphone, scrolled through her contacts, and pressed, "Call."

"Good evening, Georgette. This is Alice McComber. Happy Easter to you, too. Is William there? He had to leave? I understand. Georgette, would you please call him for me? I need to see him right away. Yes, I know he's investigating a shooting. That's why I'm calling. Tell him I have important information — vital information — about the shooting. Yes, you could say I witnessed it. Yes, he can call me, but I think he'll want to see me. I'm at home. Yes, it is a tragedy. I agree, things like that don't happen here in Laman. Thank you, my best to your family, too."

Alice put down the phone. "Georgette is William's mother. I knew he and his wife and children would be with her for Easter. You never met them. They moved here after you left.

Like you, William was one of the many children who always seemed to gravitate over here. Sean and I loved having all of you here. William's our chief of police now. I'm sure he'll be here shortly."

"Are you cold? Would you like to wait inside?"

"No, I'm fine. I'd rather wait here. You'll stay till he gets here, won't you."

"Yes." I saw Marian and Wendy standing at the window. "Would you like some coffee or something?"

"Coffee would be nice."

I made motions to indicate we'd like some coffee. They nodded. Marian came out with two steaming mugs.

"Here you go. It's getting cool out here. Sure you don't want to come inside?"

"We're fine, dear. Won't be much longer. Would you bring me the card Robert made?"

"Of course. I'll be right back."

"Alice, did you use that phone to send Kelly those text messages and photos?"

"Yes, I did."

"Does your phone have GPS?"

"I believe so. Why?"

"The police can use it to see where you've been today. And they can look at the messages you sent. They'll want that to verify your story."

"Even if I deleted everything?"

"Yes. And they'll test your coat for gunpowder residue."

"Will you and Wendy be going to see Betty Jean? I hate to think she's sitting there all alone."

"Yes, we are, but Mom's with her now. So's Aunt Libby and Clare, Wendy's mother. She's not alone."

"That's good. When you go, would you take Jenna and Jordan with you? Betty Jean will want them with her."

"Certainly. I think that's a good idea."

I took my phone and called Mom. "Hi, any updates?"

"Kelly's out of surgery and in Recovery. She's going to be

okay. They're going to let Betty Jean see her when they move her to a room. Are you coming?"

"Yes. There are still some things I need to finish first. Tell Betty Jean we'll be bringing Jenna and Jordan with us."

"All right. We'll see you when we see you."

Marian brought Alice the card then went back in the house.

"Alice, Mom says Kelly's all right."

"I suppose that's a good thing. I was tormenting over violating a Commandment. Didn't Robert do a nice job on this card?"

"Yes he did." This time Robert copied Durer's *Praying Hands*. I was amazed again at how talented he was. I passed it back to her.

"Do you think William will let me keep it with me?"

"I'm sure he will."

A car pulled up and a man got out and headed our way. He wore a heavy coat and slacks. I could tell he wasn't wearing a uniform. But then he was at his mother's for Easter and probably went straight to the crime scene before coming here.

"Good evening, Mrs. McComber. Ma'am."

"Good evening, William. Happy Easter."

"Thank you. Same to you, ma'am. Mother says you have some information about a shooting earlier this evening."

"That's correct. William, this is Rachel Cord. She's visiting family for Easter. Rachel, this is William Carnes, our city police chief."

"Pleased to meet you, ma'am."

"Nice to meet you too, but please call me Rachel. We're too close in age for you to call me ma'am."

"All right. Now, Mrs. McComber, what can you possibly tell me about a shooting on the other side of town that happened only about two hours ago?"

"I did it."

"Excuse me?"

"I did it, William. I shot the woman through her bedroom window."

He was totally surprised. He looked at me for help. I nodded in agreement which seemed to deepen his surprise. He looked back at Alice.

"Begging your pardon, ma'am. This is a serious—"

"I'm well aware, William, of how serious it is to shoot someone. Here." Alice held out her phone. "Rachel says there's evidence on my phone that shows I threatened the woman and tells where I was earlier. Also, that there's . . . gunpowder something-or-other on my coat that proves I fired the gun."

He took the phone and looked at me questioningly.

"Gunpowder residue. I smelled it when I hugged her about 6:15. She'd just returned home. The GPS on her phone should tell you where she was at around 5:25, which is when I think Kelly Richards was shot, as well as where Alice disposed of a .22 caliber target pistol—don't recall the make— afterwards. That'll be Jeffers Creek where County Road 66 crosses it. You should be able to recover text messages and photos from the phone she sent the victim since February 17th."

"You in law enforcement?"

"Professional investigator." I handed him my card.

He studied it. "Out-of-state. And you just *happen* to solve a two-hour old crime in my town."

"Wasn't my intent. I was only trying to discover who was threatening a friend and ended up here. The rest was serendipitous."

"I'm sure."

"William?"

"Yes, ma'am?"

"May I pack an overnight bag before you arrest me?"

He smiled. "Mrs. McComber, should I consider you a flight risk?"

"William Carnes. Where am I going to go?"

"That's what I thought. So, you will not need an overnight bag, as I do not intend to arrest you tonight. What we are going to do is this: you will accompany me to the station. At the station, I will advise you of your rights and take any statement you wish to give. *At the station.* I don't want to hear anything more about the incident right now. After I have your statement, I will bring you home. You'll be sleeping in your own bed tonight. Time enough tomorrow for arrests and charges."

"I don't want any special treatment."

"No, ma'am. I know that. I appreciate it. I do suggest if you have an attorney, you may want him present this evening to advise you."

"Ben Morris was our family lawyer for years. I'm not sure if he's retired or not."

"Alice, if I may. My niece Nancy Drew and her husband are out at Mom's. They're both lawyers and could at least advise you tonight."

"I remember Nancy Drew. Do you think she'd do that?"

"I'm sure she would. I can call and have her meet you at the police station."

"Thank you, Rachel. I'd like that. Would that be all right, William?"

"Perfectly all right. Rachel, I'll need you to come too and give a statement."

"I understand. Could I come and do that later? Betty Jean McComber was with Kelly when she was shot. She's the one who called 9-1-1 and also told me of the shooting. She's out at the hospital too. She's quite upset, and I want to give her some support right now. Also, her daughters are here. I was going to take them out there."

"One of my officers should be getting a statement from her now. Can I trust you not to discuss anything with her — or anyone else for that matter — about what you've learned this evening before I have all relevant statements in hand? I don't need anyone muddying the waters."

"Definitely. I understand fully."

The front door opened and Debbie's father stepped out.

"Chief Carnes? Someone said you were out here. Everything all right?"

"Evening, Mr. McComber. Yes, sir. Pretty much. Mrs. McComber called to say she saw something earlier."

"Alice, you didn't say anything when you got home."

"I didn't have time, Bob. I needed to talk to Rachel here. Would you get my purse, please? I need to go with William."

"Why? Where's he taking you?"

"Mr. McComber, sir, she needs to write up a statement officially. I'll have her back here directly."

"What'd she see? What happened?"

"Sorry, sir. Can't say. Don't need some fancy lawyer complaining I influenced a witness statement. You understand."

"Right. Right. Know what you mean. They'll do it every time."

"Yes, sir. One more thing. Understand Betty Jean McComber's daughters are here?"

"That's right. For Easter."

"They need to go to their mother. Rachel's volunteered to take them. If you could get them ready too, it'd be appreciated."

"Did something happen to—Oh, right. Can't say. I'll get them ready. Be right back with your purse, Alice."

"Thank you, Bob. And thank you, William, for not saying anything."

"Quite all right, ma'am." He looked at me strangely. "Rachel Cord and Betty Jean . . . Did she used to be Betty Jean Cooper?"

"Yes."

"I heard stories about you two back in high school after we moved here. You were pretty infamous back then."

"Trust me, I'm sure most of those stories were exaggerated. One or two may even have been untrue."

He laughed. "If we get a chance, you'll have to tell me which ones those were. Are you staying with family?"

"No, I'm at the Dogwood Street Inn. I'm due to check out tomorrow morning and go home."

"Look, about your statement," he gave me his card. "Why don't you call later and we can decide if I want you to come in tonight or in the morning."

"I can do that. Thank you."

"That's all right. I think you saved the city a lot of overtime we can't afford."

Mr. McComber returned with Alice's purse. Jenna and Jordan came out with Wendy.

"Thank you, sir. Sorry for the disturbance. Hope the rest of your evening goes well. Mrs. McComber, if you're ready, it's time we go."

"Certainly, William."

Twenty-Eight

I fell face forward on the bed and didn't intend to move for at least a week. I heard Wendy come in and put things down.

"You just going to lie there?"

I mumbled into the pillow.

"What? I can't understand you. Turn your head. You're going to suffocate."

"I said, yes. Don't wake me before Saturday."

"Well, at least get undressed and under the covers. And leave me some room. I'm getting some water. Can I bring you anything?"

I rolled over. "Four fingers of absolution and forgetfulness."

Wendy came back with her water and my tumbler of Glenfiddich. I sat up.

"You're two fingers shy."

"You want more, get it yourself."

She sat in a chair by the glass doors to our balcony. I took a deep breath of the Scotch then a sip and rolled it on my tongue.

"I am so glad to be home."

"Admit it, Rachel. Your family is not the band of ogres you've been dreading for half your life."

"Are you saying I wasted half my life?"

"I wouldn't say 'wasted.' Missed opportunities, maybe.

Missed memories. I know I have some good memories from this weekend."

"Yes, Wendy, when you're right, you're right. I thank you, again, for your wisdom and making me go. I grovel to your wisdom. Come here and let me show you how well I grovel."

"You want me to come to you? I thought groveling was you crawling to me and kissing my feet."

"I'm too exhausted to crawl. I'll kiss your feet later. And any other part you'd like kissed."

"Knowing you, I'm not sure that counts as groveling. Would you like something to eat? Let me rephrase that. Would you like some food?"

"Not right now. Maybe one of the pastries Betty Jean sent home with us later."

"I'm surprised she insisted on working today. Don't think I would have. Thought she'd want to stay with Kelly."

"I'm sure she would, but she said she needed to work. Probably needs the routine. The normality."

"Any idea of what's going to happen with Alice?"

"No. I asked Bill—Chief Carnes—after I signed my statement. He's assigned the investigation to one of his officers. He said there's a range of assault charges she faces. The most worrisome is if 'hate crime' is added to the mix. He's not in any hurry to arrest her. Wants it fully investigated before he takes it to the county DA."

"I'm sorry Debbie and Marian are blaming you for Alice's confessing. Thought you were winning them over."

"Well, Alice doesn't blame me. Even thanked me. Maybe they'll come back around by the wedding."

"Speaking of which, we need to let people know right away we have a date and see who'll be coming. Before we left, your mom said there are two locations available for the 24th. She was going to start calling local motels for availability."

"The invitations are still on the desk, aren't they?"

"Yes. We just need to add dates and where."

"Let's do it first thing tomorrow. Think I'll take a nap. If

I'm not up in a couple hours, wake me, please."

"Okay. At least take your shoes off."

The next morning after an early breakfast that included more of Betty Jean's pastries, we called Mom and settled on the location and then finished our invitations.

Rachel Evangeline Cord and Wendy Pan Devlin
Wish you to join us in celebration of our wedding
Saturday, the Twenty Fourth of April, Two Thousand Ten
Two O'Clock in the Afternoon
The Heartland Mission
Laman, Iowa
Reception to follow
Come as you are — we're all friends and family
RSVP

Wendy took most of the invitations to drop off at the post office on her way to the bank. A few she'd give personally as I had kept a few for friends I knew I'd see. That taken care of I called John Cartwright.

"Good morning, John. Hope your Easter was happy and without incident."

"It was, thank you. I trust yours was the same."

"Perhaps not totally without incident, but happy nonetheless. I don't recall if I told you or not, but I'm getting married. It'll be on the 24th in Laman, Iowa. That's about a five and a half hour drive. You and your wife should receive your invitation tomorrow or Thursday. I've also invited Matthew Marston. It's short notice, I know, but I'd love having you there, if you can make it. We've arranged accommodations, but will need to know by the 14th to lock them in."

"Congratulations. I'll speak to Ellen about it tonight and let you know. I know Matthew will be thrilled for you, but he'll be in London that week. Ellen will want to know if you have a wedding registry."

"No, we don't. All Wendy and I desire is 'good wishes' and for whichever friends who can to join us in celebration."

"Will you consider a donation in your names to a charity of your choice?"

"That would be appreciated. Our first choice would be the Human Rights Campaign, or the Southern Poverty Law Center or ACLU. Actually any group that supports LGBTQ rights."

"Consider it done. I'm sure you also called for an update on the Douglas Grimes situation."

"Yes. Anything new?"

"Some. The blood on the deck step was Cochran's. More importantly, the brake fluid in Grimes' car was corrupted. Analysis showed traces of ethyl alcohol. Also, we found where Suliman bought the resupply of liquor, and we have a list of what he bought. One item no one mentioned was a small bottle of Everclear. While any of the alcoholic drinks could have been used in the brake fluid, I'm betting on the Everclear. It's nearly pure and boils at a low 173 degrees Fahrenheit. A couple ounces of that would guarantee failure. It could also have been used to spike the rum and cokes Grimes was drinking."

"There's our smoking gun."

"Quite possibly. It's definitely something Suliman will need to explain. And if he didn't tamper with the brakes, one of the others must have. All we need now are the results of the tox screens to see if you're right about Grimes being given caffeine or some other stimulant. I hope to have those results later today or tomorrow."

"Then what?"

"I've already briefed the Washaw County sheriff and county attorney on what we have and they've agreed to reopen their investigation. As soon as I have the tox results, they'll get everything we've done to include your reports. After that, it's their ballgame. You should expect to hear from their investigator."

"Okay. Do you think Suliman suspects we know what he did? I suppose, in all fairness, I should say what we think he may have done?"

"I've no idea. Once the audit was complete, we had no reason to go back to Gimmicks. And while he knows you were snooping for Mrs. Grimes and may be worried, as far as I know, he's not aware of our investigation in Washaw County."

"Once the results are in, what are your thoughts of updating Stephanie again?"

"Part of me says we both have a duty to her as our mutual client to keep her informed. On the other hand, I'm worried she won't be able to keep from saying something to someone and jeopardize Washaw County's efforts. I think it's in the best interest of our client and the investigation to wait."

"I agree. I told her I had little left to investigate, but I think I'll do some subtle surveillance to be sure all suspect parties remain in the picture."

"All right. I'll let you know as soon as the results come in. Congratulations, again, on your upcoming marriage."

"Thanks."

I called Frank Taylor. "Hey, Frank. You free for lunch today? I'm buying."

"I'll make myself free. What time?"

"One o'clock okay?"

"One's fine. See you then."

I made one more call.

"Roger Burke, Photography. This is Roger."

"Hi, Roger. It's Rachel Cord. Not sure you remember—"

"Rachel! One of my all-time favorite models. Why wouldn't I remember you?"

I was looking at an evocative, black-and-white photo of me lying nude among driftwood at the river in early morning. It was the only time I'd posed for him or any photographer. Wendy loved it and insisted we display it in our home office area.

"Because I only posed that one time nearly six summers ago. So I hardly think that makes me an 'all-time favorite model.'"

"Here's why I think so. Eighteen months ago I had a gallery show out in San Diego. The photography curator from the San Diego Museum of Art liked my work and asked to see my whole portfolio. She commissioned and bought five photos. Two were of you."

"I'm on display at the San Diego Museum of Art?"

"I don't know if you're currently on display, but you were last fall as part of a photography show they held called *River Views*. You're now part of the museum's permanent collection."

"Not sure how I feel about that. What I wanted to know is if you still do weddings?"

"Not as many as I used to. Are you getting married?"

"Yes, April 24th. Would you be available?"

"For you, definitely. *River Views* brought me to the attention of several public and private galleries. Let's get together this week and discuss what you want. Where's the wedding going to be?"

"Laman, Iowa, at 2:00 p.m. on the 24th. We'll cover your motel and expenses over and above your photography fee. Could we meet in the evening this week? I'd like my fiancé to meet you too."

"How about tomorrow evening at 7:30? I'm still at the same address."

"That'll be great, Roger. Thanks. Oh, any idea how many people saw the *River Views* show?"

"No, but I could find out. It was up for six weeks. At least several thousand."

"That's okay. See you tomorrow."

I looked at the photo once more. Several thousand people saw me like that. There was a certain sensual sadness about the woman lying against the sun-bleached, ruined trees cast up from the misty river. Yet also defiance in her outward gaze. I couldn't remember how Roger talked me into doing the shoot, but that I'd agreed only three months after my rape I found personally life-affirming.

Time to hit the road. I headed for PJs in Lincoln Heights. PJs wasn't there but Ruth was.

"She's just having her annual physical, Rachel. Nothing ever be wrong with Mama as long as this house is full of children that need her. She'll be sorry she missed you today, but there's no way she's going to miss your wedding. Put us down as definitely being there. Give me another hug for Mama."

I finally made it into the office. Mary Farr was at her computer behind the reception desk. I gave her a box of Betty Jean's turnovers and tarts and her wedding invitation.

"Where's Doris?"

"Supply run to Office Depot. Should be back any minute. These look good."

"They are, and there'll be lots more at the wedding reception."

"Great!" Mary licked her lips after taking a bite of a lemon tart. "Can't wait. These really are 'puckery good' like the box says." She opened the invitation. "Looks like your trip home was successful."

"Yes it was."

Doris Garrity came up the stairs carrying two bags.

"Hi, Rachel. Ooh, goodies. Are those for us?"

"Yes, and here's your wedding invitation."

"Be right back. Let me put this stuff in the supply room."

"Mary, any messages?"

"Been quiet. Two calls yesterday but we referred them to Fields & Cook as you requested. A Duncan Hanratty called Friday afternoon from Buffalo, New York. Said he found the Simpson boy right where you thought he'd be. Said to give him a call when you got back. Message is on your desk."

"Thanks."

Doris came back and opened her invitation. "Thank you, Rachel. You know we'll be there." She picked up one of the turnovers.

"Don't think I *could* get married without you two being there. Just let me know by next week how many are coming so I can confirm the rooms. I'll be in the office working on reports. If you don't see me walking out by 12:15, please rattle my cage. Thanks."

In the office, I turned on my computer, picked up the Simpson file and Hanratty's message and called him.

"Hi, Duncan. Rachel. Understand you found David Simpson. He okay? Any problems?"

"No problems. The boy's fine. He was at his cousin's as you thought he would be. Took me two weeks to verify it. He was staying hidden. Called you Friday but your secretary said you were gone for Easter. I contacted the local sheriff and we called the parents. Then a deputy and I went out and picked up the boy. His mother flew in Saturday morning and she and the boy flew home Saturday afternoon."

"Thanks, Duncan. Have you sent me your report and invoice of your hours?"

"Emailed them to you as attachments. If you need hardcopies, I can send those too."

I opened my email, downloaded and glanced at the attachments. "No need. I can print out the attachments for my files. I'll send you a check as soon as I settle with the parents."

"No rush. The mother handed me a $500 check as a bonus when she picked up the boy. You going to the national convention this year?"

"It's on my calendar. We can buy each other a drink and swap horror stories. Thanks for your help."

"Any time. Stay healthy."

I read Duncan's report and it looked like he earned every dollar of his bonus. Good for him. The parents were happy and they had their son home for Easter. It didn't take long to type out the final report and invoice I bluetoothed to Doris and Mary to double-check my spelling, grammar and math. Then I called up the interim report I'd given Stephanie Grimes, made a duplicate, and used that as a new draft for a final report adding the new information I had. I was reading what I'd written so far when Doris and Mary came in.

"Rachel," Doris said, "It's ten after."

"Thanks, but both of you didn't have to come down here to tell me."

"That's not the reason. Mary and I were discussing it, and it'll be only the two of us coming to your wedding. We can share a room."

"Are you sure? It's no problem. There'll be a passel of my grandnieces and nephews there. The more the merrier. Can you imagine me having grandnieces? I'm not old enough to have grand-anythings."

"Rachel?" Mary said. "Do you know how long it's been since Doris or I had a few days away from our kids and husbands? Longer than either of us can remember. As much as we love them, this is our chance to have some 'me' time too."

I did a save and shut down. "Okay by me. I need to leave. Doubt I'll be back today. See you tomorrow."

On my way to meet Frank for lunch at Charlie's, I stopped in at Phil's. Elspeth was at the counter.

"Rachel, I was just thinking of you. Are you married yet?"

"Soon. Very soon. Here's your invitation for you plus one, if you're seeing anyone."

"Thank you. Thank you. I'm so excited for you and Wendy." She opened it. "Where's Laman?"

"About five and a half hours west north west. We're providing the motel rooms, so don't say you can't come. Is Phil still on the other side of the world?"

"She is, but she texted to tell you congratulations."

"Well here's her invitation. I'm sorry she won't be there."

"I'll let her know. And I will bring someone. She recently moved here from Abilene and has the cutest Texas drawl you've ever heard. Are you staying for lunch?"

"No, I'm meeting Frank Taylor down the street at Charlie's hot dog stand. Just stopped by to drop off your invitation. Bye."

Despite the cold weekend, today was again unseasonably warm with the high predicted in the 80s. For the second time I beat Frank to Charlie's and put in our order.

"Charlie, for all the years I've been coming here, when are you going to share your secret coleslaw recipe with me?"

"Wouldn't be a secret long if I shared it with everyone, now would it? Besides, what would keep you coming back if you had it?"

"Your chili fries."

"Can't afford the risk. You're not as addicted to my chili as you are the slaw."

Frank walked up just as Charlie handed me two Chicago dogs for Frank and my slaw dog and chili fries and two drinks.

"I see you survived the visit home."

"That I did."

"Told you so."

"Yes, you did."

I gave him his invitation and his hug alone left no doubt he and Lorraine would be there. His mood was mixed. His White Sox won their opener against Cleveland, but the Cubs got trounced at Atlanta. He held on to hope this would the year the Cubbies beat the Billy Goat.

My last invitation drop-off of the day was to Brownie and Sonny Tristan. Sonny asked if we'd like her band to come and play. I added two more rooms to my list for the band. Hang the cost. Who wouldn't want a world-touring blues band at their wedding?

I then headed to Old Town's art district to recon and stake out Suliman's place. See what he'd been up to. If he were acting normally. The breeze was up which reminded me of Linda Woodruff at Gimmicks. I wondered if she'd been out on the water today and if she could give me an idea of the present cross currents at Gimmicks. I stopped at The Daily Grind for a latté and called her.

"Hi, Rachel. Still snooping?"

"Just a bit. I was wondering how things are going in the Rubik's cube."

"Still tense and out of sync. The partners seem to be at loggerheads which isn't helping the situation."

"So they're all there?"

"Why wouldn't they? It's just we need them stable and in control. Stop roiling the waters."

"Speaking of waters, have you been out on the lake?"

"Yes, and today is particularly nice. Planning to go out again later. As for me, my title's been upgraded to Special Projects Manager. Meaning everything Doug was handling and I get to use his office."

"Good for you. I'm sure you were probably handling a lot of it for him already."

"True. True."

"Thanks for the update. Happy sailing."

So the partners were arguing? About what and to what degree?

I finished my latté and wandered through some of the galleries Suliman frequented. Using last week's soirée as conversation, I found out he'd been in and out and acting his normal self. At The Madsen Gallery, I saw the Balson painting mentioned to Wendy and me. It was a little smaller than the one at Suliman's but I liked it better. A "SOLD" was attached to it. Gregg, who'd been playing bartender the other night, came over.

"Nice painting, isn't it?"

"It certainly is, but I see it's sold. You were telling my friend and me about the artist the other night at Suliman's."

"Yes, I was. I thought you looked familiar."

"Is Suliman adding it to his collection?"

"No. He was interested. Came in yesterday to ask about it,

but I'd sold it already. The next morning after the party, in fact. I'm waiting for—" His eyes went slightly wide and he briefly paused. "I'm waiting for the buyer to arrange delivery."

"I know my friend wanted to see it. Did she come in?"

"Ah. Yes. She did."

"Was she too disappointed it'd been sold?"

It was hard to read his expression. "Ah, no. I don't recall so. I remember her saying she was happy to see it though."

"I'm sure the new owner is happy too."

"Yes, I'm certain they will be. If you'll excuse me?"

"Certainly."

It was good to know Suliman was acting normal away from the office. Hoped it meant he wasn't feeling like a suspect. As I left the gallery, I stopped to look at a sculpture in the window. I saw Gregg on the phone and he was looking my way. He waved. I waved back.

When I got home that evening, Wendy was pensively wandering looking at the walls.

"Hi, something wrong?"

"Wrong? No. Not at all. What could possibly . . . that is . . . I was just realizing that for as long as this has been our home, that in some way, in less than three weeks, that word is going to have a more special meaning to me. To us."

She came and hugged me, but strangely, for no reason I could explain, I didn't feel she'd been thinking that at all.

Before eating, we went over our guest list and marked off those who'd confirmed they would come. It came to 13 rooms already. We called Mom and gave her the names. She said she'd handle the room confirmations. She'd reserved 20 rooms at the Laman Super Motel and another 10 at the Chieftain across the street. She said not to worry. Both managers said they could probably provide more rooms if needed, and the owner of Little River in Terryville said she'd hold five in reserve until the 16th.

After dinner Wendy and I relaxed with wine in the living

room. I told her of our appointment with Roger Burke. She was still staring at the walls.

"By the way, while I was checking on what Suliman was up to the last few days, I stopped in at The Madsen Gallery."

"Really?"

"Yes, I saw the Balson painting the bartender told us about."

"Is it still hanging? I thought it sold. Did you like it?"

"Very much. I liked the tonal pattern. I'm sorry someone beat you to it."

"*C'est la vie*. I thought it would look nice hanging there. What do you think?"

I looked where she pointed then at the other walls picturing what we'd need to move.

"I agree. It would have looked nice there."

Twenty-Nine

It was another warm day and I got an early start. I was parked where I could watch the parking garage at Suliman's loft with a thermos of coffee and a turnover. At 8:23, he drove out of the garage and headed south. I followed. I figured this would be my routine until Suliman was arrested. I couldn't totally dismiss the others from suspicion yet, but Suliman was definitely involved.

He made no stops and went straight to Gimmicks. When he turned into the drive, I continued on, made a U-turn, and went back toward town. I had a few more invitations I wanted to deliver personally. I'd find a reason later to call and check on his schedule.

As Tanya Waverly was the lead anchor now at Channel 3 TV, I didn't expect her to be at the studio this early in the day. I'd planned to leave a note with her invitation. So it was a pleasant surprise she was in and had a few minutes before an interview.

"Rachel, congratulations. I wish I could be there, I truly do, but I'm going to be in New York on business that weekend."

"Job interview? One of the networks?"

She nodded and held up crossed fingers. "Possibly. They called me and are paying for the trip."

"This town will miss you — I'll miss you — but I wish you the best."

"Thanks. This might not go anywhere, but it's exciting

they'd like to see me just the same." She held up a finger to an assistant who was trying to get her attention. "My interview's here. I've got to go. Congratulations again."

Andy Walther met me in the lobby of the *Daily Record*.

"Hi, Rachel. Is this about the advance copies of *Still A Bitch* I sent you? I haven't heard anything from you."

"Is that what's in the box you sent? Haven't opened it yet. I'm still amazed there was a *Life's A Bitch*, much less a sequel. No, Wendy and I are getting married in Iowa on the 24th. We hope you and your wife can join us."

He opened the invitation I gave him. "The 24th? That's right around the corner."

"Short notice, I know, but we only decided when and where a couple days ago. We're holding a room with your name on it."

"We'll definitely be there. This'll be great for the next book."

"Absolutely not! Don't even think about it. I must have been crazy to let you write one book about me, much less two. Never! Never again. Understand?"

"Completely. How many people are you expecting?"

"Why?"

"Just curious."

"Andy? I'm warning you."

"As you said, Rachel, 'Never again.'"

I was still fuming about Andy wanting to use my wedding in a book when I arrived at my lawyers' offices. I could just picture the kind of title he'd come up with: *Bitch Bride* or maybe *The Bitch Wore White*.

Carmen and Truman put me in a better mood after I vented about Andy and actually had me laughing when they suggested even tackier possible titles. Best of all, they were happy for me and would be there with their spouses.

Kerri's invite was my last personal drop-off. We met at Preston's Restaurant for coffee around the corner from Police Central and Kerri's Sex Crimes Division. Her husband wouldn't be available, and her oldest would probably have plans of her own. "Seventeen-year-olds. They're from another planet. I'll bring the other three. Just need one room with two queen beds."

My personal errands complete, I headed for the office to continue working on my final report for Stephanie. I'd barely started it when Ed Buchanan called.

"Rachel, your rings will be ready Friday for a final fitting and pickup. Just need to know if you want your wedding date engraved on the backs."

"That's great, Ed. Yes. The date will be April 24th 2010."

"Numerals okay, or would you prefer April spelled out?"

"Numerals are fine. When on Friday?"

"Your choice. Remember I'm retired."

"How about noon? That's Wendy's usual lunch hour."

"That's fine. Noon on Friday."

"Thanks, Ed. We're excited about seeing them."

I called Wendy to let her know then returned to my draft. I was going back through all of my notes to be sure I hadn't forgotten anything when I came across the death of Cochran's fourth wife, Kimberly. I'd never checked beyond the news articles for a copy of the accident report or any investigation if there'd been one. I fretted over whether it was important or not. Fretting made me hungry and I decided to pick up a slaw dog at Charlie's. My phone rang, as I was ready to leave.

"Rachel? John Cartwright. First of all, Ellen and I would be honored to be at your wedding."

"Great, John. I take it you also have other news."

"Yes. Test results did show Douglas Grimes had high levels of caffeine in his system at time of death. I notified the Washaw County sheriff and he's sending his investigators to pick up everything. They'll be here late this afternoon and would like to discuss the findings this evening. Could you be here at seven to take part in the meeting?"

"I'll be there. I've been working on my final report as well as keeping tabs on Suliman. I'll bring copies of everything I've got to date. See you then."

I called Wendy again to let her know I'd be in a meeting most of the evening and not to wait on me for dinner. She reminded me about meeting Roger Burke. I called Roger and changed our appointment to Thursday night. Then headed out for my slaw dog—might even get two—and an order of chili fries.

We met in one of the small conference rooms at Marston & Marston. There was a lot of paperwork spread out on the table already. John, Bob Hammond, Bill Roberts and a secretary were there, and I was introduced to Detective Vernon Reed and Deputy Jack French from the Washaw County Sheriff's Department. Both men were in their early forties and wore suits. I handed out copies of my report.

"Do you mind if we record this, Miss Cord?" Reed asked.

"Not at all, and please call me Rachel."

We spent three hours going over the background and how the investigation progressed. No one was interested in CYA or how or why certain things weren't done to begin with. We were strictly focused on moving forward. I told them of the disparities in Grimes personality as well as my other findings. Reed and French were interested in Kimberly Cochran's similar accident.

"Were you able to find anything beyond the newspaper reports, Rachel?" French asked.

I noticed they both had the habit of always saying the name of whoever they were asking a question. That way there'd be no confusion as to who answered when they played back their recording.

"No, I got stonewalled this afternoon. I was told to submit a FOIA request."

We shared a smile and continued on to other issues. Finally, Reed leaned back and stretched.

"Rachel, what's your assessment of the current situation?"

"They all tell consistent, credible stories from their own

perspective. There are similarities, but nothing sounds rehearsed or coordinated. At least to me. If they're colluding, I haven't spotted it. Yet, the evidence shows the car was tampered with, and Grimes had levels of caffeine he would not knowingly take. At least one of them is lying. From opportunity alone, Suliman stands out. And it bothers me he didn't mention buying the Everclear. Whether he's doing this alone or in tandem, I can't say. And despite the fact we're talking about one hell of a lot of money, I can't prove it's sufficient motive in this case."

"I wonder," said French, "if the brake tampering happened before Grimes agreed to the deal. Maybe someone thought he'd never agree. On those twisting roads, drunk or sober, without brakes the probability is high he'd have a life-threatening accident. When he did agree, there was no way to untamper them. I mean, it's possible one person tampered with the brakes, while someone else tried to keep him drunk and agitated enough to drive off and get killed in a drunk-driving accident. Two people working independently toward a common solution."

We pondered awhile and came to no conclusion. Reed leaned forward.

"Rachel, do you happen to know their schedule for tomorrow? Will they all be there at Gimmicks?"

I checked my notes. "According to Linda Woodruff, there's an important meeting of the partners and senior staff at 10:30. They should all be there before that. McManus normally comes in before eight; Suliman by nine; Cochran anywhere between nine and noon."

Reed nodded. "At this point in an investigation, I like suspects feeling comfortable and confident, like they're in control. With these three, I think that's their offices. Where they're the boss. I appreciate your describing their offices. It can tell a lot about a person's personality. How they interact with others." He nodded to himself, again. "Rachel, John, I think this is Jack's and my job from here on out. Greatly appreciate all you and your team have done and would appreciate if you'd hold off updating your client until Washaw County's ready."

We nodded and I asked, "Vern, if you'd like, I can shadow Suliman in the morning as I have been, just to let you know he is in fact going into work?"

"Okay. But once he's there, you're out of it." He wrote out two phone numbers next to his and French's names and gave it to me. "Jack and I can split tailing the other two. Think that's it for the night. Thanks, again, for all your help."

Thirty

My morning was a repeat except the weather turned seasonally normal and 20 degrees cooler. Suliman left at 8:20 and drove directly to Gimmicks. Like the day before, I continued past and made my U-turn. Then my Nosy Parker raised its head and I turned into Gimmicks and found an unobtrusive spot between two SUVs in an upper employee lot with a bit of view. I called Reed to let him know Suliman arrived.

"Thanks, Rachel. You were a big help. If you like fishing, give me a call some time and I'll show you the best trout streams in the state."

"Might do that. Hope you and Jack catch a big one today."

I poured some coffee, settled in and waited to see what the day brought. I could see some of the lake. The water looked choppy and there weren't any sailboats out. Except for a pack of four stalwart runners there was no one just out and about.

At 10:10, a silver Lincoln MKX pulled up to the entrance and Harold Cochran got out and entered the building. The Lincoln pulled away. A nondescript blue Toyota sedan had followed the Lincoln in and pulled into a visitor space. Det. Vernon Reed got out. A minute later from somewhere else in the parking area, Deputy Jack French came and joined him. They walked to the entrance together.

At 10:30, I wondered if the important staff meeting started on time or not. I called Linda Woodruff to see if she'd answer.

Besides, I was beginning to feel the need of a potty break.

"Hi, Rachel. I recognized your number. Wasn't expecting to hear from you."

"Hi. Wasn't sure if you were in a meeting or not."

"Should have been, but it was suddenly postponed. Don't know why. What can I do for you?"

"I'm down your way, and thought if you were free, I could stop in for a chat and a hot cup of coffee."

"Sure. Why not? Nothing happening here. It's too cold to go sailing. I'll call down to reception to give you a pass and we can meet in the cafeteria. See you in a few."

I really didn't need the coffee, but the "Ladies" was welcome as well as just being in the warm. Linda met me, we picked up coffee—I added a sugared cruller—and we went and sat by the south windows to take advantage of the radiant heat of the sun on the glass.

"What brings you out this way, Rachel? You still working for Steffi?"

"No, that job finished. I was supposed to keep a guy under surveillance today but lost sight of him. What happened to your meeting?"

"Not sure. We were waiting on Harry, when Ray and Darren got called away. Then someone called and said the meeting was cancelled and would be rescheduled. Then you called. When I called reception about your pass, I was told there were two detectives here seeing the partners. So tell me again you're no longer working for Steffi."

"It's true. It's no longer my investigation. All I owe Stephanie is a final report after those detectives do what they're here to do."

"Are you saying Doug's death wasn't an accident?"

"Linda, promise me I won't regret saying this, but his brakes were tampered with. There's no way he wouldn't have gone off the road. Whether or not he would have died, I can't say for certain."

"Oh, God. That's terrible. So you're really here to back up

the detectives?"

"No way. I'm here because I can't tame my curiosity. I need to know what's happening. It's a fatal flaw. You know what they say about the cat."

"Yes, but I also heard satisfaction brought it back. Do you like your job?"

"Mostly. I've been doing it a long a time. I apprenticed and worked for someone for three years before striking out on my own. It's now another 12. Yes. I like—"

There was the muted sound of gunshots coming from high above. We both looked up.

Linda looked at me. "Was that—?"

I distinctly heard two more shots. Alarms started going off.

"What's that?"

"Fire alarm. We need to leave the building."

"Where are the stairs?"

"That door over there."

"Call 9-1-1. Report gunshots fired." I ran for the stairs.

Going up four flights of stairs at full tilt is agony at best. When I reached the top my knees were screaming and I was huffing and wheezing. At least someone had turned off the fire alarm. I took a moment to get my breath back. Leaving the stairwell I was totally disoriented. The partners' offices were in the four corners, but I had no idea which way to go. An elevator opened and two people from the company medical clinic rushed by with a medical kit and headed left. Two security guards ran past in the opposite direction. I followed the guards.

When I caught up there were five security guards and Jack French standing at the entrance to one of the offices. I looked around to get a clue as to whose. The nameplate on the nearby desk read, "Ms. Davies." Cochran's office. I didn't see the lioness anywhere. Jack saw me and came away from the doors.

"What are you doing here?"

"Being nosy and having coffee downstairs. What

happened?"

"We were talking to Suliman in his office. He didn't like some of our questions. Said Cochran could explain. We started over here when he pulled some kind of martial arts shit, grabbed Vern's Glock and shot him. Then he ran this way and fired at me a couple times. I fired but don't think I hit him. Now he's squirrelled away in there with Cochran and some woman."

"Probably Cochran's assistant, a Ms. Davies."

A security guard holding a two-way radio came over.

"Detective, we'll have those floor plans for you directly. There is an emergency staircase in the office that leads to the floor below. We have guards standing outside it now."

French nodded. "Under no circumstances does anyone go up those stairs. I don't need some hero wannabe making matters worse. Understood?"

"Yes, sir." The guard turned away, said something in the radio and then listened. He turned back to French. "The Sheriff's SWAT team and hostage negotiator are on their way."

"Good. Can you get me an update on my partner?"

"Yes, sir. Right away."

We heard shouting from inside the office, but couldn't distinguish individual words. French moved to the double doors to listen. I followed. Still couldn't tell what was being said. I saw a refrigerator and a stack of water glasses in the alcove. I grabbed two glasses and handed one to French. He looked at me questioningly. I put the open end of the glass against the door and my ear against the bottom.

"Saw this in a movie when I was a kid. It really works."

Some of the sounds were still garbled but I could make out most of it. French made shushing motions to keep the guards quiet and put his ear to the glass.

"He wasn't supposed to die, Harry! He wasn't . . ." I thought it was Suliman shouting.

". . . the gun, Ray. This isn't . . ."

"Get him drunk . . . That . . . you said . . . he's dead! Dead!"

"Ray, you're scaring Pamela. Put down the gun." It sounded like Cochran was close to the door.

"Away from the door! I'll shoot!"

French and I instinctively jumped to the side and against the walls. Nothing happened. We waited then moved back to the edges of the doors so we could listen. It sounded like Suliman was right against the door.

"They told me his brakes were tampered with, Harry. Said it wasn't an accident. I didn't do that."

There was a loud "Thunk" against the door about head high. A moment later three more. I made a motion to French suggesting a head hitting the door. He nodded.

"I shot a cop, Harry. I panicked. This is his gun. Oh, fuck fuck fuck fuck." More thumping against the door in time with each "fuck."

"Give me the gun, Ray." Cochran must be close to the door too. We could hear him better. "Give me the gun. We can work something out."

"There's nothing to work out, Harry. Doug's dead. I did what you said. I spiked his drinks. 'Keep him drunk but awake. Keep him confused.' That's what I did. Just like you wanted. And look what happened."

"Stop pointing the gun, Ray. You don't want to shoot anyone." Cochran's voice was fading away. "You're not a killer."

"Aren't I, Harry? Who screwed the brakes, Harry? Was it you? Wasn't me. He wasn't supposed to leave. Wasn't supposed to drive. Did you really try to stop him? Or did you want him to leave? Was that the plan?"

The guard tapped French on the shoulder and whispered in his ear. French nodded. He looked at me and gave a "thumbs up." I hoped that meant Reed was okay. The guard listened to something on his radio.

"SWAT's here. On their way up."

French nodded again and returned his ear to the glass. We

heard nothing for several moments. Felt like an eternity but was probably only seconds.

"It's over, Harry. Over. We killed him. I killed a cop."

"Ray, I'm begging," I could barely hear Cochran. "Begging. Put down the gun."

French lightly tapped on the door. "Suliman? Ray? This is Jack French. Listen to me." French spoke calmly, quietly through the door. "The cop's okay. You didn't kill him. Detective Reed is okay. You didn't kill anyone, Ray. It was an accident. Ray, listen to me. You got Doug drunk. That's all. You didn't make him drive. You didn't fix the brakes. You're not a killer. That's not on you. Put down the gun, Ray. Please put down the gun. You're not a killer. We can work it out. Open the door, Ray. Put down the gun and open the door. Do it for Doug, Ray. Think of him. You didn't kill anyone. This is your chance to make it right. Think of Doug. Is this what he would want? Open the door."

I heard the thunk of something hitting the floor. The door unlocked. I moved out of the way. The door opened. Rashid Suliman was standing there. French was still talking quietly to him.

"Thank you, Ray. It'll be all right now. You didn't kill anyone. Face the wall, please. That's right. You're doing good, Ray. Put your hands behind you. Very good, Ray. Very good." French put cuffs on him. "Okay, Ray. We're going to walk away now. You and me, Ray. Just you and me. It's over. It's over."

French said something to a deputy in a SWAT uniform. Two of them went into the office. I heard Cochran say, "I want my lawyer."

Thirty-one

Det. **Vernon Reed was propped** up in bed. He looked more pissed than hurt.

"How you feeling?"

"How do you think? Like a damn fool. Shot with my own gun, for Christ's sake. Sheriff'll have me standing out as a crossing guard at the Elementary. Where's Jack?"

"Questioning Suliman, I think. Cochran's been arrested too. Bad wound?"

"They're all bad. You ever been shot?"

"Yeah."

"Then don't ask. Thanks for stopping by, though."

"Sorry about this. Feel like it's my fault."

"How's it your fault? You pull the trigger?"

"No, but Jack said something about 'martial arts.' Thought I missed something I didn't put in my report. You weren't prepared."

"Martial arts, my ass. The guy panicked as we left his office. Hip checked me into a desk. We grappled. He got my gun. Don't think he meant to shoot. Saw the surprise in his eyes when it went off. Anyone else hurt?"

"No. You're the only casualty. Jack sweet-talked Suliman into surrendering."

"Yeah, he can do that. Should see him with a spooked horse. Calm it right down. He's got the knack."

"Can I get you anything?"

"A shot of Old Overholt, but I doubt it's on the prescribed list. Thanks anyway. I'm good."

"I'll see what I can sneak in later. I'll let you rest."

"If you get a chance, tell Jack this wasn't his fault either. Got the feeling you and he are the type to feel guilt beyond your need. Shit happens."

I knew what he meant and knew he was right, but that didn't stop the woulda shoulda couldas and iffas scrambling my brain. I left a message for Jack French as he couldn't come to the phone then called John Cartwright to let him know what happened and asked him to call Stephanie Grimes and update her before she heard something on the news. I couldn't at the moment. Didn't want to do anything at the moment.

What I did do was go to a liquor store and bought a bottle of Russell's Reserve 6 year old rye and sneaked it in to Reed an hour later. He only had a sip to taste it but appreciated the gesture. I put the bottle in a drawer for him. Then I went home and drank two fingers of my favorite guilt suppressant.

By the time Wendy came home and we had dinner my feelings of inadequacy were gone or at least covered by rationalizations. So I was in a much better mood when we headed for Roger Burke's.

He was waiting for us at the top of the stairs much like I'd first seen him. A few years older, but the same thick dark hair held back in a ponytail; the radiant smile and dark bedroom eyes; the tan I'd thought sprayed on but real; and the polo shirt, khakis and bare feet.

"Roger, this is Wendy."

"Welcome. Come on in."

Instead of taking us to his customer area, he ushered us past the "Private" sign into his personal living space. On his walls were the marvelous black and white photos I'd first admired. I saw I was there now too. Wendy was drawn to the photos immediately.

"These are beautiful. Of course, these two I know already, but the rest, I'm overwhelmed. Wow."

"Thank you. Would you like some wine?"

We said yes. The wine was a German Riesling, crisp and slightly sweet like the one I remembered.

"I know you want to talk about wedding photos, but I wanted to give you this first. It's the catalog from the *River Views* show."

He handed me a glossy magazine and I was stunned. He'd said my photos were in the show, but he hadn't said the one of me I'd looked at two days ago was the cover. Thousands saw the show, but hundreds had this in their homes. Never thought I'd have that much exposure.

Wendy looked. "Would you sign it for us?"

"Be happy to."

He wrote, "To my favorite model. Roger." Wendy put it carefully in her bag. I gulped my wine. Finally, we talked about the wedding and different ideas and when he'd drive up to scout the area for off-site poses. When we were done, Wendy went back to admiring his photo display. I had more wine and saw Roger eyeing Wendy with the same critical, examining gaze I'd found so disconcerting the first time. He kept looking back and forth at the two of us.

"Rachel, Wendy, would you consider posing nude together for me?"

Before I could say, "No way," Wendy said, "We'd love to."

"We would?"

"Yes, we would. What are you thinking of?"

"A series I call, 'Couples,' taken in natural settings. They have cornfields in your part of Iowa, don't they, Rachel?

"Yes, but you won't see any growing in April."

Friday, Wendy decided to stay home until we picked up our rings. There was an article in the *Daily Record* of the shooting at Gimmicks and the arrests of Suliman and Cochran. Suliman was being held locally for shooting Detective Reed, while Cochran was taken to Washaw County in connection with the death of Douglas Grimes. There was no detail as to the reason for Cochran's arrest and only regurgitated the details of Grimes' accident and life from earlier reports. Another article in the business section speculated how the successful software company would be affected by Grimes' death and the arrests of two of the remaining partners.

Our rings were as beautiful as we'd hoped and fit perfectly. Ed reminded me that as we were wearing them on our right hands until the wedding I should use a teeny bit of olive oil before the ceremony so mine would slide off easily. We particularly liked that he used a Celtic eternity knot as a symbol of marriage on the inside engraving between our initials much like the "R heart W" and "W heart R" on the original bands.

We had lunch at Phil's where Elspeth and the staff oohed and aahed over the rings. Elspeth took a picture with her phone so she could send it to Phil.

Wendy got a call. "Yes? Okay. Perfect. Thank you."

"What was that?"

"Just business."

"Do they need you back at the bank?"

"No, everything's running smoothly there until the next crisis. I'm taking off the whole day. Let's go home."

At some point I needed to complete my final report to Stephanie, but not necessarily immediately. I knew John had spoken with her. She'd taken the news hard, but Yvonne and Nasha McManus were with her. I realized someone should break the news to Penelope and Jason Grimes. As soon as we were home, I dropped my stuff on our home office desk and called Beverly Norton.

"Norton residence."

"Hello, this is Rachel Cord. Is Mrs. Norton available?"

"One moment, please."

" Ms. Cord, hello. How may I help you?"

"I don't know if anyone has contacted you or your children or if there have been news reports, but two of your ex-husband's partners have been arrested in connection with his death. I didn't want Penelope or Jason—but particularly Penelope—hearing about it third hand or from some nosy reporter."

"I agree. So Doug's death was not an accident?"

"Not entirely. I don't know what the exact charges will be, but the partners contributed to his death. I'll ask Stephanie if I may share any of my report to her with you, but I thought you should know at least this much now."

"I appreciate it, thank you. I'll warn Jason. Pen is here with me, so that's not an issue. Thank you for calling."

"You're welcome. My sympathies to your family."

I turned and saw Wendy standing across the room smiling at me.

"What do you think?"

"I think you're beautiful."

She cocked her head and raised a hand toward the wall.

"I meant, 'What do you think?'"

On the wall beside her was the Balson painting from the Madsen Gallery.

"*You* bought the painting?"

"Surprise. I thought we needed one wedding present and this is mine to us."

I went and hugged her. "You're getting awfully sneaky these days. I can't match that."

"Oh, but you do. Your love has been more than a match for anything I'd wish for."

The last two weeks before the wedding were almost restful.

The Douglas Grimes story faded quickly from the news cycles. Unless there was an outside chance I was needed to testify at trial—which was months away at best—it was no longer my concern.

Everyone on our lists either confirmed or sent regrets and best wishes. There were dozens of donations to our favorite charities. My biggest disappointment was that Helen Abernathy, my former Army commander and later friend, couldn't be there. However, she made us laugh by including with her "Best Wishes" a small wooden statuette of an African fertility goddess.

Wendy's tax return assistance program was a great success. They signed up nearly 300 new account holders by tax day.

I was leery after we drove up to Laman on the 22nd to learn that 11 tornados touched down the same day over in Kansas. I had visions of our wedding turning into an OZ story.

Two more, touching down just 70 miles away and only a couple hours before our ceremony, did nothing to relieve my anxiety.

Thirty-two

"**W**elcome. **We are gathered here** in the sight of God, family and friends to bear witness to the joining of Rachel Evangeline Cord and Wendy Pan Devlin.

"Marriage is a special relationship. It should not be entered into lightly, but thoughtfully. With it come both deep joys and responsibilities.

"Marriage is different from other relationships. We do not confuse it with friendships, business partnerships or caregiving, although all of those are part of being married. Marriage is so much more.

"It makes people kin, it celebrates intimacy, and it ties a life long knot. It is the most significant contract a person will make in their lifetime.

"It touches the heart more deeply than any other action people take. It strengthens communities in ways too numerous to list.

"Please remember your miracle lies in the path you have chosen together. Enter into marriage knowing the true magic of love is not to avoid changes, but to navigate them successfully.

"Commit to the miracle of making each day work together, for no human ties are more important, more tender.

"What say you, Rachel Evangeline Cord?"

I turned to face Wendy. "I say to you, Wendy Pan Devlin, I love you unconditionally and without hesitation. I accept you as you are, not as I would make you or wish you to be, and offer myself in return. I choose you as my wife, to care for, to stand beside, to share all life's adversities and joys as one unit, one family, all the days of my life. And now I take from your right hand the ring I gave and you wear as a symbol of love and place it on your left hand as my pledge, my signal to the world, that from this moment you, Wendy Pan Devlin, are my wife and life."

"What say you, Wendy Pan Devlin?"

"I say to you, Rachel Evangeline Cord, I love you unconditionally and without hesitation. I accept you as you are, not as I would make you or wish you to be, and offer myself in return. I choose you as my wife, to care for, to stand beside, to share all life's adversities and joys as one unit, one family, all the days of my life. And now I take from your right hand the ring I gave and you wear as a symbol of love and place it on your left hand as my pledge, my signal to the world, that from this moment you, Rachel Evangeline Cord, are my wife and life."

"By the exchanging of vows and tokens of these vows as witnessed by God, family and friends, and by the laws of the State of Iowa, you, Rachel Evangeline Cord and Wendy Pan Devlin, are bound together in marriage this day, April 24th 2010. May joy, hope, love and peace follow you all the days of your lives. Amen."

www.ingramcontent.com/pod-product-compliance
Lightning Source LLC
Chambersburg PA
CBHW070737180626
46818CB00007B/2886